Poppy Kisses

A RETURN TO COAL HAVEN NOVEL

MARIE JOHNSTON

LE PUBLISHING

I need a husband. Jensen needs a business makeover. A marriage of convenience should solve both our problems.

Moving back to Coal Haven should have been simple—start my tutoring business, settle into the historic house my grandmother left me, and move on from my past. But there's a catch: I can't claim the house unless I'm married.

Jensen Hollis. My childhood rival. The guy I spent years trying to outdo. The one who married our mutual friend while I watched from the sidelines. Now he's divorced, a single dad, and—somehow—my only option.

It's a perfect arrangement. A temporary marriage. One year with no feelings involved.

At least, that was the plan...until playing house starts to feel a little too real.

Dear Reader,

I've seen statistics say that dyslexia affects one in five individuals. But since it's hereditary, that rate is higher in a lot of families. In mine, it's two out of three. Four out of my six immediate family members have it and countless more if we expand out to the grandparents, aunts, uncles, and cousins.

All the examples of life with dyslexia I used in this story are from my or my loved one's personal experience or as much of a parallel example as I could make it. From fumbled words to the help needed with professional communications, to years of speech therapy and tutoring that have cost tens of thousands of dollars, to the lack of understanding and support in the education system. I was that mom accused of not reading to her kids enough and that must be why they struggled with both reading and writing. There is so much more I could've included.

This story is only a snapshot, and everyone's experience with dyslexia is different.

With that, I hope you enjoy Poppy and Jensen's story. Dyslexics are some of my favorite people. I love their magnificent brains, and if there is ever anything to assemble and it has 3D diagrams, I can hand it off to my kids. They will have it put together before I've finished reading through the instructions.

Happy reading,
    Marie

Chapter One

Poppy

My online remote tutoring student, Auggie, tapped at his screen, his gaze narrowed as he concentrated. The words he was writing appeared in the program on my end.

"Good," I encouraged him, using the time he worked to study the rest of the house behind him. He was working at his kitchen table. Despite the high ceilings and dining room attached to the kitchen, it had an aged look. An old farmhouse? So much more room than the tiny, outdated motel room I was in.

If I'd had a better space to work, we could've met in person. I was back in Coal Haven, North Dakota, and that was also where Auggie lived. But my office situation was a work in progress, and I would be relocating to my brother's house until I found something more suitable. Whenever and wherever that was.

"How's that?" Auggie asked. He was bouncing. Probably swinging his legs. We were almost done, and he was about to jitter out of his chair.

I used the cursor to point out the tail on a *P* he'd flipped. "Not bad. Correct that and keep going—you're on fire."

He puffed out his lips as he worked. There was something familiar about Auggie and the way his short, dirty-blond hair stuck up in spikes. He'd run his hands through the strands, and something tickled my memories.

My family had moved from Coal Haven to Billings right before I'd entered high school, but I sort of remembered some students I'd gone to school with. Several of them probably had stayed in the area. They might be married and have kids Auggie's age. Those kids might even be in fifth grade with him.

Would I know his mom or dad? Both?

Did I want to know until my employment and housing situations were secure?

I had worked with a private school in Casper, Wyoming, before I'd quit my job—before I would've gotten fired. Now, I was subbing for an old college friend with her dyslexia tutoring company. Right now, freelance work was the best option unless I wanted to be thirty and moving in with my parents in Billings. Which was why I was ogling a nice house from my dark motel room.

A vacuum fired up in the room next door, and I grimaced. Could Auggie hear it?

He continued writing like he hadn't. Debbie hadn't told me his last name. She'd given me a quick rundown of his personality—upbeat, hardworking, and full of energy—and where he was in the Barton System tutors like us used to teach our dyslexic students. Then she'd turned him over to me for the summer, deliriously happy to have some help with her bursting schedule.

Her business had grown fast, and she had waiting lists of students needing help. Amazing but not surprising since dyslexia was considered a learning disability, and families didn't get help from their health insurance. But Debbie hustled hard with fundraisers, and I got paid a decent wage when I took clients for her.

I looked at the notes she'd sent me for Auggie. Nope, no last name, just that he preferred Auggie to August, and he liked to be read to during brain breaks.

Auggie tipped his head down as he worked, his tongue tucked into the corner of his mouth. His bright-blue eyes faintly triggered a memory, as did the rodeo shirt he wore. He lived where ranching and rodeo were as common as the windmills dotting the countryside.

Auggie rubbed his eyes and squinted at me in the camera. "Are we done yet?"

"Almost. Finish the sentence and then you're done."

The material was harder for him. The signs were in his heavy sighs and tired eyes. We'd just started a new level in his lessons.

One of his sighs gusted over our connection, and he slid to another chair around his table, dragging the computer with him. The room behind him whirled through the screen. I was used to my remote students moving around when they moved spots or took their computer to a parent so I could update them.

During our hour, I'd spent the entire time in the same chair. Auggie was on his fourth seat around his dining room table. I'd seen the cute old house had been well cared for. The living room ceiling arched behind him, and the kitchen was an open square. There were sliding

French doors on one wall. I think he was across from them now. I got a peek at some cabinets that were nicer than I expected to see in an old farmhouse.

"I need a drink." He pressed a knuckle into his eye.

I checked the time. We were almost done, but he was struggling with the last word. "Remember the happy rule you and Debbie went over?"

His lips pooched out again. "No short vowels at the end."

"Right. They need to be closed off."

His world-weary sigh puffed through the speaker, but he completed the word.

"You did it! Get yourself some water."

Relief crossed his little face. The screen lurched again as he took the computer with him.

I chuckled. "Do I get some water too?"

"What?"

The world dipped and spun as he grabbed a cup off the counter. Ice clattered. He must be standing at the fridge with an ice and water dispenser. He was holding the laptop in the crook of his arm. I saw his shoulder and the house behind him. An enclave was off the living room, and a man passed through, wiping a rag over his trimmed hair, and disappeared into one of the dark rooms.

I choked on a cough. I'd only seen the guy from the side, but he was in gray shorts and a white T-shirt. His wide shoulders had flexed and bunched under the material of his shirt. Whoa. Either the camera loved him, or Auggie's dad was a smokeshow.

The light flipped on in the room he'd gone into, flashing bright and then settling into focus. A bathroom. He was leaning over like he was washing his hands or inspecting a face I really wanted to fill my screen.

Auggie shifted his hold, and I craned my neck like I could look around him from my small motel room.

"One more glass," Auggie said after gulping the first one down. My view jostled again. He must be filling the water.

"No problem," I muttered. *Just shift to the left. My left, not yours.*

Wait, it would be his left, too, from the way the laptop was cradled in his arm.

The guy behind Auggie turned his back to us and yanked the shirt over his head. This time, I was the one letting out a gusty breath. Two things registered. Auggie's dad had a delicious-looking bubble butt, and wow, his back was ripped. What were his abs like?

Then the man turned, and a quiver traced through my belly. His features weren't the clearest, but I didn't need detail to see that he was hot. Besides, his washboard stomach was on display. I'd been single for too long. I was riveted.

He spun around, exiting the bathroom and running a hand through darkish blond hair the same shade as his son's. His biceps bulged with the movement. Then his gaze lifted to pin me in place right through the screen. His eyes widened.

Embarrassment filled me like I'd been caught peeping. I kind of had.

"Auggie, bud." A man should not have that smooth and deep of a voice. "You've gotta warn a guy when you're on the move with that thing." He looked around like he was trying to find the shirt he'd tossed in the laundry basket. "Hi, Debbie," he called.

The world spun as Auggie turned around. My back thumped against the wooden back of my chair. Whoa. I didn't recall going to school with someone that hot, but they'd all been just entering their puberty-ridden years when I'd moved.

"Sorry, Dad. It's not Debbie, remember? I have a sub." I got a good look at the refrigerator as Auggie walked toward what I can presume was the table. The thunk matched the shaking of his screen, and he spun the camera to face his dad. "Poppy's teaching me today."

The dad looked like he was about to duck into the bathroom, then he gave me a double take and tilted his head. My screen filled with impressive pecs as he approached the table.

My mouth went dry, and I pushed back farther in my chair. "Hello," I said weakly. What did swooning feel like? Was I doing it?

He braced a hand on the edge of the table and leaned in. The same chisel that formed his chest had been taken to this guy's jaw. Even his nose was a bold slash on his face. His hair stood up in spikes, and his dark brows were drawn together. He studied me with stormy blue eyes.

"Poppy?"

I swallowed and nodded. "Nice to meet you. Auggie sure was fun to work with."

His eyes narrowed for a heartbeat, then a slow grin spread across his face. "Hot damn, I'd recognize those freckles anywhere. Poppy Duke. How the hell are ya?"

My mouth turned into the Sahara for a different reason. He knew me. He knew my freckles. Not many people had pointed out my freckles when I was a kid, except for the boy who constantly challenged me and told me over and over again I'd never be the one he crushed on.

"Jensen? Jensen Hollis?"

"Yeah!" He laughed and slid the chair out to sit where Auggie should've been. Instead, he tugged his boy toward him to perch on a knee. "Auggie, Poppy's an old friend of mine."

Friend was stretching it. Pals, maybe. Buds. There'd been moments we'd been as close as best friends and then as acrimonious as exes, only we'd never dated. No. He'd had eyes for one girl only. He'd made it known every chance he could.

I bet if Hassie had freckles, they'd be cuter on her. Just one of the many ways he'd compared me and the other rung in our wheel of three who used to play together. Hassie Heart captured his heart in kindergarten.

Auggie blinked at me, then looked at his dad. "Okay." He scrubbed a hand down his face. There were drips on his shirt from the water. "Can I eat breakfast?"

A lot of my morning students rolled out of bed and in front of the computer. I was no different. I refrained from attempting to tame all the strands that escaped from my hair.

"You two done? Did I interrupt?" Jensen asked.

No, your abs did. "Nope. Auggie finished everything he set out to do."

Auggie slipped off Jensen's lap and trudged into the kitchen and out of my view.

A beat of silence passed before the corner of Jensen's mouth lifted. "Small world, huh?"

"Yeah, right?" I was in his small world. I'd enjoyed being out of it for the last twenty years.

"How's Billings?"

Surprise curled through me. He'd remembered where my family had moved? "It was good." I'd made a new friend group and it'd been freeing, but I'd also missed him and Hassie. "I'm in Casper now. I mean, I was. I'm relocating."

"Where to?"

"Uh, I wouldn't mind settling in Coal Haven. I'm in town, actually."

"No shi—kidding." His gaze slid sideways. Auggie must be in earshot. "Auggie finally gets an in-person tutor?"

Debbie's center was out of Dickinson. Unless Jensen wanted to drive Auggie on two-hour round trips twice a week, his only choice was online lessons. "I don't know. I'm subbing for the distance students." Her waiting list was so large she'd almost begged me to start my own center. And after one too many glasses of wine, I had agreed.

What had I been thinking? What made me think I could pull this off? Debbie had all the faith in me even after I told her about my failure in Casper. We'd gotten our master's together in occupational therapy and then she'd recruited me into the dyslexia tutoring world, along with several other OTs we'd trained and worked with. I'd done it as a side hustle throughout my career, and now, I hoped it could be my career. At least I could work without having an official base.

Jensen clicked his tongue. "Shame. These online sessions get long for him." He ran his hand over his hair, mussing it until it stood on end like Auggie's. Now I remembered. "I did cabinets for Alder. Did he tell you?"

"No, but he was probably distracted by getting back together with Daisy." I loved my brother, but until he and

Daisy had remarried, we hadn't talked a lot. He'd been my uptight oldest brother, and I probably topped his list of annoying sisters.

Jensen frowned. "They were married when I did the installation."

Right. They had been. But they hadn't been back together. "Yep." Before I ended up explaining about my grandma Annie's trust and the property my siblings and I were each left—if we were married—I scrambled for a subject change. "How's Hassie? I heard you two got married."

His expression went blank and his gaze darted in the direction Auggie had gone. "She's, uh, probably in Oklahoma. Maybe Nebraska. Or Nebraska and then Oklahoma."

"Oklahoma," Auggie called from the direction a cupboard had just banged.

Jensen's jaw went tight. "She's on the barrel racing circuit but also teaching lessons too."

"Teaching barrel racing?"

"Yep." He popped the *p*.

Hassie had been the rabid horse girl growing up. She raised horses, talked about horses, and spent all her time out of school on horseback. For a while, she'd been my best friend, but as we neared middle school, even at my young age, I could tell Hassie had my back only as far as it served her. I'd say no one could love Hassie more than she loved herself, but she'd been the center of Jensen's world for as long as I'd known them.

"We've been divorced for five years," he said.

"Oh." If I had paid attention to more than the muscled caps of his shoulders, I'd have noticed he wasn't wearing a ring. That didn't always mean anything, but if

Jensen didn't have a Hassie Heart tattoo, I'd lose a year of wages to my next youngest sister, Clover. "I'm sorry."

He shrugged, but his expression remained void. Auggie must be listening in. What other subject could I touch on that would be less awkward?

"How's your mom?" I had liked Erin Hollis. The day of his dad's funeral ran through my head. One of the saddest days I'd ever known to that point in my life. For Jensen? I couldn't imagine, and he hadn't talked much about it except for one time after the funeral service. It was the only time he hadn't looked at Hassie like she'd hung the moon and stars.

"She's good. World's proudest grandma."

I laughed. His mom had always brought goodies to school. Our class had looked forward to class parties and holidays because that meant Erin brought her treat bags. "I've never been able to find anything to compare to her cookie pizza."

Jensen's grin spread wide. "If I tell her that, you'll have a batch delivered to wherever you are." He squinted at the screen. "Where are you? Alder's?"

"I got a motel room. Daisy and Alder offered, so I'm going there tonight. Lily has little ones that'd make it hard for me to have quiet sessions. Same with Violet, but they just have wee little Willa. Still, a baby crying is too distracting for the students."

He folded his arms in front of him and *gawwdd*. His muscles. Did the cabinets he made install themselves if he called them a good girl? Where was the scrawny boy who helped me work on my cone drills while also telling me it was lucky he didn't play soccer or I wouldn't have a chance?

The man in front of me could decimate me at everything.

"So three of your siblings have moved to Coal Haven and you're next?" he asked.

The timer on my phone blared and I jumped. I tapped it off. "Sorry, Jensen. I have another session."

"We need to catch up."

Fear climbed into my throat, choking out the *yes!* He might be divorced, but he could still be hung up on her. It'd been hard enough to hear the comparisons when I hadn't thought he was an Adonis.

"I'll be around," I said noncommittally. "I'd better get going. Nice to talk to you!"

I clicked out of that session and grimaced. Could I have sounded more insincere? It had been nice to see him. Was I curious to know more? Yes, but also, I'd had enough of people like Hassie Heart. Wait, or did she go by her married name? Hassie Hollis?

Jensen might be tight-lipped around his son, but I had no wish to learn he hadn't changed in the last twenty years. The way he'd been smitten, I didn't have to hear the story to know the divorce hadn't been his idea. He'd have gone to hell and back eight times and asked her if she'd needed anything on his next trip.

Someday, I'd find a man like that. But it wasn't Jensen Hollis.

●●●

Jensen

. . .

I stared at the "session ended by host" flag in front of me. Poppy Duke.

A fondness welled up inside my chest. Poppy had been part of the "Sporty Spice" crowd, as one teacher had called us. A group of us who'd played together at recess. We'd eaten lunch together, and sometimes we'd hung out. Hassie had competed in horses, Poppy had been big into soccer, and I had played football and ran track.

Auggie plopped into his chair at the table with his bagel in front of him. I didn't have to look behind me to know that two cupboards and a drawer were probably left open. "Was Poppy nice?"

"She was real cool." Memories surfaced, and I stared at the screen, seeing her face where there was only Auggie's background of Hassie curving around a barrel on one of her horses, Gone Girl. "She made me laugh, and she didn't put up with my shi—you know."

Auggie gave me the same dubious look his mom would shoot me when I would suggest a date night that didn't include buckles, bronc riders, or barrels.

"She's a soccer player," I said. Did Poppy still play? Her light-brunette hair had been pulled back, but those big hazel eyes were the same. It was how I'd recognized her beyond her name. Her freckles, too, but those eyes always told me how she was feeling. They flashed fire when she was pissed, turned cold when her stubbornness kicked in, and sparkled like a lake on a gorgeous summer day when she was happy. Today, she'd been guarded. Her enthusiasm hadn't matched mine. I'd been fucking thrilled to see a friendly face again.

"Cool," Auggie said. "I like soccer."

He was obsessed about it. When I was trying to relax at night, he was doing drills with the soccer ball in the living room. The toe taps and penguin warm-ups I'd taught him had come from Poppy. "Yeah. You ready for school?"

"I haven't finished eating!"

"I know, but is everything else ready?"

"My backpack's not."

I pinched the bridge of my nose. "You're supposed to do that before bed."

"You told me to shower." His bagel was abandoned. "I fed Luna."

He loved our black Lab, so I didn't worry about feeding her.

"Eat, or we're going to be late." I had to give up on the bus. He—*we*—were perpetually late, and I had to drive him most days. This way, I didn't have a *shame on you* call from the driver or the school. The chidings were valid, but it had sucked. Especially if it'd been done by email and my replies had been littered with typos.

Auggie pouted, but he dug into his bagel. I kept an eye on the time. We had fifteen minutes. The drive to town took eight. Another two in the drop-off line while he gathered everything. I didn't want to add up getting in and out of the car and what Auggie would inevitably need to run back into the house for before we'd even left.

I inhaled a steadying breath. If I rushed him, it'd only delay us more. I opened my email app.

A reply from an estimate I'd sent a couple days ago waited for me.

Thank you for the information. We're going to have to pass.

Damn. My cabinet business was like a goose with a busted wing, flopping around on the ground and not really taking off. I'd had a good feeling about this couple.

They'd bought a house built in the seventies and had contacted me for a refacing. Easy enough and I had a good portfolio. Five years' worth, but my independent work outside of contractors was spotty. At least I could make my own hours, and with Auggie, I needed the timing down.

I typed out a reply. *No problem thanks for letting me know.* I typed my name and reread it. Read it again. Then sent it.

I tucked my phone into my pocket. "Time to go, bud."

"I'm not done!"

"Eat and run." I had a little leeway. His teacher, Miss Whitfield, knew he had tutoring this morning, and she was easier going than his past teachers. She hadn't assumed shitty parenting for my son's reading struggles like his last teacher had.

Two minutes later, I was in jeans and a fresh T-shirt, and we were on the road. A dust cloud kicked up behind me. The pastures around my house were leased out. The cattle roaming them weren't Hollis beef. Mom shut down the ranch not long after Dad died. The fenced-off area by the old barn no longer held horses. I missed the sight. I had always thought I'd bring my family back and raise them where I had grown up. I had, only it was just me and Auggie.

The familiar pang of longing tugged at my heart. I missed being married, but I didn't miss the arguing. Or the long absences. The lack of communication. The suspicion. I didn't miss my ex, just the idea of marriage.

We passed the motel. A metallic-blue SUV was sandwiched between two dusty white work trucks that were probably oil field workers of some sort. It had to be Poppy's.

How long was she in town? Had she changed since we'd been friends?

Who the hell hadn't? I'd been through the wringer thanks to my ex. I was finally settling into a quiet life with my son. The familiar scratch of panic scraped across the back of my neck. But I'd be driving one of those work trucks to the mine, the refinery, or the oil fields if I couldn't grow my cabinet business.

I pulled into the drop-off lane at the school. Three other cars were turning and burning at the same time, all of us butting up against the morning whistle. The playground attendant narrowed her eyes at me. I gave her a wave as Auggie scrambled out and I pulled away.

Before I went home to work in my shop, I had to stop at the grocery store. I went through the aisles, my empty cupboards and sparse fridge shelves flashing through my mind. I was combing through cereal options that didn't feel like I was giving my kid dessert for breakfast when I heard, "Have you tried Jensen Hollis?"

I pulled to a stop. Me?

"Yeah." The woman didn't sound thrilled. Her voice was vaguely familiar. "I mean, I liked his work and he has good recommendations, but he writes like a fourth grader."

Shame burned hot in my chest. My handwriting had been critiqued longer than how I strung a sentence together, and the sting never went away.

"He doesn't need good grammar to work with wood," the other woman said.

"He even spelled his name wrong."

I winced. Fuck. Had I? When?

"And he kept calling me Isabull when he took the measurements," the second woman continued. "Even this morning, he had no punctuation in his one sentence with his misspelled name."

"Wow, that's too bad."

My cheeks were burning and a brush fire swept over my skin. Childhood embarrassment mingled with adult humiliation. If they saw, I'd feel ten times worse. Biting back a groan, I pivoted with the shopping cart.

I had not called Isabel *Isabull*.

Had I?

I'd check that damn reply.

This wasn't the first time I'd lost a job because I'd jacked up something I'd written. An email, a promotional brochure, typos on my website. It was like Whac-A-Mole, only half the time, I didn't notice the mole.

Since my divorce, I'd had to bootstrap expenses. I had done my own printing materials until I realized I was hurting myself more. Then I had relied on word of mouth, but the more new people moved to Coal Haven, the less they knew my real reputation. I could build the shit out of anything. I might have nearly failed high school because of English, but I never messed up a measurement.

Well, not never, but the customer wasn't usually standing right next to me to see me fix my mistakes.

I grabbed a brightly colored box of cereal and tossed it in my cart before beelining to the checkout.

Delores beamed at me from behind her horn-rimmed glasses. "Howdy, Jensen. How's it going?"

"Oh, you know. How 'bout you?" I dug out my wallet. Down the aisle across from the register, two women sauntered around the corner, pushing carts. One had a baby carrier and the other had a toddler playing with cans in her cart.

Isabel glanced at me. Her eyes flared, and her gaze skated away.

I clenched my jaw and tugged the brim of my hat down. Delores chattered about how busy it'd been all morning and she couldn't wait to see her grandkids.

"They're going to help me move," she said.

That got my attention. Delores had been working the checkouts for as long as I could remember. "You're moving?"

She beamed, the apples of her cheeks pushing her glasses up. "To Indiana, where Kellie and the kids are. She has crazy hours, and I can watch the kids."

"That'll be nice, but we're going to miss you."

She shrugged and hit the total. "I want to give her the help I wished I had when I was younger. We could all use an extra hand, and you know, we all deserve it."

I tapped my debit card on the machine and tucked my wallet back. My gaze caught on the retreating back of Isabel.

Isabull. How had I said it wrong? "Thanks, Delores."

"Anytime, Jensen, and if I don't see you again, take care. Good luck with Hollis Cabinets. I tell everyone about you." She'd been saying that for years. Hearing best wishes about my cabinet business would have left me with more optimism any other day, but after overhearing why I'd lost a nice contract, it was a dash of salt on an open wound. Now I was down one more advertising avenue.

"I appreciate it. Have a great time with your grand-kids. Tell Kellie hi."

I pushed my cart out.

How did I keep fucking up? I checked and triple-checked my work. And errors still got through. Errors that didn't matter with the work but with the customer service. I was nice, dammit.

Yet it wasn't enough.

Where did a guy go to get help with shit he should've learned in school? With basic speaking and writing?

How fucking humiliating.

I had not said Isabull.

At least Auggie was getting help so he wouldn't face these issues when he grew up. I got in my pickup and drove toward home. I hit the highway, and as I passed the motel, the blue SUV caught my eye. Was that Poppy's?

Poppy, my son's tutor. Poppy, who might be moving to town. Poppy, who might have some insight on how to keep me from sabotaging my business.

Chapter Two

Poppy

If I sat in my car any longer and stared at this house, the renters would call the police on me.

I chewed on my lower lip.

This place was called the Perez house, thanks to the original contractor and occupant who'd lived here long ago. He'd made it the classiest farmhouse around, with two stories and proud peaks on the roof. Quaint shutters added to the homey feel, but overall, it had a run-down air to it. Still majestic, just old.

But it would be perfect. I could live here and work here. The patio would be ideal for those summer days when kids were going nuts inside. The overhang would provide enough shade to see our computer screens while the side of the house blocked the north wind.

It used to be Aunt Linda's home before she married Darren. My grandparents had bought the place after

Linda and Darren had moved out, and it was one of the several included in my grandma's trust.

This house would go to me. If I was married for at least a year. I could live there now—if I was already married. I checked Linda's message from weeks ago.

Linda: The renter is moving out at the end of May, and I'd like to have another renter in by the end of June.

I had no husband, yet I'd quit my job before I could get fired and left Wyoming on a wing and a prayer that I'd land a husband between now and the end of May. That was barely over a month away.

Of course that hadn't been why I'd uprooted to start again. But it hadn't not been the reason. The distant possibility of a decent home had been enough.

Yet, here I was, staying with Alder. He and Daisy had three spare bedrooms, but the one across from where I was sleeping was getting turned into a nursery. Daisy wasn't due for six months, but the clock was ticking. I loved Daisy's little girl and I enjoyed witnessing my brother get used to fatherhood through his stepdaughter, but I couldn't overstay my welcome. They'd only just rekindled a romance that hadn't burned out since they'd been high school sweethearts.

Would Jensen and Hassie reconnect?

I couldn't believe they had divorced. Jensen would've grown his hair to his waist and developed a taste for death metal if Hassie had wanted it. His tidy home came to mind. Hassie had been a diehard horse girl, and Jensen had said she was a professional barrel racer. Yet there were no pictures of horses.

Didn't he have a closet full of Ariats and a dressy pair

of Tony Lamas? Wranglers and Carhartts? A set of chaps that he wore whether he rode a horse or not?

Jensen had grown up in the country, and his family ranched. To be with Hassie, he'd had to have adopted her rodeo lifestyle. There would be at least one picture of a horse and something made out of horseshoes somewhere in that tidy farmhouse.

I pushed Jensen out of my head for the millionth time. Every time I let my mind wander, it landed on his abs. I was better than that!

Western flair or not, he had a nice body. A pleasing, deep voice. Puberty had done that man all the favors. I'd been left with pimples, more freckles, and a set of hips that made pants shopping a challenge.

Thankfully, it was a mild spring, and I could wear short pants with elastic waists.

I'd recognize those freckles anywhere.

I had to close my eyes. My body had never reacted this way when he'd tease me about connecting the dots in fifth grade. In seventh grade, there had been that one time he'd said it and my stomach had gone all jelly wiggles, but I'd also gotten the flu pretty bad that year. Must've been that.

My phone pinged. I took one last wistful glance at the house. The biggest bedroom was up in a corner, and it overlooked the expanse of property that came with the place. Aunt Linda never used to let us in there, but I'd snuck in when she'd been tied up chatting with my parents or grandparents. The windows were huge for such an old place, but they'd let in so much welcoming light. I'd fallen in love. Grandma Annie must've known.

So why all the stipulations?

Irritation scratched across the back of my neck. I checked the message.

Debbie: Auggie's dad wants to hire you.

"What?" I set the phone down and put the car in drive. I used voice control to ask the car to call Debbie.

"You made quite an impression, young lady," Debbie playfully chided.

"I'm so lost. Why is Jensen calling about me?"

"He said you're old friends."

"I guess you could say that," I muttered.

"Aren't you? Oh god, I'm sorry. I shouldn't have assumed he was telling the truth. I didn't give him your information."

"No. No, it's fine. Yes, we were old friends, but that was all." Except on the playground when he and I used to square off for kickball. He'd had a powerful kick, but I'd practiced twice as hard to kick farther. Or when we had a group project, and he and I were the only ones pulling our weight. When we'd laugh together while waiting for the bus. Hassie's mom always picked her up. Did they still live in town?

"He's from Coal Haven?"

"I'm not sure he ever left." I'd only been to his house once, after his dad's funeral. The place had been packed with mourners and I'd gone outside after I'd seen Jensen sneak out. I'd found him sitting on a hillside. Hassie had avoided him much of the day as if dealing with the deep feelings of a friend losing a parent was an inconvenience, but we all dealt with the discomfort of loss differently. I hadn't liked seeing him by himself that day, so I'd sat with him. We'd talked. No teasing. No joking around. No boasting. I'd never felt closer to a friend than I had that day.

"Maybe he's into you."

I snort-laughed. "No. Trust me. I grew up with that man, and he had eyes for one girl only. Auggie is theirs."

"He's married? I've only ever dealt with him. I mean, Auggie talks about his mom and horses, but never like she's around."

"They're divorced. You had to be there. Adoration like that doesn't go away. Since kindergarten, he said he was going to marry her. He asked her out in third grade." I used to get so annoyed. Like, *my dude, let the girl play The Ground is Lava*. Then I'd thought it was sweet in sixth grade when Hassie had started to see him as a maybe. By the time my family had moved, I'd been glad to leave them and that toxic, one-sided romance behind me.

It'd been freeing to no longer be compared to Rodeo Barbie.

"If he wants to contact me, that's fine." I wouldn't go out of my way though. When it came to Jensen Hollis, he'd shown me that when he had eyes for someone, no one else's feelings mattered as much. We were adults now, but that hurt girl who'd been compared to Hassie and found short was still inside me.

Almost twenty years had passed. I should get over it. But one thing Jensen's single focus had shown me was that he'd never have my best interests at heart.

●●●

Jensen

I parked in front of Alder's house. He'd done some work on the outside over the spring. The flower beds were turned up and white tulips were blooming. The path to the front had been freshly swept, and the grass had been trimmed away from the stones leading to the steps into the house.

I got out and tugged the sleeves of my long-sleeved shirt down. At least I was wearing one this time when I was seeing Poppy. Even as kids, she hadn't seen me without a shirt.

We'd been friends for years. Whenever I thought of elementary and middle, Poppy was there. She used to wear her hair pulled back or in a single brown braid with curls spinning out.

Would I get a similar cautious look when she answered the door?

I ran a hand over my short hair. It needed a trim. I hated feeling shaggy, and the longer it was, the more sawdust stuck to the strands. It was why I stayed clean-shaven no matter how much Hassie had gushed about the beards of the cowboys on the circuit.

Dusting off my pants and shirt, I made my way to the door. When I glanced up, the curtains fluttered. Satisfaction spread through me. Had she been watching?

I knocked on a solid metal door, warm from the sun. I tilted my head, but I heard no movement on the other side. Finally, the door creaked open six inches.

Poppy peered out. A pale-yellow cloud surrounded her pupil. She squinted in the daylight. "Hey."

"How's it going, four-ten?"

Her left cheek twitched. My old nickname from when she'd been stuck at four feet ten inches while I'd soared over five feet had seemed like a good icebreaker. I was a little over six feet, and she had to be only six or seven inches shorter than me now.

Uncertainty flooded me. Was I wrong about how close we'd been? That last time we'd really talked, when she'd kept me company on a side hill during one of the worst times of my life, had been shortly before she'd moved.

"Debbie said you wanted to talk?" She sounded cautious, like I was going to convince her she could get rich on the latest multilevel marketing scheme.

"I need your help." There. I came out with it. As embarrassing as this was, it was better than another grocery store incident. Yet the sense that she'd turn around and tell me to drive off hung heavy in the fresh spring air between us.

The door swung a little wider.

Yes.

"What can I help you with?" she asked.

Embarrassment flooded my chest, puffing it up. I wished I could float away from it. If I couldn't talk to Poppy about this, then who? Debbie might help, but I hadn't tried asking her. I'd figure out why later. "My business."

Her brows drew together. Once Hassie had said that she was glad she didn't have plain brown hair like Poppy. I might've been thirteen, but even I had noticed the way some of her strands sparkled like spun gold against the darker brown.

She flicked her tongue out to lick her bottom lip. A part of me I'd kept dormant for a long damn time roused, noticing how pink her tongue was, how plump her bottom lip. Damn.

"What about it?" she asked. "I don't know anything about construction or cabinets."

"I know Weston Duke taught you how to wield a

hammer." I'd known her dad by reputation mostly. Our tight group had talked about family as much as we had talked shit to each other.

A smile lifted both sides of her mouth, but then it was like a gate slammed down. She flattened her red lips. "If you're looking for precision measurements, it's not me."

This was an uphill battle and I didn't know the route to the top. I had no clue why the path had gotten treacherous. "Can we talk? For real?"

Her puffy lips stuck out as she considered my request. "Yeah, of course. Sorry." She pushed the door open. "Come in. Alder and Daisy are at work, and Laila's at school."

"Laila's a couple of grades behind Auggie." I stepped into the house and stuffed my hands in my pockets.

The old farmhouse was familiar. The hardwood floor was the same, nicely polished, but the walls were painted a soft shade of off-white. There weren't more than a few pictures on one wall and a picture of a sunset on the other. Poppy's mom had adorned the walls when she'd lived here. Pictures, sayings, and artwork had been like wallpaper.

I'd been here once for Poppy's birthday party. One of her sisters, Clover, had tried to push her way into the festivities the whole day. I had tried to be Hassie's shadow. A familiar burn of resentment branded the inside of my ribs. That me had long since learned a lesson.

"We can sit in the kitchen." Poppy waved me after her.

My gaze dropped to her butt cheeks, which looked like they were fighting under her black athletic leggings.

Firm and round, I bet they jiggled when they were slapped. My fingertips tingled.

I tore my attention off her ass and was caught in a cloud of sunshine and peaches. I suppressed a groan. She smelled like peaches with an ass like that?

Inhaling, I should regret cementing her scent to memory. Was I being creepy? I had no idea. Had she always smelled like a late summer day? Didn't kids smell like wet, sweaty dogs on late summer days?

We weren't kids anymore. Poppy was all woman, and I noticed every inch.

As she led me through the kitchen where my knotty alder cabinets were mounted, I admired my work. I didn't often get back into a house to see the lived-in version of my efforts. I took pictures when I finished and that was it.

I ran my hand over the counter. Damn, I did good work.

"They really like them." Her gaze was on me. She'd tucked her hands into the thin hoodie she was wearing. Just like her scent, the fabric was a soft peach color that brought out the color in her cheeks. Tendrils of hair stuck out around her head, escaping the hold of her ponytail like a rogue halo.

She lifted her brows and ducked her head. "Jensen?"

Shit. I was staring. She was angelic in a rumpled, athletic way. Like she'd played a couple games on the pitch and came to torment me about the bad decisions I had made. "Sorry. I don't usually get to see them after they've been used."

"They get abused with Alder too. He's always in the kitchen."

"He never used to be?"

"Nope." She pulled out a high-back chair from the

table and plopped down. She gestured to the seat on the end. "What's up?"

I sat and blew out a breath. I couldn't look at her. The conversation in the grocery store hadn't been the first time it'd happened. It'd been the only time I'd gotten confirmation. "I lost a job because of my emails."

"How?"

"I think I'm dyslexic."

"It is hereditary." There was no surprise in her tone.

I clenched my jaw as memories clashed in my brain. "Hassie said it couldn't be her and pointed out I was the one who did poorly in school."

A flash of sympathy ran through her gaze a moment before irritation set in. "She always liked rubbing it in how good she was at spelling."

"She spelled d-i-v-o-r-c-e easily enough."

Poppy let out a huff, then studied me, curiosity in her eyes. "You've never been told you have it?"

"No, my reading teacher told my mom she didn't read enough with me and that's why my fluency suffered." Mom had tried to read to me for an hour a night after that. As a young boy with too much energy, that nightly hour had been sheer torture. And it hadn't helped.

"Mrs. Groggins?" Poppy rolled her eyes. "I never liked her. How could she think that was true at all?"

"She didn't like me, that was for sure. But wouldn't she know? If I was dyslexic?"

Poppy shook her head. "I mean, if it's something she'd been educated about. They're only just starting to get legislation in the state moving to get more dyslexic awareness and learning tracts in the schools. Don't get me started on screening that should happen much earlier. It's frustrating because dyslexia affects, like, twenty percent of the population. One in five kids. Can you imagine? In small communities like ours, it could be more prevalent because of the hereditary factor. Other locations' ten percent incidence could be our thirty."

Her vehemence soothed the chastised kid inside of me. The boy who had never pleased his teachers. Who'd hated reading out loud so everyone could give me sideways looks when I stumbled through the passage.

It gave me the courage to tell her everything. I swallowed my humiliation. "I had some typos in an email, and I, uh, got my name wrong."

A brow cocked up. "Did you switch a couple of letters around, but it looked right?"

Story of my life. "The punctuation was off too. Maybe I should make that my tagline."

A chortle burst out of her. "Maybe. How do you know that cost you a job?"

"I heard the client tell a friend when I was at the store." Sympathy welled in her eyes, making the yellow shine. I looked away. "If I can't spell my name right, then how can I build decent cabinets? Even when I replied, I fucked up something." I rubbed the spot between my brows. "I triple-check my emails, but I get my promotional ads wrong. If someone doesn't proofread for me, I'm screwed."

"You compensate." She whirled her index finger by her head. "You've adapted. Your brain's got your back, but in doing so, it's also sabotaging you. Just a little."

"How do you mean?"

She fluttered her hands around. There was that energy she'd been known for. Maybe she'd just needed to warm up to me again. "You had to strong-arm your way through an educational system that's not set up for people who learn like you, so your brain adapted, but it's hard. Does Auggie get cranky after school?"

I snorted. "When doesn't he?" He could be quick with his temper and tears, and getting him to help with chores would become a meltdown.

"But it's gotten better since he started tutoring?"

I thought for a moment. "He's not zombified until he breaks down. Not as much."

"His brain was working overtime. But tutoring is giving him rules to read by so it's not so hard. Then he doesn't come home with glassy eyes and meltdowns."

"How do you know all this?" My relief at hearing her describe what we went through gave way to astonishment. "You're not dyslexic, are you?"

She shook her head. "Parents tell me."

Talking with her was fascinating. She'd only worked with Auggie once, yet it seemed like she knew him better than me. "He used to ask me to shut off the lights when we had dinner."

Her smile was kind. "Some of my students say it gets better, but I work with teens who say they still want a dark place after a tough day in school. One of the moms said she can tell when her middle schooler with dyscalculia has a heavy math day as soon as he walks out of class."

She tapped her fingers on the tabletop, her intelligent gaze on me.

Just like before, when she looked at me, I felt seen. Not exposed, just seen. For a guy who'd futilely dogged a girl who had shared little of her effort with him, the sensation was unique. And welcome. Like it was now.

"Do you use an extension or an app to proof your emails and texts?" she asked.

I clenched down, the corner of my jaw going rigid. I rubbed a hand down my face before resting it on the table. I came to her for superficial help, not realizing how deep my issues went. Like Debbie had told Auggie, his brain worked differently. And here I was, talking about apps and tutoring for myself. "So I guess I'm dyslexic."

"Oh." Dismay crossed her features. "I'm sorry. I work with it every day, and I didn't think about the fact that it's just been dropped on you."

"No, it's..." A relief. Something I'd really always known. "Don't I have to get diagnosed or something?"

"You could try, but from what families have told me, it's frustrating to get a diagnosis. Debbie usually just meets with the kid and the family. She can't officially diagnose, you know, but if she says a kid 'needs to be here,' then that's as good as gold. Usually, families have all had similar experiences." She shrugged. "It's bizarre. Generations struggle in school, get treated awful, and it never changes, yet we know all about dyslexia and we have tools for it. Despite that, the cycle repeats. So infuriating." She inhaled and shook her head. "Sorry. I hear a lot of horror stories from the families. Debbie started a center based on her experiences with her three kids."

"You really love what you do." I'd always admired her passion. "And you like working with kids."

"I never set out to, but I got used to working with kids when I coached soccer."

I sat back, my arms crossed, grinning. "You ended up coaching?"

She tucked a stray curl behind her ear. "Yes." Tension infused her body. "So, about the help. Do you want to do some research first? I can set you up with those programs on your phone and computer." She ducked her head. "There's tutoring."

"Tutoring?" Alarm piped through my veins. If yesterday morning hadn't been so humiliating, I'd have laughed it off and figured out something else. Maybe I could sit beside Auggie and go through his lessons where no one else could see me, not even Debbie.

"We have adult tracks." She screwed up her face. "Debbie does, I mean. I haven't taken on any clients officially. I have to find a place to work out of first."

"Got any in mind?" I needed her help to keep my brain from sabotaging me, but I wanted to know more about her. Poppy Duke was right in front of me after two decades, and I didn't want it to end.

"One." She rolled her eyes, then shook her head. "It won't work though. I have to start looking."

"What place?"

She went still, her gaze searching mine. What was she looking for? I waited under her warm perusal, hoping she'd judge me up to her standards. A spark of bitterness flared deep in my chest. I was tired of waiting for a girl to find me worthy.

Just as I tore my gaze away, she cleared her throat. "My grandma Annie passed away and left a trust behind. Me and my siblings each get a property. This house was Alder's."

"Each of you?" I thought for a moment. "Isn't Lily in town? In your grandma's old place? Violet?"

I'd seen Lily around, but she'd been busy with her kids. She might not even recognize me. She was the youngest Duke and had been a few years behind me in school. Violet had also gotten married to a guy who'd been several years older than us.

Poppy nodded. "I get the old Perez home on the edge of town."

The Perez couple had retired as snowbirds decades ago, but their old farmhouse had been one of the first in Coal Haven. "Nice."

Her lips thinned. "It would be. Linda used to live there, and my grandparents bought it. But several years ago, Grandma Annie changed her will and trust. She put all the property in a trust with these bizarre rules. I have to be married."

"And you're not?" I had assumed not since I'd only seen just her, but I caught myself leaning forward. She wasn't wearing a ring.

"Nope. Never got married," she said flatly.

Never? She and I were almost thirty-five. No one had captivated her enough, or had she dated losers?

I glanced at the cabinets. A thread of suspicion fluttered in my brain. Didn't Lily get married a couple of years ago? Then Violet? Alder had called Daisy his wife when I'd installed the cabinets. Was the timing fortuitous? Or more than a coincidence?

"Wait—is that why Alder— That's not— He didn't —" I snapped my teeth together.

Poppy's eyes were wide. "No." Her voice pitched up. "He's always wanted Daisy back." She bit her bottom lip. Why'd she seem suddenly hesitant to talk about it?

"It's not my business."

Poppy blew out a breath. Her shoulders hunched. "They're all in love," she said as if she'd heard all my questions loud and clear. "Lily and Eliot are so in love. Violet and Evander. Alder and Daisy. The trust just sped things up. Or created it in the first place," she finished with a mutter.

I mulled over her information. I'd seen them all around town. Not a lot. But they'd been in love. The looks between each couple, the shared smiles, the body language. It'd all showed me what my marriage had lacked. "And you?"

She held her palms up and gave me an empty smile. "No husband, no house. And in four years, any unclaimed property gets sold. Aunt Linda gets the money."

Maybe Linda needed the money, but it seemed like a waste of an inheritance. "It's in her best interest if you stay single?"

"She says she doesn't care, but she does have to believe the marriage is real and sign off on it after a year. Dad too."

"Your boyfriend isn't interested?"

She wrinkled her nose. "I'm not seeing anyone."

Her tone was so disgusted I laughed. At least she didn't bust me for probing for information. "Okay, no guys. What about a girlfriend?"

"I'm not into girls, but if Debbie wasn't already married, I would one hundred percent ask her to marry me for a year to get that place." A gust of breath left her. "It's beautiful. I could put the office upstairs and look out the big window. That property is so breathtaking."

My mind spun, but I was pleased that boyfriends weren't off the table. For no reason. My gaze dipped to how well her athletic shirt clung to the swells of her breasts. Damn, she had nice tits.

What were we talking about? Oh, right. "You need a husband to get the house of your dreams?"

She nodded, and her gaze strayed to the window like she was imagining working in the home that could be hers if she had a wedding ring. "It probably needs some work. Linda's been renting it, and the current tenants are out at the end of May. She said the place could use some updating, and I don't have the time or the funds."

She needed a husband and a contractor. I needed a proofreader and a project that could really get my name out there. The Perez house was a gem in Coal Haven. If I could tie my name to those renovations...

No. That was crazy.

Or it was the leap I needed to finally secure the job that would give me the stability and flexibility I needed to be a single dad to my son. "I have an idea."

Chapter Three

Poppy

"Can you believe it? Marry him as if I didn't grow up seeing him lust after another girl?" I reached the far wall of the living room, pivoted, and stomped in the other direction. My angry pacing resonated through Alder and Daisy's house.

I'd told Alder what Jensen had proposed and he'd only cocked a brow, said it might be worth thinking about, and went outside to play with Laila. Daisy was tucked into the corner of the couch, already in her pajamas at seven at night. Her head oscillated as I went from wall to wall.

"It's been a long time," she said gently. "And he's divorced."

I scoffed. "He's hung up on her. I know it."

"To be fair, you've never known him to not be hung up on her. But a lot of time has passed. He's raising their kid, and I haven't seen her around." She tipped her head. "If it makes you feel better, he never mentioned Hassie once when he was putting in the cabinets."

The sound of an engine came from outside. I continued my back and forth, my hands on my hips. I could have the house. It could be mine. I'd just have to marry a guy who might still be obsessed with his ex.

It wouldn't be a love arrangement. Just because it'd worked out for Lily, Violet, and Alder didn't mean it would be the same for me. I wasn't interested in Jensen anyway. Or his abs. Those broad shoulders. That ass I could bounce a quarter off of.

I shook my head just as a knock resounded at the door.

Violet poked her head in. "Alder said we could just come in. I want to make sure."

I stopped with a stomp. "He told you?"

"I'm the guilty one," Daisy said with a timid raise of her hand. "I thought all the experts could weigh in on this one."

I couldn't be mad. The only reason I hadn't texted all of them was because Alder had arrived home right after Jensen had left. Then I'd ranted to Daisy. She must've sent an SOS text to my sisters when she'd changed clothes. Had I been that unhinged?

Violet entered, and Lily was right behind her.

I waved a hand toward the couch and recliner. "Might as well sit."

When they were settled, I dropped to a cross-legged position on the floor. "I can't marry him."

"I thought you two used to be tight," Violet said.

"Not tight." We'd been each other's biggest competition as kids. Who could kick farther, run faster, throw harder. Who did the best on a test. Who told the funniest story. "I was never a girl to him."

"I bet you are now." Lily chortled. "You were wearing those pants today?"

I frowned at my leggings. They were comfortable. I never did go for my run today, but I'd kept them on. "Yeah?"

The smile still played along Lily's lips. "And that shirt?"

"If his eyes could leave prints," Violet said, "I bet we'd find evidence on your *T* and *A*."

I pulled my shirt out. When I let go, it clung to my torso. "Why would he?"

"Your ass is fire in those," Lily said. "You might as well not be wearing anything." She waved her hand like she was clearing a cloud of smoke. "Regardless, he offered a deal. What was it exactly?"

I took a steadying breath. "If he married me, he could renovate the house and use it for marketing material and brochures." The Perez house was a piece of local history. If he did good work, and if Alder and Daisy's cabinets were an indicator, he was excellent, it'd go farther than a few typos. "I'd get the house, but in turn, I proof the pamphlets and brochures. Get him set up with some software."

"That's it?" Violet asked.

I nodded, unable to tell them specifics. Jensen could tell them, but not me. I couldn't reveal that I tutored Auggie without risking my reputation and my job. My sisters wouldn't tell anyone, but I had enough on my mind.

My oldest sister inspected me.

I wrung my hands together, trying not to wither

under her scrutiny. "We ran into each other. He was more excited to see me than I was him." They all nodded like they had bought my story. "I can't do it. It'd be crazy."

A little giggle left Daisy. Her eyes flared. "Sorry. You sound like I did after Alder proposed his bargain. I thought he'd lost his marbles. It was crazy," she agreed. "It was also the right decision. Even if we didn't fall back in love, it would've still been my best option."

She'd had to move and had nowhere to go with Laila. Alder had wanted the house. The difference was that he had really wanted Daisy back. There'd been no falling back in love. They'd never been out of it. This house was a nice bonus.

"I can't," I said weakly. Jensen wasn't a stranger, but this was marriage. Living with him. Hearing about Hassie.

Concern crinkled Violet's brow. "Why not? What bothers you so bad about it? Don't you feel safe with him?"

"I'd probably be the safest," I said bitterly. "I'd probably be one of the guys to him. He was all about Hassie. Always comparing us. I never measured up."

Daisy's mouth formed an *O*. Lily did a slow nod.

"I see." Understanding filled Violet's voice. "You think it'll be a year of 'Hassie did it this way'?"

"I couldn't compete with her at seven or eleven. Or fourteen," I said. After looking her up, it still held true. "Now she's a professional barrel racer, sponsored by some boot company—*and* hat brand, and she's on posters." I held a hand up. "I don't want to compete with her. I'm not interested in Jensen."

The three of them exchanged knowing looks.

"What?" I snapped.

"Not interested?" Violet asked. "Or afraid you'll be too interested?"

The image of him in nothing but running shorts that revealed impressive quads shimmered in my brain, crystal clear. "It doesn't matter. I don't need to hear that Hassie looks better in a dress than I do."

Daisy's scandalized gasp echoed in the room. "He told you that?"

"We were twelve, but yeah." I rubbed my temples.

"Damn," Lily said. "He must've been afraid he'd lose his crush if he looked too hard anywhere else. It's still wrong—and he was wrong."

I shrugged, but my confusion lingered. That didn't make sense. Jensen had been devoted. He'd been a devoted classmate; he'd just kept me in my place. "It's insane. I can't get married to a stranger."

"I married a stranger." Lily's smile was indulgent. "It was pretty nice, honestly."

I scowled at her. "You're not helping. None of you are."

"We can see the big picture better," Daisy said. "Personal feelings about him and Hassie aside, we can see that you're disappointed that you might not get the Perez house. You're frustrated that you can't find a decent place to set up your tutoring center. And trust me, I've seen the places to rent around Coal Haven and Crocus Valley. It's rough out there."

"Alder doesn't have any open units?" He'd invested in a ton of property. Technically, none of his purchases had turned into investments yet. He'd put a fair amount of money into renovating them. Daisy said they got snatched up as soon as the paint dried.

Had he used Jensen for any of his rental improvements? Had Jensen asked, or had his flubs made him hesitant to put himself out there?

I flicked away the thought of Jensen. I was not worried about his business. I needed to concentrate on mine. I had no job, and I couldn't rely on Debbie to send me her scraps forever.

"And we see the bonus," Violet said gently. "You're not marrying a total stranger. You just don't know the adult him." She set her phone on the armrest. "Did you get all that, Clover?"

"Oh my god. Jensen actually married Hassie and then they got divorced?" Clover's scandalized tone rang through the living room. "And now you're marrying him?"

Shocked but pleased I wouldn't have to catch Clover up and repeat all of this, I shook my head. "I'm not marry—"

"You have a chance to own the Perez house," Clover cut in. "The *Perez house*. Remember when we trick-or-treated there after Aunt Linda moved out and you were so upset with her? You wanted it to stay in the family."

Our grandparents might've owned it, but the house had been as good as gone. It wasn't like the new renters would let the owner's grandkids wander through whenever they wanted.

"Is he hot?" Clover asked.

I huffed. "That's not the point."

"He is." She squealed. No wonder Violet called her. If they wanted me to consider the opportunity, Clover was the one who'd cut through the haze and get me out of my head. "He must've turned into a snacky snack if Hassie married him."

"He's okay." I ignored the way the three women

exchanged another round of looks and bit back smiles. "He makes cabinets for a living." It showed in his biceps.

"So, dad-bod hot or could he have a calendar of his own?" she pressed.

"You mean is he one month in a calendar or all of them?" My question was a cover for an instant answer I refused to say.

A whistle came over the line. "He's that good-looking."

"I think he has a lot of muscles," Lily said, loud enough that Clover would hear perfectly.

Daisy crossed her legs under her. "Would he be the one I heard one of the playground monitors say could strip her down like he stripped her grandma's cupboards?"

Violet snickered. "That's gotta be him. Look, I'm all in with Evander, but I think we can all agree that if Jensen made a Cabinet of the Month calendar, he'd raise some money."

"Maybe he can do that for your center," Clover suggested.

"You guys are not helping!" I said indignantly.

"I think we're helping, just not the way you hoped." Clover was suddenly serious. "I think you knew the decision that would work the best, and you wanted us to agree. But, Poppy, you hated being so far away from family. You love Coal Haven as much as the rest of us, and you light up when you talk about forming your own center here. Even Debbie's willing to throw you clients."

She had said she'd hire me, or I could start my own clinic. I'd been too enraptured by the idea of being my own boss to get hired again. There was a niche in the area, and she'd even had to turn down the school's requests for her to hold workshops for the teachers.

"You know what you want to do, and you know what you're afraid to do," Violet said. "But it's you who has to decide."

●●●

Jensen

I put the lid on the stain and admired my work. The cabinets were mine, for the shop I was trying to keep functioning and filled with projects. As it was, I had four old chairs—none of them matched—and two tables I was refinishing for a previous client. Bit projects like that helped supplement income, but they wouldn't sustain a career.

I'd found an old set of cupboards at the thrift store in Dickinson. The irony that I was staining them to later mount so they could hold all my stains wasn't lost on me. The small dose of humor kept the dread at bay.

Job hunting sucked, but I was getting closer to filling out applications. Much of it was seasonal or required that I be away from home before school and beyond. I had Mom to help, but she went south for the winters, and if I told her an inkling of my issues, she'd cancel all her plans. I couldn't have that. I would not be the adult son holding his mom back.

I took my phone out and snapped a few photos of my efforts. My website needed new blood—and a fresh set of eyes, but I hadn't heard from Poppy. I had looked forward to hearing from her again—about an answer of course.

I couldn't believe I'd suggested we marry. Who'd have thought I'd entertain the idea of saying vows again? I didn't have an issue with the vows themselves. It was that the other party hadn't been interested in upholding them, but the agreement Poppy and I would have mitigated that.

An engine sounded from outside.

Had Mom stopped by? She usually waited for when Auggie was out of school, but maybe she needed to talk to me about something private. Like that "friend" of hers in Phoenix she constantly referred to. Dad had passed almost twenty years ago, and Albert was the first man I'd heard her mention.

I popped my head out the door. Poppy paced next to her SUV.

My heart sank, yet I soaked her in. She wore a different set of pants today that didn't mold over her ass nearly as thoroughly as her running tights. They were black sweats that cuffed at the ankle that she paired with a long-sleeved shirt. Now that thing hugged her curves, draping over her tits to pool around her generous hips. Poppy looked like she had thighs that could crush a man's head while he begged for it.

"Hey." I might as well get the rejection over with. After the radio silence for the last two days, I had assumed she was avoiding me and I'd never see her again. She'd decide she couldn't live in a town where she might run across a guy who'd rather marry her for tutoring than pay her.

Poppy jolted and spun around. "Hey." Her gaze jumped from the house to the shop. The old farmhouse was white, but between Mom and then me as the owners, it'd been well cared for. The floors inside creaked like an old place, same with the stairs, but it had all its charm.

She twisted her fingers together. "Can we talk?"

"Come on in." I pushed the door open wider and waited for her to enter.

When she did, she slowed to a crawl, her wide gaze taking it all in. I had different sections of cabinets. All served a purpose, but had also been for marketing images to show off my skills. Her attention landed on a bar in the corner with an immaculate granite countertop and a TV mounted over it. Rows of juice packets and mineral waters lined the back instead of liquor bottles.

The corner of her mouth tipped up. "A juice bar?"

I laughed. "I never made that connection, but yeah. It keeps Auggie entertained when he's home. If he's home sick, I have a chaise lounge under that tarp he can lie on."

"Oh, that's a good idea." She crossed her arms, pulling her shirt tight over the swells of her breasts.

I waited for her to start, but she just rocked on her heels, a nervous energy circling her.

I'd rather have an answer than wonder how much better I could do if I didn't fuck up my name in emails. "It's all right if you say no. I mean, it's a wild proposition, right? I just thought, you know, two birds, one stone. I'd hate to see that house—"

"I'll do it."

I shook my head, making sense of her words. Just like that I was engaged again, and I had no fucking clue how to feel other than I was glad it was with a friend this time. "You'll do it? Get married?"

Color leached from her face, but she nodded. This had to be just as weird and confusing for her, but her reaction made her look ready to vomit. Mutual benefits weren't enough if the idea made her miserable.

"Poppy, clearly you don't like the idea—"

"I haven't had... Men have let me down." She swallowed, and vulnerability shone from her eyes. "I was never what they wanted, and I'd resigned to never getting married. But this is a business arrangement. Right?"

Her earnest question caught me off guard. She sounded like she needed it to be nothing but a business deal. It was.

So why was there an emptiness inside my chest? "I've been through one empty marriage before," I said carefully. "I don't care to do it again. So, yeah, just a contract. We each hold up our end and we're good."

"We go our separate ways after a year?" she asked cautiously.

But she'd still be in Coal Haven? My neck was tight when I thought she could leave at any time. "In a year, we go our separate ways."

"Okay."

"Okay."

We eyed each other.

She cocked a hip out. "I'll let Aunt Linda know. And I'll have to tell my parents. My siblings know what's up, but everyone else will have to believe it."

"Except Auggie." My son had already seen one failed marriage. I wasn't going to let him think I'd let down another woman, nor could he start thinking he wasn't enough for the women in his life.

A crease formed between her brows. "Of course. I wouldn't want him getting hurt in the process. Whatever you need to tell him, I support."

Her care when it came to him hit me down deep. "Okay."

"Okay." She nibbled on her lower lip.

Could a guy do that while kissing her? Just pull that plump flesh between his teeth and—

"I should tell my parents first. How should we say we met?"

"Won't the truth work?"

"Your son is a client. Confidentiality."

"It's fine."

"Would Auggie care if people knew? Some kids are really private."

He might not. He'd been doing sessions for two years. It was a normal part of life for him now. But that she asked? My appreciation grew. She'd shown him more consideration than his own mom. "We can just say we met through Debbie and let people fill in their own blanks."

Relief crossed her face. "Yeah. That'll work. And we don't have to live in the house. Aunt Linda won't rent it out if we're renovating. I just have to have been married at least a year to get ownership, but I'm sure she'll let me work out of it if I'm married."

Wild rules. "You can live here until the year is up."

Her mouth dropped open. She closed it. Blinked a few times. Had she not thought about living arrangements? Had wrapping her head around marrying me been that overwhelming?

But then I'd been married before. She hadn't. "Will you want a wedding?"

"A wedding?" A look of horror crossed her face. "God no. All that planning?" She shuddered. "Lily, Violet, and Alder all did a *justice of the peace* wedding. Well, Violet and Evander had an early ceremony so they could get the house faster and had a reception the next summer. So no. No need for a real wedding."

She might not want the planning, but there was a longing in her expression that suggested she'd like something more than stopping in an office downtown.

"So?" she asked. "Are we doing this?"

Her gaze stroked down my stain-splattered hoodie that read "Hollis Cabinets," then lower to my carpenter jeans with a hole in the knee. I leaned against my workbench and crossed my arms. "You don't want to."

"I don't want a relationship, but it's hard to separate the idea of a marriage with one. Feels wrong."

"Why?"

She scrunched that pert nose of hers. "I thought you would understand."

I scratched behind my ear, muddling through her retort. The curiosity was apparent, but the bitterness was a mystery. Had she been hurt before? "Because I'm divorced?" When she nodded, I shrugged. "I still believe in the idea of love and marriage, but I've also seen that love doesn't make it work alone. Now I have Auggie and he's my main concern, so no, I'm not after a relationship either."

Her gaze was stricken. This wasn't easy for her, but she wanted the house. I could help with that. "I get a house. You just get some proofreading."

"I get a respected project under my name." I pointed to the Hollis Cabinets sign. In case that wasn't enough, I had more. "Mom spent much of my early years in school defending me and herself. I couldn't read well. I shouldn't be obsessed with graphic novels. My books shouldn't have so many pictures."

Poppy held her hand up. "Who the hell said that? Who complained that you weren't reading and then when you were, in fact, reading, complained about the format?"

"Mr. Gilding."

Poppy rolled her eyes. "He needed to retire before we even started school."

"That." I pointed at her. "That's why I'm willing to do this. I've never had to prove myself to you."

"We were in competition all the time."

"Because you were intimidating as fuck."

She barked out a laugh. "I was not."

"You were smart and you could kick my ass on the playground. I never could kick as far as you in kickball." I'd tried. "I used to practice at home, and Dad would help."

"I learned to boot from soccer. And I used to practice too."

Pleasure infused me. I'd gotten to her enough that she'd put in extra time to show me up? "Yeah, well, it was impressive and I'd tell Dad that you made it to the swings."

The corner of her mouth tipped up. "Should I admit to practicing with Clover because you were getting better and better?"

A chuckle burst out of me. "My whole life has been trying to keep up with women." The humor slowly dwindled. My time with Hassie had been nothing but me trying to keep pace with her, be good enough for her, only to fail over and over. "Anyway, it's a year, and like kickball, we both have a goal and are using each other to improve. I'll refurbish the Perez house, and you'll fix my company. Maybe my brain while you're at it."

"Your brain doesn't need fixing," she said earnestly. "I can't fix your company because I doubt it needs fixing either. And we can start lessons whenever. I'm subbing for Debbie. I'd like to talk to the school about doing some workshops over the summer and next fall, but I haven't been trying to build a client base until I knew which zip code I'd land in."

"You're in my zip code now, four-ten."

Her left cheek twitched. "I'm a little taller than that these days."

"You sure about that?"

She scowled, her lips forming that mutinous pout that brought back memories. "I'll call my parents and tell them the news."

"I'll talk to Mom. She'll have to know the truth." She had been supportive of my marriage, but she wasn't Hassie's biggest fan. "I can't let her think I'm just going to ruin another marriage."

"Fair. Then we'll talk to Linda about when we can get into the house."

Her use of "we" wasn't lost on me. Us. We. I had been single for years, but before that, those words had been more like a manifestation. In reality, there had been no us. No we. Just her and whatever she wanted.

No. As much as Poppy fascinated me, I wasn't ready to dive into a relationship. But maybe I could at least experience a marriage that was balanced for once.

Chapter Four

Jensen

Mom sat at my kitchen table, worry lining the corners of her eyes. I'd asked her to come because I had to talk to her and Auggie together. Mom was worried, but I couldn't deny the lightness inside of me. I had a chance to improve my business, and I got to hang out with Poppy more.

I gave Auggie a ham sandwich and set the plate with the other two between me and Mom. When she'd first been adjusting to the life of a single working mom, we'd had a lot of sandwiches. I'd never touch bologna again, but I still liked ham on toasted sourdough. It'd been her Friday night meal. A little reward, with chips, after getting through a week of work, school, and practices.

"I know I've said it's not good to lie, Auggie, but I'm going to have to ask you to do a little bit of it."

Auggie nodded and picked up his sandwich. His eyes were glassy. I'd kept the light off over the table. I had opened the blinds as wide as possible instead. Poppy's words ran through my head. He must've had a hard brain day at school.

Mom didn't touch the food. The bag of nacho Doritos was open next to her elbow. She only ate them with us, but she hadn't touched those either.

She tucked a strand of graying blonde hair behind her ear. "What's going on?"

"You remember Poppy?" I asked.

Confusion formed a line between her brows. "Poppy Duke? Yes, of course."

"My tutor?" Auggie asked.

"Yep. Remember I said we're old friends? Well, we both need a little help with something, and in order for me to help her, I need to, uh, marry her."

Mom's jaw fell open.

"You're marrying the tutor?" Auggie asked and took a bite of his sandwich.

Auggie was chill, but I'd have to ease Mom's shock. "In order for her to inherit the Perez house, yes."

Incredulity filled Mom's expression. "The Perez house? Marriage?" She slumped in her chair. "I didn't realize you and Poppy kept in touch."

"We didn't. We haven't. She subbed for Auggie's normal tutor, and afterward, we got to talking." I didn't tell Mom I tracked her down because my business was suffering over my typos and the way I talked. She'd feel responsible because some asshole told her she wasn't reading to me enough. "I could do some work in the house and use it in my promo materials and on my website. Even new people moving to town admire that house."

"She needs to be married?" Mom gave her head a shake.

"A stipulation of the trust her grandma left behind. So we marry for a year, she'll live here, but as a guest, and when her parents and her aunt Linda are around, we'll pretend to be a happily married couple until they sign off on us."

Mom folded her arms. "I always liked Weston and Magnolia. Linda too. I don't like lying to them."

"I know." There was no way around that part. I liked Poppy, but neither of us wanted a relationship. So there was no chance of this being real. I had to build a stable future for me and my son, just like Poppy had to do the same for her.

Auggie grabbed a handful of chips and crunched through them. "Okay. Does she get the room upstairs?"

There were two open rooms. The smaller of them was across from Auggie's room upstairs. The bigger one was across from mine. "I think she'd like the bigger one. Upstairs can be her working office until I'm done with her place."

"I can't…" Mom snapped her mouth shut. "A marriage of convenience?"

"That's all it'll be." It'd have to be. I wasn't putting myself out there again. "But we'd have to pretend it's for real to everyone outside our circle."

Mom's gaze darted to Auggie. How could I expect a ten-year-old to play along with something so important?

It was worth the gamble.

My phone vibrated. I glanced at it and did a double take. Poppy's name was on the screen. "Excuse me."

I ducked into the laundry room that was also the entry from the garage, a mudroom, coat closet, and catchall for Auggie's sports equipment.

"Hey," I answered, hating the way I anticipated her

voice on the other end. I wasn't going to be that guy again.

"They're coming to Coal Haven." Her panicked reply carried over the phone. "They're coming to meet you."

"Who? Your parents?"

"Yes," she hissed. "They said Aunt Linda could meet us and talk logistics."

I recall liking Magnolia and Weston Duke. A small tendril of anxiety wound through me. Like Mom, I didn't want to lie to them either. "Okay. When?"

"I don't know! This weekend. Tomorrow."

"Poppy, are you losing your shit?" She'd been detached at times when I'd talked to her before.

There was a moment of silence. "Yes."

"Why? You knew this would happen."

"I didn't know it'd be this soon."

That didn't change much. "I can grill. We can do sandwiches. Wraps. Whatever."

A squeak came over the line. "You don't care?"

"We're pretending for a good reason, and we're both too old for your dad to be all *you gonna treat my girl right?*" As a dad, I would understand any protectiveness, and I'd treat Poppy right. Hassie might've smashed my pride, but deep down, I knew I hadn't done anything wrong except expect her to grow feelings where none could take root.

She let out a long exhale. "It's happening."

"I'm telling Mom and Auggie now."

"How's it going?" She was back to the professional tutor I'd talked to before.

"I'm in the entry talking to you."

She chuckled. "Touché."

I grinned, not minding at all that I was squirreled

away with her on the phone. "I think Mom's reeling, but I told her most of the deal."

"Most?"

"I didn't want her to feel bad about, you know, the typos."

"Ah. She always had such a soft heart."

"Soft but strong," I agreed.

"I'm nervous, Jensen." Vulnerability filled her voice, and I wanted to soothe it all away.

"It'll be fine. It's just another game. We play until the whistle blows."

"I can still kick farther than you."

"I'd be disappointed if you didn't, four-ten. I haven't played kickball in twenty-five years." I thought for a moment. She was nervous about the meet and greet. How could I ease that for her? "Wanna invite your siblings?"

"Which ones?"

"All of them."

"All? Jensen, it's tomorrow."

"You saw my impressive juice bar."

Her light laugh went right into my ear and curled around my heart. As a kid, I had liked a fired-up Poppy. Hearing her laugh? A new goal formed in my head. Make Poppy laugh more. And see her boot a ball across the yard again.

"Are you sure?" she asked.

"I'm still in. I won't be the first to cave."

"Oh, I'm not giving up."

"Good to hear. Tomorrow. Tell me the time, and I'll get the food ready. Auggie will love it if any other kids show up. Oh, and, four-ten, bring your ball."

"I have a whole bag of them in Alder's garage. Thanks, Jensen."

"Anytime." I meant it. Poppy had always given as much as she took. Another thought occurred to me, one that shadowed my growing excitement for tomorrow. "I'm not, uh, going to talk to Hassie until she calls next." Which could be tomorrow or next year. "We need to deal with people who are actually here."

"Sure. No problem. I'll take your lead with that. Oh, and tell your mom hi. She should come tomorrow, too, if it's not too awkward for her."

She was thinking about Mom? Appreciation warmed me from the inside out. "I'll let her know."

"Hey," I rushed out before she disconnected. "I'll grab some rings."

"Oh." Seconds of silence ticked by. Did that thought sit heavy with her too? We needed a symbol, but the rings wouldn't mean a thing. Did she like diamonds? "O-okay. I'll get yours."

"Don't worry about it. I did some work for a jeweler, and he can set me up. Just let me know your size."

"Yeah. Sure. Don't spend too much—but don't get one that turns my hand green."

"Deal."

We disconnected. I was grinning at the sheer absurdness of buying wedding rings again. Then I caught myself staring at my phone. I stuffed it into my back pocket. Not once had my ex given my mom that much consideration. But then Poppy had always been different from Hassie. A fact I hadn't appreciated so much until now.

●●●

Poppy

·   ·   ·

I knocked on the front door. Jensen's house looked the same as I remembered—a two-story, white farmhouse with green shutters. Pounding resounded from the other side of the door and it whipped open.

A 3D Auggie grinned at me. "Hi!"

"Hi, Auggie. Nice to officially meet you." I held out a hand. He stared at it for a moment before putting his small fingers in mine and giving me a sturdy shake before letting go. Now, I could see both of his parents in him, but he definitely reminded me of the boy I used to race on the playground. He was probably as fast as his dad had been. "We got you a ring!"

"Sorry." Jensen appeared behind him, crossing the living room, and nerves exploded through my belly. This whole day had me twisted inside out. "Auggie beat me to the greeting."

"Can I give her the ring, Dad?" Auggie jumped up and down.

The air thickened between me and Jensen, but Auggie's energy defused some of it. Jensen dug in his pocket. I had offered to buy them, but he said he'd done some cabinetry work at a small clothing store in Crocus Valley that had a jewelry counter. The place was close enough to Coal Haven that if someone saw him, the rumor mill would work in our favor.

He held his hand out to Auggie. A simple diamond ring was nestled in his palm. I'd told Jensen just to go with simple. People could have their opinions, but there was no need to waste money on something that would be worn for only a year.

"That's not real, is it?" I sounded as alarmed as I felt. It was gorgeous. Just my style. A legit diamond was just too much.

"The lab-grown ones are reasonable," Jensen said, and it matched the band I could get for myself. "I couldn't let your parents think that I skimped on your ring."

My heart was pounding. Auggie was holding the ring out like he wanted to put it on. "They wouldn't care as long as I didn't care."

Jensen only shrugged. His reputation was on the line, so I wouldn't argue. Besides, I could return the ring when we ended things.

But it was so pretty, sparkling in Auggie's grip.

I held my hand out. There was a slight tremble. The diamond might be real, but this marriage wasn't. Auggie was excited, Jensen was satisfied, and I would get to enjoy the shine of a gem.

The warm metal slid on. Satisfaction spread across Auggie's face. Jensen's brow furrowed when the ring was fully seated. This had to mess with his mind.

Guilt ate away at the earlier nerves. I brandished my newly bedazzled hand. "Guess it's official."

Auggie's eyes lit up. "Dad said you have lots of nieces and nephews."

Jensen ruffled his hair. "He's excited to finally have other kids here to play with."

"I get more every year. What can I do to help get everything ready?" I asked.

"I'm cutting strawberries." Auggie rushed away.

Jensen pushed the door open, a wry smile on his lips. "Now that we're engaged, you can come in."

I laughed, the tension easing. "Leveling up." I went inside to help get food ready.

Only an hour later, everyone milled in and out of Jensen's shop. The main rolling door was open. The

April day was gorgeous, with a breeze that hinted at the warm weather on its way. I'd almost worn jeans, but Jensen wouldn't back down on a boot-off.

I didn't want him to. I spun the simple band on my finger. I was getting used to the rock.

Lily and Eliot were perusing the cabinets inside. I'd heard Lily gush about the colors and how our grandma's old house could use an update. Evander hovered over a newly walking Willa while Violet frolicked with Cali and Kellan. Daisy sat on a lawn chair, her hand resting on her rounded belly. Alder was kicking my soccer ball around with Laila and Auggie. Jensen's mom cheered them on.

My other brother, Jasper, hadn't been able to make it. If I had been getting married for real, he would've carved out time. Maybe. It was calving season. Clover hadn't been able to make the drive in time, but she insisted on being one of the witnesses.

A twinge of longing dragged through my chest. I'd love to have all my family at my wedding. But it didn't matter. This didn't mean anything.

I rubbed the center of my chest. I just enjoyed when my family was all together. They were my favorite people.

As soon as I'd heard about the trust three years ago, I'd been drawn to Coal Haven. Hadn't thought I'd move here. Apprehension filled me. What had I been thinking? I wasn't even sure I could open the center and keep it that way, yet here I was, planning to get married to just get a space to work in. Without insurance reimbursement, lessons cost a fortune. Who'd pay me for that? Who'd donate money? I'd need a lot. Debbie had generated tons of community support, but fundraising was almost a full-time gig for her.

Hadn't I learned my lesson before? Twice?

I was stubborn to a fault, and I was dragging Jensen in with me.

I tightened my ponytail. I was standing next to Jensen as he and Dad talked about the work he'd done on the house and what he planned to do to my place.

Our place. I could not fuck that up today.

Linda hadn't arrived yet, but nerves rattled inside me. I must crackle when I walked.

Jensen had a mineral water in one hand as he talked to my parents. He slid an arm around my waist, and I stiffened. The muscles in his arm twitched against the small of my back.

Relax. This was supposed to be natural between us. I soaked up his heat and relaxed. Just a little.

"So it started out as long distance?" Mom asked. Her dark hair was pulled back, the gray in it looking like intentional highlights. I had told her that I hadn't wanted to say anything since I'd had a string of duds. She hadn't pushed, and if she was hurt by my lack of transparency, that was actually a lie, she was hiding it.

I nodded, the thought of lying to her sticking in my throat.

"Auggie has a bad habit of walking around with his laptop while in a lesson," Jensen answered. "He was getting a drink, and there she was."

I smiled, more from the memory of being glued to my screen when Jensen had been wandering shirtless behind Auggie than from his story.

Dad considered me, then Jensen. "You all had a pretty tight group, but I didn't think you were that close into adulthood."

"I'm old enough to know what I like now," Jensen

said, his tone confident. "Old enough to know when it's right. It's never felt right until Poppy."

My knees went weak. God, if he meant that for real? I'd melt into a lovestruck puddle. "Makes you wonder what would've happened if we hadn't moved."

A twinge of regret darkened Dad's eyes. "Now that you're all coming back, I wonder too." His smile was tight. "What would've happened if I had never gotten to know Gentry King well enough to hear the story of his late wife's trust funds and then pass the tale along to Mom."

"It's all working out." Mom patted his arm. "But I agree. Would've been nice not to have stipulations." She beamed at me. "Do you have a date set?"

Jensen and I had talked about this. We'd go to the justice of the peace two weeks after our announcement, so it'd look like we put some planning in versus rushing through vows to get into the house faster.

Still, the question hit differently when his strong arm was around me and my shoulder butted into that defined chest I'd seen a week ago.

A car rolled down the drive. I froze, watching the silver sedan park at the end of the line of cars in my driveway. Uncle Darren got out first. He squinted at us and dipped his head. Aunt Linda stood up. She gave us a nervous wave. My tension returned.

"There she is!" Dad bellowed. He turned to us. "Excuse me."

He strode to meet my aunt and uncle. I let out a long breath.

"You're doing good," Jensen muttered. "Except for turning into a statue when I touched you."

"I was not a statue."

He flattened his hand on my side and brushed up until his thumb scraped the underside of my boob. I jerked.

His deep chuckle vibrated right into me. "Point proven."

I glared at him, but he only slid his hand back down to my waist, his strong fingers curling along my waistband. Butterflies unfurled in my belly, lazily stretching their wings and deciding they liked his hand on me. A lot.

"I'm not used to PDAs and..." I swallowed. "I haven't dated in a while."

"Same."

"You haven't dated since the divorce?" Incredulity distracted me from my approaching aunt and uncle. Had Jensen and Hassie been separated longer than the five years they'd been divorced? Dismay curdled the acid in my stomach. Was he waiting for Hassie?

Of course he was. It was Jensen.

"Hard to do as a single dad." His tone said there was more.

Like that it was hard to date when he was still obsessed with his ex-wife?

Dad clapped Darren on the shoulder and the group started for us. Alder jogged toward them, and the crew stopped. I struggled not to wring my fingers together. I'd love this gathering—for any other reason. I adored family get-togethers, but a giant lie sucked the fun out of it.

"What are my red-light touches?" Jensen asked close to my ear.

His breath tickled loose strands of my hair and a shiver traced down my spine. So far, every touch had been a blazing green light. Which meant warning bells should be ringing.

"Uh..." Words weren't coming. All that came to mind was what he could do with those big, hot hands.

"What about a peck on the cheek?" His lips were close to my face. He dipped his head more. "On the mouth?"

"I don't know," I whispered. My instinctive answer was *yes!*

Violet had joined my parents and my aunt and uncle.

His hand shifted down lower on my hip. "If I touch your ass, is that too far?"

"No," I breathed. *Do it, please. Just grab a big handful.*

Slowly, his thumb stroked up and down the crest of my hip, right at the zone where it could be considered my ass.

Eliot and Lily exited the shop in front of us. They waved at the new arrivals, and the group started moving.

"You're still stiff." His low voice rumbled in my ear. "Deep breath in."

I inhaled.

"Deep breath out."

I pursed my lips and exhaled.

He put two fingers under my chin and tilted my face up to his. I'd never been this close to him before. We'd spent recesses together for years. Had classes together. I even had to work on a group project with him in seventh grade about climate change. He tried to get me to include a volcano just so he could make a model of one.

None of those times had I ever admired the dark flecks in his eyes. Or really studied the spot of hyperpigmentation at the edge of the iris. The mark nearly blended into his blue eyes, but this close, I could map it out.

"I'm going to kiss you now," he said only loud enough for me to hear, and my breath caught. "They're all talking, and it'll look like I'm sneaking it in. You good with that?"

I was a mess inside. I nodded.

He touched his lips to mine, a soft press that lingered for one second. Two. Just as I was about to sway into him, striving to get closer when I was already plastered to his side, he pulled away. His gaze met mine, searching.

A small puff of air escaped me. A simple, chaste kiss, yet my lips tingled. My whole body did, all the way down to my toes.

"Jensen," Dad broke in. "You know my sister, Linda, and her husband, Darren?"

Jensen narrowed his eyes like he was making sure I was okay, then casually looked away. "Yes, I've seen you both around."

He pulled away from me, briefly pressing his hand to the small of my back. I needed the steadying. My heart rate sped up until I got lightheaded.

I should've panicked more telling Mom and Dad I was getting married to a guy they hadn't known I was dating. But at this point, after Lily, Violet, and Alder, they probably took it in stride. Besides, they loved love. They'd been married for almost four decades, and they wanted everyone as happy as them. Then there were my happily wed siblings. Why wouldn't Mom and Dad think that Jensen and I would be living the dream?

Linda was harder to read. Darren as well. There were no emotions worn on their sleeves. No warm and fuzzy. Just distance and silent appraisal.

"Hey, guys," I said after Jensen was done shaking their hands. "Thanks for coming on such short notice."

Linda folded her hands in front of her. "Short-notice weddings seem to be par for the course."

Tension rode down my body. Jensen slid an arm around me again. This time, I leaned into him. My warm compress for the stiffness.

"I told him we had some time yet," I said, holding back my wince at the way my voice pitched up. "But he said why delay what was meant to be?"

A snort came from Lily. Everyone turned toward her, but Eliot had already blocked her. Violet shot me a knowing look.

"Doing okay, Lily pad?" Eliot gently patted her back. "Swallow a bug?"

There were no bugs out yet, the nights got too cold, but I appreciated Eliot's efforts to hide his wife's laughter.

"That's sweet." Linda's expression was unreadable. "And when is the wedding?"

"Oh, yes." Mom clapped her hands together. "We were just asking that when you arrived."

Darren folded his arms across his barrel chest. "I was telling Linda that it's probably another drive-through wedding."

She chuffed. "I was beginning to think that you've all snatched people off the street to meet the demands of the trust."

A squeak left me. Just my luck. I'd be the one busted after my other siblings got away with it.

Lily's cough rang out, but it sounded suspiciously like a laugh. She buried her head in Eliot's chest. He kept his back to us, but his shoulders were shaking as Lily "coughed."

"I'll get you some water," Alder said. The responsible oldest brother. But when he turned toward me, mischief danced in his eyes. "Does your random man want a drink too?"

I glared at him. What an obnoxious prick. But he schooled his features like the frustrating older brother he was.

Another snort sounded, but Violet covered her mouth. "Oh my goodness," she said, muffled. "It's like the cotton's already been released."

Jensen had all of two cottonwood trees on his property and they were across the drive and behind the house.

"No, it won't be a quickie wedding," I blurted out. Jensen whipped his head toward me. "Not that quick," I finished weakly.

He stared at me for a moment while everyone's eyes were on us. Laughter from the kids rose around us. Was he letting me take the lead? I didn't know where to go with it!

"It's whatever she wants," he said carefully. "Naturally, I'd like to get started on the house to get her office up and running, but if we've gotta wait, it's no big deal."

It would actually be a big deal. I wouldn't feel like I was accomplishing anything while working in his upstairs bedroom. I'd be under his roof, with his ring on my finger, for longer than planned. Longer to keep the ruse. More time to fumble the plan.

Linda waved his words away. "If you're doing work there, I'm sure you can get in just fine. It's only if you want to live there that you have to be married." She paused and took in the property, her gaze swiveling to the big, white farmhouse, then the shop. "Are you selling?"

This time, it was Jensen going rigid. This was the house he'd grown up in. All his memories of his dad were in this house. We hadn't talked about what we would tell people. I'd stay here until our year was up. Even pretending to sell must be stopping his heart.

"No," I said quickly. "No immediate plans to move." Not until after the year was up when I'd move into my own place. The Perez house.

"Oh." Again, Linda's expression was unclear. "So... when?" She shook her head. "Sorry, don't feel obligated to invite me. I just want to calculate when the year requirement will be fulfilled."

"No, of course you're invited." My invite wasn't to put on a show. I liked my aunt and uncle. She was hard to get to know, but I didn't want her feeling left out. "We'll have it at the Perez house even."

Jensen's gaze was on me. What was I saying?

I was coming up with a wedding plan on the fly. I looked to Jensen. If he minded, he didn't show it.

He gave me an encouraging nod. "I like that idea."

Emboldened, I let the floodgates down. "The backyard is really pretty. We can do it at sunset and have a cozy reception in the house."

Aunt Linda's face lit up. "That will be beautiful. A summer sunset in that yard is one of the things I miss."

I'd almost forgotten the house used to be her home.

"Then we have time to go dress shopping," Lily suggested.

Delight warmed my insides. I hadn't been able to do any wedding shopping with my sisters, and Clover wasn't engaged. Even when Daisy and Alder married the first time, it was a simple wedding. Daisy hadn't needed or asked for much help. "That would be fun."

I snuck a peek at Jensen and found him staring at me, curious.

"What do you want me in?" he asked.

Running shorts and nothing else. "A tux would be too fancy for a backyard sunset wedding." I nibbled the inside of my cheek. "What do you want?"

"I've been through this before. It's what you want."

He said it like he wanted to reassure me, but a part of my growing enthusiasm deflated like a week-old balloon. He'd done it all before. He'd had his dream wedding with his dream bride. This wedding would be mine, and any excitement I got out of it would be for me alone. Jensen would go through the motions. Would he be fending off nostalgia the whole time? The wistfulness and the what-ifs? He'd be remembering when he'd gotten everything he'd wanted.

"Slacks are fine," I said woodenly, and his gaze flickered. A slight divot formed between his brows as if he heard the tone change but couldn't figure it out. "I don't want a fancy dress. We can even do snacks and refreshments."

"Both Rattler's and the Purple Petal cater," Alder said. "Let me take care of the food. Our gift to you two."

Daisy nodded.

"Lily and I can handle the decorations," Violet said. "And Clover will tell us what she's going to do when she's in town next."

I missed Clover. I was close to my sisters, more so since they'd settled in Coal Haven and it was easier to gather us all in one place. But Clover and I were Irish twins, and we'd acted like twins growing up. Our curfews had been the same, our clothing styles, our personalities. Clover and I were the middle kids of middle kids.

I could talk to her about Jensen's comment. It wasn't his rodeo, and he'd been left by his rodeo queen.

Chapter Five

Jensen

The older kids were spread out so far they were in the pasture beside the shop. Poppy was warming up her legs for our kickoff. She rotated her foot while her toe was stuck in the ground. Then she did slight knee bends before doing circles with her hands on her thighs.

I should get my head in the game and quit ogling her. I hadn't played a sport since I graduated high school, so I swung my arms a little to make it look like I cared.

I did care, but not about our kickoff. Poppy had gotten quiet during the wedding planning. Her expression had lit up when she suggested the idea of a Perez house wedding. First, I had feared she'd feel cornered. Our little elopement had turned into a full-blown wedding. The guest list might not be large, but the ceremony might upset the balance of our bargain. When did reality and fantasy mix?

She'd perked up at the thought of having her family

attend, of gathering everyone to enjoy a day that was supposed to mark the beginning of everything together instead of acting like we were beginning a countdown. Then she'd gotten quiet when the details started coming together.

Her family had scattered ahead of us. My mom was standing by Magnolia, laughing. Alder and Weston were chatting together. Linda and Darren had eaten and left. Mom had loosened up immensely once that happened. She'd given them a wide, guilty berth. Linda assured us that in a month, when the renters moved out, she'd give us the key. She had even seemed to look forward to the wedding.

Did I?

I liked seeing Poppy light up and relax into me, but my stomach churned at the idea of walking down the aisle. This time, I knew the bride would be leaving me. Wasn't that better?

The heartburn left behind after my burger told me differently.

I was getting married again. The plan to elope hadn't felt fake, but it had registered in my head as transactional. Now I'd be a groom, standing in front of people I loved and respected, speaking my vows loud enough for them to hear. Only, unlike last time, I wouldn't mean it.

Was that what was bothering me?

Were the same questions plaguing my bride? She hadn't been married before, but she'd be doing the same —vowing 'til death do us part in front of family and friends.

Poppy started doing lunges and rocking back and forth.

Too many eyes were on us, or I'd talk with her.

Instead I took a step back and snuck a peek at her ass. I could argue it was to help believability. I was supposed to be smitten with this woman, and truthfully, I was enamored with her.

Perhaps that was fucking with me. I couldn't quit picturing her at the wedding, in the fading light, the sky painted with pinks and purples, facing me with those luminous eyes. Would she wear a dress with a skirt that draped over her hips and hinted at those muscular thighs?

She started trunk twists, and I had the perfect view of the way her shirt tightened against her chest. If she continued her warm-up, I'd be doing a kickoff with a kickstand, and I'd boot the ball all of five feet.

"Poppy, are you stalling?" I teased. I was so losing this challenge.

"Why would I be?" She gave me that same smug look she used to shoot me when we were younger. She knew she had this in the bag, and I was goddamn excited to see how badly she wasted me.

"Taking your sweet-ass time with that sweet ass of yours."

Shock filled her face. "W-what?" She turned as if she was trying to see if I was really talking about her butt.

"Yes, your ass, and I'll be watching it the whole time you're kicking."

Pink dusted across her cheeks, and her eyes shone. "You're trying to mess with my mind."

I was being one hundred percent serious. "If I was doing that, I'd also tell you that when you do your torso twists, I can tell whether your bra has lace or not."

She sputtered and glanced down at her shirt. She hunched her shoulders. "Quit getting in my head."

If she wanted to think I was lying, I wouldn't argue.

This was the stuff we should be doing in front of her parents. The problem was that I meant it.

"I'm gonna go first," I said. I tapped her white-and-yellow soccer ball to the cone she'd used for a starting marker. "Keep those sweet cheeks out of sight, or I'll think you're a cheater."

Her scandalized gasp rang out. "You know I never cheat, marble chest."

The ball was forgotten. "What now?"

Her cheeks flamed. "You said sweet cheeks. I said marble chest." She rolled her lips in, refusing to admit how ridiculous that was.

I grinned. "You were checking me out?"

"Was not!"

Everyone was watching us, but no one was closer than twenty yards. Still, I leaned in. "Do you flush red, like your name, everywhere?"

Her jaw fell, but she snapped it shut. "You're the cheater, trying to throw me off." Glaring at me, she stomped away several feet. Then she jumped up and down a few times. I jerked my gaze off her chest before she narrowed her eyes. "Better kick the ball before that epic warm-up of yours wears off."

Oh, I was warm. I was also having fun. Except for her thinking that I was flirting with her to throw her off. No, my question about her flush happened to be one I wanted to very much know the answer to.

* * *

Poppy

· · ·

Jensen lined up behind the ball, going farther back than I would before a kickoff. I tried to catch my breath.

In that little conversation, he'd referenced my butt and my breasts. He was teasing. The hurt trickling into my consciousness wasn't necessary. I should be glad he hadn't followed it up with, *but you'll never have cheeks as sweet as Hassie's*.

A quiver ran through my belly.

Jensen concentrated on the ball for several seconds before taking a few loping strides and kicking. His attempt landed in front of the fence to the pasture.

"Good job, Dad!" Auggie shouted.

It wasn't a bad shot. We were going for distance, and that hadn't been my best trait. I could do power and I could curve, but straight yardage? Not as good.

My years of experience had to count for something. Years I hadn't used in a long time.

Laila kicked the ball, but it only went as far as Dad and Alder. My brother tapped it to Lily and she punted it toward me. It lifted into an arc through the air.

"Oops!" Lily called. "Sorry."

"No problem." I stopped the ball with my shin and set it in place with my foot.

Alder whistled and Violet clapped for what was basically a drill I'd done a million times. The old thrill I used to get when I played reared up, and so did the shame from the last time I coached and tried to act like I knew what I was doing. I stuffed it all down. I was enjoying myself, and I didn't want to stop.

Jensen turned toward me, but instead of a gloating look, excitement sparkled in his eyes. "Show me what you can do, Boots."

I should've been prepared, but I made a choking sound. "Boots now?"

He winked as he backed up to give me space. "I have a feeling it's going to fit."

"I had a cat named Boots."

This was officially the weirdest challenge I'd ever taken on, and that included all the ones between me and Jensen as kids. He was almost complimentary. Impressed. And I had barely touched the ball.

I backed up opposite Jensen. I liked a curved path for penalty kicks. I was aiming for the direction Jensen's kick had landed. Only farther, naturally. Visualizing the action, how it'd feel, and the length it'd fly, I concentrated. He'd done well, and my nerves had noticed.

I looked from the white-and-yellow ball by the cone to beyond the fence. Damn. I mentally laid a soccer field out in front of me. This would be like a Hail Mary kick to get the offense as far away from our goal as possible. A last-second chance to keep them from scoring before the clock buzzed.

I sprinted, speeding up as I went, then I clenched my abs and channeled all the power of my core into the kick. An oomph left me and I straightened to watch.

"Hot damn," Jensen said. "That's a good one."

The ball crested, going straight. Some of my stomach acid settled down. I'd done well too.

After a few seconds, the ball hit the ground several feet beyond the fence. I threw my hands in the air as my family cheered.

Strong arms wrapped around my waist, and I was lifted off the ground. Jensen swung me around. "Helluva kick, Boots."

Laughter bubbled out of me, but electricity charged across my skin.

"Let's play kickball!" Cali shouted.

Jensen set me down, but he didn't let me go. I could've spent an eternity smashed against his hard, strong body. "I knew you'd demolish me."

He said it like he hadn't doubted it. Touched, I put my hands on his shoulders, willing him not to let go. "You had me scared, not gonna lie."

He grinned. "We could try throwing a football."

"I'd have to give up right away. My legs are my weapons. My arms are for show."

He barked out a laugh, and his Adam's apple worked up and down. Unadulterated joy filtered through me. What was this?

It was Jensen. And me. We didn't act like this.

We also weren't kindergarteners. Or fifth graders. Or eighth graders. This was us as adults. We were getting married. In a real wedding. The reality check pointed out that he was still holding on to me.

Auggie skidded to a stop next to me. "Dad, can I be on your team?"

Jensen put a few inches of space between us. That was the awareness I needed. We had to pretend while also not confusing Auggie too badly.

He smiled at his son. "Should we do boys against girls?"

Shouts of "yeah" rang around us, and Auggie sprinted away.

Jensen considered me. "What happens if we win?"

I lifted a brow. "You want to make a bet?"

"We didn't for the kickoff. Seems like you missed an opportunity."

Me? Because he knew I'd win. That soothing warmth spread deeper into me. "I clean your house for a week if you win?"

"Mm, the place is pretty clean. I'm more partial to going out to eat."

Ah. "You want me to babysit Auggie so you can go out. Wait... We can't see other people if we're—"

"No, you and me go out to eat—for the next year."

Oh. I opened my mouth to speak, but surprise froze my vocal cords. A year? A year of what was basically a date?

"And if your team wins," he continued, "I'll give you a year of massages."

I scoffed. "Are you serious?" He couldn't be. There was nothing in it for him. I'd be buying him dinners.

Those massages though... "You got me. Two *weeks* of massages or two *weeks* of date nights. I'm not made of money."

"Six months."

"One month."

"Two."

I wouldn't survive one massage session. His hands on my bare skin? A flush swamped me just thinking about it. I'd have to pretend that I wasn't turned on, and we'd be doing enough faking until the wedding ceremony that turned into a real ceremony with a very false motivation.

Disappointment slowly sunk in. He knew my team would win. It was why he'd made the bet. What made the most dangerous part of this bargain was that I was tempted to throw the game.

Chapter Six

Poppy

I pulled up in front of Jensen's house. It was move-in day. He was in the shop, but he'd told me to park as close to the garage door as possible. The small garage was apparently filled with Auggie's bikes and toys, yard tools, and an old car that had belonged to Jensen's dad.

My chest grew tight and breathing turned into a struggle. I was moving in with a man. I'd known Jensen most of my life, but in total, our years together were a small window. Add in our ages, and there wasn't much history there.

At least there would be no massages.

The game had been close, my ego had waffled a little, but the kids had fun, and I had a date Saturday night.

Not a date. A bet I had to settle.

I got out just as Auggie ran out of the shop. "Hi, Poppy!"

"Hey, Auggie. Long time no see." It'd been two days.

I had stayed at Alder and Daisy's a couple more nights so they could have their own night out. I'd gotten to know Daisy's daughter, Laila, a lot better, especially since she was a little carbon copy of her mom.

I held my hand out for a fist bump.

He bumped knuckles. "Dad said I had to help you carry everything in."

"Right on. I don't have much." All of my furniture was at my parents' place in Billings. They joked that they would keep a portion of the garage empty to store their kids' items when we moved. I wasn't the first who had stashed belongings there.

Auggie grabbed my laptop bag. I hitched my duffel bag onto my back and extended the handle of my rolling suitcase. "Lead the way."

He took me inside. I had been in the house when we'd had the gathering, but again, I was hit with the fresh-cut-wood-and-citrus scent of Jensen.

Home sweet home. For the next year and two months.

I followed him to a cove with three doors. There was the bathroom I first saw Jensen shirtless in and a bedroom on each side. He turned to the one with the open door. A nice queen-size bed greeted me. A small closet was tucked in the corner and two dressers lined the wall on either side of it. I'd get a nice view of the shop out the window.

I could stalk my future husband if I wanted to. Only I didn't have to. I lived here now. Would I get used to referring to Jensen as my fiancé? My husband? I'd have to. I'd even changed my address at the post office. I'd get mail in Jensen's mailbox. We were doing this.

It was for the house. For my job.

"Where do you want this?" Auggie asked, yanking me

away from the mounting stress. I had the place to live. Now I could work on the steady and reliable employment.

"You can put it on the dresser to the left."

He went to the one on the right.

"Your left is the other one," I said gently.

He let out a frustrated noise. "I always get that mixed up."

That was a pretty common challenge for dyslexics. "Has Debbie worked with you on ways to help?"

He shook his head and stuffed his toe into the floorboards. "My teacher always tells me to hold my thumb and finger out and whichever one makes an *L* is left." He did it and squinted at his fingers. "Doesn't help."

Because he would be trying to figure out the way an *L* usually looked on top of determining right from left. "That's because you know your right from your left, but you get them mixed up sometimes. There are some games we can play. Some people also wear a bracelet. I knew this one girl who has a little mole on her right hand, and she'd use that to help her."

He studied his hands. "No moles."

"Want me to ask Debbie?"

He ducked his head. "Yeah. I guess."

The heavy resignation in his voice broke my heart. I lined my suitcase up by the wall and dropped my backpack on the bed. Then I perched on the edge. "Gets frustrating, doesn't it?"

"Yeah."

"Wanna talk about it?"

"Nah. It's better now. Debbie's helped."

"Good." I stayed quiet. He'd talk if he wanted.

He glanced at the window. Jensen was walking across

the drive, his long-legged swagger in his carpenter jeans enough to give me several fantasies.

"Kids used to ask why I can't spell easy words," Auggie said.

I tipped my head. I could probably guess which words. Any sight word, for one. Sometimes, the words that could be easily sounded out weren't so easy for kids like Auggie. "That sucks."

"Now I tell them, shut up. I'm dysplex-dysl..." He worked his jaw like he was straightening out his tongue. "Dyslexic. Teacher's helper told me to quit saying shut up."

I bit back a smile. Shut up was easier to say than dyslexic. "Did she also tell the other kids to quit asking you why you can't spell?"

He shook his head.

"You should tell your dad so he can talk to your teacher. You shouldn't tell others to shut up, and they shouldn't make you feel bad." Some was natural curiosity, but without education, the cycle would continue.

"Hey," Jensen said from the doorway. His gaze fell on his son and concern grew in his eyes. "Everything okay?"

"Talking about spelling," I said.

"Do you have trouble with right and left?" Auggie asked his dad.

"Sometimes," he answered. "Not as much as when I was your age."

Auggie nodded like he'd conducted an experiment and the results were as expected.

"Getting our girl settled in?" Jensen asked.

My insides went dangerously liquid at the casual *our girl* comment. "This is a nice room."

"Wanna see mine?" Auggie asked. "I have a tool set like Dad's."

"His is plastic," Jensen clarified.

"Absolutely, I want to see." I followed them to tour the second level. I'd follow Jensen up twenty flights of stairs if I could have that butt flexing in front of me.

I stopped in the doorway. "Whoa."

"Yeah," Jensen said almost apologetically.

The floor of Auggie's room wasn't completely covered with toys and school papers but close. Pictures of horses and cowboys filled his walls. Cartoon cowboys covered the far wall. In a line across from his twin bed with the comforter full of horses and horseshoes were four pictures of horses.

Auggie pointed to the one on the farthest right. "That's Midnight Reins, Mom's favorite horse."

"Favorite from when?" I had to moderate my tone. It had seemed like Hassie had had a new favorite horse for each season. Her parents bought and sold horses faster than I could learn their names. She'd bragged about each new purchase and then had boasted about how much her parents had sold them for. I'd heard her mom tell mine that her new car hadn't cost as much as one of her barrel-racing geldings.

"Last year," Auggie answered. "He won her eighty grand in one month."

I gaped at Jensen and mouthed *eighty grand?*

His lips thinned, and he nodded. "She had a good year last year."

Auggie dug in his dresser and withdrew a magazine. "She sent me this." He opened it to a full-page spread of a gorgeous, blue-eyed Hassie smiling at the camera with her pearl-white teeth. A beige cowboy hat was on her head, with her long blonde hair streaming out behind her. The headline read "Barrel Sensation."

"Wow. Okay." I took the magazine, wishing I could close it and toss it in the trash. Even on paper, she was captivating. "I used to be friends with your mom."

Auggie's face lit up, and he adopted a toothy grin. "Were you best friends?"

I had to answer carefully. Jensen's gaze weighed heavily on me, but he didn't speak for me.

"Early on," I said, finally. "We met in kindergarten and were inseparable." Until she'd left me behind. It wasn't until fifth grade that I had noticed a change. Our friendship wasn't equal. It was her telling me how great she was. "Then she got into horse shows and competing, and I moved to Billings." I handed him the magazine. I didn't need to read about her accomplishments, not when I was marrying her ex-husband in order to open my business. "You must be proud of her."

Auggie nodded. "She's going to call soon."

Jensen's expression was stony. He swallowed and looked away.

"Thanks for showing me." I meant it. I didn't want to see Hassie, but Auggie could've had major issues with this arrangement. Yet he'd been cool. He was a good kid. I hoped for his sake, Hassie called him soon.

There was a bark outside. "I'm going to play with Luna." He tossed the magazine into the drawer and didn't bother closing it before he ran out.

Jensen propped his hands on his hips. "He's not the neatest kid."

"Are many ten-year-olds?"

He gave me a small smile. "I don't have much experience with ten-year-olds." His gaze strayed to the magazine. "His mother has even less."

Ouch. If he was smitten with her, he at least realized that she put her career over their kid. "She's doing well."

"She dropped baggage so she can really fly," he said bitterly. His smile turned empty. "It says so in the article."

Outrage heated my cheeks. "What? And Auggie read it?"

"I was two days away from hoping he'd forgotten about that damn magazine so I could throw it out. Now I have to start the clock again."

Sympathy rose up. For Jensen and his worry for his son. For Auggie. The familiar tug of frustration toward Hassie for only thinking of herself. "That's gotta be hard."

"Yeah. Especially when he keeps this room like a shrine to her." He shook himself and scrubbed a hand down his face. "Anyway, you get all settled? Sorry I wasn't there to help you haul everything in." He spread his hands out. "I had to wash up. I didn't want to risk getting stain on any of your stuff."

"I'm tougher than a little stain. So are my things."

"Would've bothered you before, four-ten."

A lot would've bothered me when it came to him back then. He was a lot more now. Bigger. Stronger. Kinder. He'd never been mean unless he was comparing me to Hassie. No, a little stain wasn't what would get me worked up about Jensen. "Well, I don't have a feature in a magazine, but I can figure out something for dinner if you have to work. I don't have any sessions today."

"Auggie asked for spaghetti. It's his favorite meal, so he wanted something special for you. If you cook, he's going to be upset with me. You get the night off."

"Aw, he's a sweet kid." I tapped my chin. "Who does he get that from?"

Jensen's smooth grin sent all sorts of tingles down my spine. He had to go past me to leave the room, and he stepped closer to me to miss a stack of books.

My breath caught as he leaned in. He put his mouth by my ear. "The real question is, how sweet can I be?"

●●●

Jensen

Poppy stopped beside me at the sink, her sunshine-and-peaches smell wrapping around me, tightening my gut. Fuck, she was like my very own summer day. Her presence brought me back to a day spent outside, doing nothing but having fun, tossing a ball around, playing in the pool.

"I insist on helping with the dishes." She opened the drawer with the ladle and spatulas, closed it, then pulled open another drawer full of knives. "Where are your dish towels?"

"Right here." Auggie tugged one out for her on my other side.

"You're not doing dishes your first night in the house," I insisted.

"I'm not sitting and watching you," she said and accepted the dish towel from Auggie.

"You haven't changed at how well you listen."

She snickered. "And you haven't installed a dishwasher, cabinet man?"

I ticked up a brow at her moniker. "I had to make a

decision about destroying the old cupboards and messing with old plumbing. Decided the two of us don't make a lot of dishes."

She took a step and studied the cabinets. "Seriously? These are the originals?"

She sounded impressed, and goddamn, that made me glow inside. I washed and rinsed a plate, setting it in the drying rack. Auggie had taken advantage of Poppy's offer and vanished. "I painted them. I might regret it later, but the cabinet style is just dated. An eighty-year-old house is going to show its age no matter what. I wanted to preserve some of that and did it by using the shape but making the color bright." I looked around at the pearl of the cabinets, the opalescent tile backsplash, and the pale-blue walls. "Farmhouse chic."

"I like it. It's bright." She dried another plate and guessed the correct cupboard to put it in.

A lump formed in my throat. She was learning my home, making it hers. Temporarily.

But I liked it. I hadn't had this with Hassie. Auggie got his energy from her, ping-ponging from task to task, barely sitting idle. I'd been alone while I'd been married. I wasn't alone now.

She leaned against the counter and twirled the towel while waiting. "I'll test out the office tomorrow. I have a few sessions."

"Recruiting your own clients yet?"

She didn't look at me. "Not yet. I'd like to be able to get into the house first."

Made sense, but also, wouldn't she want to be recruiting her own client base? It wasn't my business to run, but if she wasn't successful, she might decide to move. My roots were here. Hers could be anywhere. "What are you calling your center?"

"Um…"

I stopped with my hands still in the water, halfway through washing the pasta pot. "You don't have a name yet?"

"I had to find a place to live and work first."

No office. No name. Had something happened to make her jump in with half a plan? "Was this a sudden decision?"

She scowled at me. "No."

I bumped her shoulder, my hands still buried in suds. "The four-ten I used to know liked to have a plan. She planned the shit out of a science project."

"I'd like you to know that I got second place in the science fair in sixth grade."

"After the girl who tested different flavors for medicine?"

"When it's something that's already out there and tested?" Outrage filled her face. Just the reaction I was going for. I chuckled, and she shot me a glare. "I'm still mad."

"You don't say?" Her anger had been epic the next school day. She'd ranted so long that the playground monitor had to threaten her with detention if she didn't quit holding audience and go inside. "So? Your decision wasn't sudden. Was your move?"

I wanted to know more, and I'd keep scrubbing the already clean pot to make it happen.

"No, I planned it." She shifted her weight on her feet. She was still wearing shoes. What would it be like to see her in her pajamas? Or would she treat her room like a hotel? She'd leave fully dressed, and I'd never see her less than presentable?

Did she wear a nightshirt? Would it be long, to her knees? Or short enough that her ass cheeks hung out? Heat curled through my blood and headed south.

I rinsed the pan. "Then why do you make it sound like you packed up and moved on a whim?"

She didn't look at me when she shrugged. "Kinda felt like I did when I didn't have a secure income before leaving my job and breaking my lease."

"Why didn't you open officially if you can remote work?"

"Are you going to compare notes with my dad?" Her tone had an edge that went beyond joking. This was a sensitive subject.

I finished a saucepan and rinsed it. Then I took the towel from a startled Poppy and dried it, keeping my attention on her. "I'm not criticizing you, Poppy. I just feel like we should get to know each other if we're going to be living and working together."

She considered me with wary eyes. Her sharp mind was working. "I want to make sure I get it right," she finally said. "I've heard all of Debbie's horror stories. Did you know that Debbie had to move almost as soon as she opened?"

I hadn't seen the place she worked out of now. "Doesn't she work from home too?"

Poppy nodded. "So do all of her full-time tutors. It can be hard to get people to trust a company based out of a house, to pay all that money to a tutor they've never met. Most people don't have experience with Orton-Gillingham-based teachings like Barton uses, so they don't know how to verify the center isn't scamming them. It can take time to see improvement in their child at school."

"Why'd she quit renting the space?" I preferred having my own shop. I had assumed Debbie functioned as she did because it worked best for her. Mostly I wanted Poppy to keep talking. She had moments where she was open and I got to see that fearless girl I knew. Then other times, she closed up. A riddle I wasn't supposed to solve.

"A law office was on the lower floor of the office she'd set up," Poppy continued and I soaked up her lilting voice. "An accounting firm was next to them and then some sort of certification office was on the other side. No one who was used to kids who maybe can't monitor their volume and want to do wind sprints down the hallway."

I would've been one of those kids. Auggie too. "They complained."

"Debbie furnished an office with a waiting room and two tutoring rooms only to be told to leave when her six-month lease was up. You know how much that set her back?"

A lot. And now Poppy was driven to have her own place. She was also scared of failing. The girl who used to take on any challenge must've had a few hard knocks on the way.

"Well, dishes are done." She brushed her hands down her leggings. Could I write the makers of athleisure wear a thank-you card? The way the material clung to her legs and I could witness the flex of her quads was a vision I'd never forget. Then she turned, and I nearly groaned.

Her ass. My palms tingled to touch it, to run my hands over those globes and feel how tight her glutes were. The room grew uncomfortably hot, and I was so busy getting myself under control that I almost missed what she was saying.

"...for the night. Let you be and have your house to yourself." She threw a parting wave as she headed for her room.

Having this place for just me and my son had never been the plan. "What do you normally do?" I stopped myself from speeding after her. I was casual. Nonchalant. Not at all hoping she wouldn't squirrel herself away for the entire evening.

"Hey!" Auggie charged in from upstairs. "Can I play outside?"

He knew he could go out whenever he wanted. We'd talked about the rules, and I would often go out with him. As an only child, he could get bored and ten-year-olds with nothing to do usually found trouble.

"I'll go out with you." Then I wouldn't pant after Poppy like the lonely fucker I was.

If only I could blame loneliness. The blood gathering in my dick and my inability to take my eyes off her round ass and her high tits might be an influence.

"Mind if I go out to play with you?" she asked timidly, like she was afraid we'd tell her it was boys' night.

I'd never exclude her. Every night could be a Poppy night.

I found Poppy Duke sexy as hell.

Shit.

This was a problem. She trusted me. I had to be a good roommate and keep my lusting to myself. But it'd been a while since I'd taken notice of a woman. Sure, my body had been telling me that it'd been more than a minute since I'd been with anyone, but there was no one particular person I fantasized about. That had changed with Poppy under my roof.

Chapter Seven

Poppy

I entered the house and its already familiar warmth surrounded me. I needed a shower after sprinting through the yard for the last few hours. Auggie had been delighted when I said I'd play outside with them and then he and Jensen had dragged out the sports equipment from the garage.

Jensen set up a net for badminton. When we realized the wind was too strong, he'd set up a net for batting practice and weighed it down with a couple of sandbags. First, Auggie had been at bat, and I'd played the outfield. Next, I had goaded Jensen into batting with Auggie pitching. While he might've taken it easy to keep from line driving a hit into his son, he'd still kept me running with pop flies in every direction. Then it'd been my turn, and, well, I wasn't as good at sports that used my arms.

After batting practice, we'd shot some hoops and then Auggie had the bright idea that Jensen and I should race. There'd been no contest other than how long Jensen could make me think I had a chance.

Mostly, I had wanted him to charge ahead of me so I could watch him. His sweats didn't leave nearly enough to the imagination, as if I needed more reminders that the boy I had known was all man. Powerful legs, thick shoulders, and that voice. When we'd been talking at the sink, the dishes hadn't been the only thing wet.

I should've dated more. I turned the last guy down because he'd been half-lit when he'd hit on me. Clover had come to visit me in Casper, and we'd been out for the night. After I'd turned him down, he'd asked Clover out. I made a few good calls here and there.

I wouldn't have to worry about that with Jensen. Just like I didn't have to worry that he was attracted to me. That magazine article of Hassie showed me I wasn't his type.

"Go get ready for bed, kiddo," he said to Auggie. "I'll be right up to tuck you in."

"Do you need the bathroom down here?" I asked. "I can wait until you're done. My first appointment isn't until ten tomorrow."

"Go ahead. I don't get started in the shop until Auggie's off to school anyway." Jensen went to the cupboard and dug out three glasses. He filled them with water at the fridge.

I stole one last look at his broad back. A man running shouldn't be such a turn-on, but here I was, salivating over a guy getting me a glass of water. When did my bar get set so low?

More importantly—why was Jensen raising my bar so high?

"Night, Auggie," I called as he charged up the stairs.

"Night, Poppy," came his muffled reply.

I snuck another glance at Jensen and caught him watching me as he downed his water, his throat working over each swallow. He pushed out one of the glasses he'd set on the island.

"I'll shower first." Otherwise, I'd linger around him like a dog in heat.

He was not interested.

I turned my back on him and went into my room. By the time I gathered my toiletries and clothing, he had left the kitchen. The floor creaked upstairs, and Auggie's slight weight couldn't do that.

I set all my things on the sink counter. Swallowing, I took in the view. His razor and shaving cream were tucked in the corner. The toothpaste and his toothbrush were haphazardly tossed next to them. A bottle of mouthwash sat in the corner. That was all guy. It had to look like I lived here.

Nerves fluttered through my belly. I'd been prepared to pretend, but I hadn't been ready for the intimacy it required. He might have any guests over, or Aunt Linda could come here next week and use this bathroom.

As soon as my things were laid out on the other side of the counter, I spun toward the bathtub. Seeing our personal items mingling...did things to me. Made my belly flutter. Images of me and him intertwined flashed in my head.

Oh god. I couldn't have that. I was getting too awkward, too aware, around him.

I showered and dried off, feeling better. The low burn deep inside me didn't let up, but I was close to the reprieve of my room. I could call Clover and distract myself. I would not tell her I was hot for Jensen. Those confessions needed some alcohol and a place where he wasn't.

I lifted my pajama top and was mid-shrug into it when I stalled. Crap. I didn't bring a bra or underwear. All I had were my sweaty clothes, and I wasn't putting them back on. Oh well, it was just a few steps to my bedroom. I finished dressing and then my gaze caught the mirror. I'd picked my white pajama top and bottoms. The thin material clung to my breasts, and my hair dripped wet spots right over them.

I was all out of my routine. I could wrap my hair in a towel, but I didn't want to hang the wet fabric on a dresser. I already had this shirt, and I'd change and hang it up. I'd have to get a clothes basket. My hair dryer was in the room, so it'd be fine.

Just a few steps. I could hold my toiletry bag in front — No. That was staying in here until I bought some holders and baskets for my hair products and moisturizer. It had to look like I was doing more than staying overnight. I bundled my dirty clothes together, stuffing my underclothes into my pants.

I cracked open the door and stopped to listen. No more footsteps sounded from upstairs. I would be quick, and maybe he wouldn't see how short my pajama bottoms were. Jensen was just turning into the little hallway nook. I ran right into him and my clothing dropped.

"Shit, sorry." He stooped to pick it up, but his gaze landed on my legs and he stopped. "Jesus." He recovered and grabbed the pile of clothes. My yellow underwear fell out. He paused for a second, enough for pure mortification to swamp me, then he quickly stuffed it back into the clump.

His head was so close to my legs. When did I last shave? "Sorry."

He rose, slower than when he'd bent. "'S all right," he said gruffly. He jerked his focus off my legs, hit my boobs, and heat smoldered in his stormy gaze. With a choking sound, he tore his attention away.

I looked down at myself only to see both of my nipples poking right through the sodden fabric. Shit! I snapped my clothing from him and hugged it to me. He propped his hands on his hips, then stuffed his fingers through his hair, and finally rested his hands back on his hips.

So...this was getting uncomfortable. "I, um, should get a few things for the bathroom. To make it look like I live here."

"Sure, yeah. Whatever you need." His voice was rough. "Night, Poppy." He pivoted away and shut himself in his bedroom.

"Night, Jensen," I uttered, whether he heard me or not.

I hugged my dirty clothes. Then I glanced around before shimmying my shoulders. My taut nipples scraped against my shirt. What would his calloused fingers feel like? Had that emotion clogging his gaze been for me?

What was I thinking?

I shook myself and scurried to my bedroom, closing the door and my growing attraction to Jensen on the other side.

●●●

Jensen

· · ·

I sat on the couch after getting Auggie to bed and stared at a show I wasn't paying attention to. Poppy was in the shower again. It'd been an entire goddamn week of having the image of her full tits pressed against a damp shirt haunting me. Seven days of going to bed hard and trying to sleep when I knew she was only across the hallway.

Each day, I went deeper into hell. The last week had been the most excruciating of my life. I could only escape her in my room. The bathroom smelled like sunshine and peaches. Each time my gaze landed on her lotion, I imagined her bent over, toned leg extended, and rubbing it all over.

Now I was hard again. Pulling a blanket over my lap, I pressed down as if my dick would listen and winced just as she was coming out of the bathroom. But I didn't look away. Was I going to get another view of that sweet, lush body?

She'd wrapped a towel around her hair, but she was in different pajamas. The navy-blue shirt was looser and definitely less peep-friendly. I approved of the short shorts. When did I become such a leg man?

She hesitated, and anticipation shot through me. Was she going to hang out for a bit? We'd been like ships passing in the night. I was up first, or at least out of my room before her, and got Auggie up. Then she got ready while I took him to school. Two mornings a week, she tutored Auggie and got me set up with some proof-reading programs on my computer and my phone.

In the evenings, she retreated to her room, except for last night when she'd gotten a sandwich from the store and ate outside on the porch. Auggie had joined her, but for some reason, I'd held back.

Auggie didn't get special attention from a mother

figure. While I would never shove Poppy in that role just because she was a girl under our roof, the more he was treated like he was special, the better. Deep down, his mom's half-assed caring had to affect him.

"Do you mind if Clover comes to visit?" she asked.

Was that what she was nervous about? "No problem. This is your place for the next year." A little more —thirteen more months. I got her for longer than a year.

She twisted her hands together. Was she wearing a bra? Damn. "She's going to bring a guy. But they won't stay here," she rushed out.

"Not a problem. When?"

"Saturday."

Perfect. "That's our date night."

She blinked a few times. "What?"

"Aw, come on, you remember the deal." My team had lost that day, fair and square. But I'd made sure that no matter what, I'd won. Since she'd been moving, I hadn't bugged her about it, but I still planned to get my two months' worth.

She rolled her eyes, but a smile played along her lips. "It can be a double date."

I was growing into a desperate man. "You and I double-dating with Clover? Who'd have thought."

"It's not my first time double-dating with her."

My irritation started to rise. It should damn well be her last. For a year. I didn't have a say after that. Add in her tits being practically invisible, and this evening was starting to suck. "They were all losers though. This'll be the first time you wow her with your choice in men."

The corners of her lips lifted. "There were some losers."

I settled into the corner of the couch. "Grab us a couple of beers, darling, and tell me all about them."

She crossed her arms. Yep. Bra. But those tanned legs couldn't be hidden. "Doesn't seem fair to tell you about my tragic dating history."

"Why not?"

"You can't exactly complain to me about the mother of your kid."

I could. A lot. "There's not much to say." That was the truth of it. There wasn't much to tell, and that had been the issue. "She loved her career more than us." Sympathy crossed her face, but I wanted to keep this lighthearted. "Was one guy an emo?"

She barked out a laugh and went to the fridge. "What about me makes you think I'd go for the emo type?" She withdrew two cans of my favorite pale ale. Good. She was going to accept my invite to hang out for the evening. "His name was Leif and I met him in college."

It was my turn to laugh.

She crossed to me and handed me a cold can before dropping onto the other side of the couch. "He played in a band. That's supposed to be hot."

Supposed to be. Now that was better. "Not hot?"

She wrinkled her nose. "Unfortunately, not after I heard them play. Then there was the guy right after I graduated. He texted his ex the whole time. He told me that they hadn't really been serious."

"But?"

"But his sister dropped the fact that they'd been engaged, and not only that, his ex was thinking of getting a restraining order against him. He kept helping himself to her apartment and waiting for her outside of work."

"Shit." I had little dating experience before Hassie

had finally gone out with me. Perhaps that was why I was hesitant to go out with anyone, but after hearing only one of Poppy's bad experiences, maybe I'd been right to lean into my single-dadness. "Did he cause problems with you?"

"He wasn't obsessed with me."

I was glad she didn't have to deal with that fear, but he also had bad taste if he wasn't obsessed with her. "He clearly didn't see you in a wet T-shirt after a shower."

Her eyes flew wide and her face went fire-alarm red. "You weren't— What— You didn't react."

I'd reacted, and I'd had to hide it from her. "You're a guest, and I shouldn't have said anything. I don't want to make you uncomfortable."

"I mean, it was a little insulting that you practically ran away." She took a drink.

"I'm just a guy, Poppy, and you have nice tits." She sputtered over her beer, and I grinned. Teasing her was fun, but I didn't want to push my luck. "Did you ever date a finance bro?"

The look she gave me said *don't get me started*. "I went out with a hedge fund guy, and he was nice. No chemistry. But then I dated a financial adviser, and between critiquing me about spending money on my morning coffees while he casually dropped that he had a gambling problem, I ran by the third date."

Did I feel bad that she'd had such poor experiences dating? Yes. Was I happy that all of them had been dreadful? Also yes. But she was only telling me the fails, and I wanted to know about the ones who got to experience the full Poppy effect. "What kind of guy made it past the third date?"

Fondness filled her face, and fuck, I didn't like that

one bit. At least there was regret there. "I was with Dillon for two years." Her brow furrowed as she twanged the top of her can. "I thought we were endgame, honestly. We liked the same things, had fun together, and I even thought he'd propose."

A knife twisted in my gut. If she'd married, would we have ever reconnected? "You don't have to talk about it."

"No." Her expression turned thoughtful. "It helps. I lamented to Clover after the breakup, but a few years have passed and…I can see better that it was a good thing he never bought a ring."

The jackass hadn't bought one. I was up to two. I never imagined I'd get a second wedding ring for someone. Was it better or worse that I knew the marriage would end going in? At first, it seemed better. But the thought of seeing Poppy pack her bags and leave made the beer sour on my taste buds.

"He wasn't good for you?" I asked, knowing damn well the answer was no. Poppy deserved someone amazing. There was one other time I had thought that. One time I had seen her as a girl who had a lot to offer. More than competition. More than friendship.

"No, he really wasn't. It was the insidious things. The 'my ex never would've worn a color like that, but you have confidence' comments. Not real compliments that didn't have an edge, and when he normally saw how I dressed up"—she waved a hand over her outfit—"I guess I thought there'd be more. But that was the thing. There was nothing, so I didn't even notice."

The only thing she would look better in than what she wore would be nothing. I couldn't finish that thought and not tent my pants. "You deserve compliments when you wear pants."

"What kind of pants?"

"Any."

Her eyes flew wide again. "My ass *and* my boobs?"

I was pushing it, but I continued to say stuff around her I shouldn't. "I'm a man sharing a house with a sexy woman. So let me get that out of the way and assure you I'll behave myself."

She studied me for a moment like she was deciding what to say. "Maybe that's the thing. My competitive side. I want to be the sexiest and not have it pointed out in small ways that I'm not. I've gotten picky."

"Be picky, Poppy. Don't settle." No asshole had better make her feel small again.

The corner of her mouth lifted. "Except for when I'm getting something out of the deal, like free work on an office space?"

"Even then. If you don't like something I do, tell me." Poppy deserved to feel good. She deserved pleasure. A lot of it.

"You might regret saying that."

"Eh, I've heard worse."

Curiosity entered her gaze. "Is it the work stuff you told me about?"

I hadn't talked about my marriage to anyone. I'd made mistakes. That had to be clear from my flagging business compared to the fact my ex-wife's got magazine features. "Yes and no." I scrubbed a hand down my face and took a long pull from my beer. "Hassie's a perfection-ist. You probably remember that."

"I do," she murmured.

"I came up short. A lot." I hadn't been able to please my ex. I wasn't into horses enough, I couldn't travel enough, I wanted a home life and not to live out of a trailer on rodeo grounds. I didn't want to raise our kid on the road or push horse culture on him when he was more interested in dinosaurs and playing catch.

I had wanted to be the husband my dad had been, to be a man he would've been proud of, but nothing I did had made Hassie happy. "Let's make another deal."

She gave me a wary look. "I don't know. I ended up with a husband and weekly dates after the last two bargains we struck. We're not negotiating with fruit snacks anymore."

I couldn't let her down, but then Poppy had never made me feel that way. "We aren't married. Not yet. And you still owe me the first date. After this, I'll give you compliments."

I thought she'd continue to be flirty, but her expression shut down. "I don't need compliments from you."

"I just wanted to—"

"It's fine, Jensen. It's not the same if we *have* to give them, right?" She guzzled the rest of her drink.

I knew what she meant, but her sudden shift felt personal. She was protecting herself. From me?

"I'd better get to bed." She rose before I could say anything.

"Poppy, I didn't mean to upset you."

"You didn't," she said lightly and tossed her can in the recycling closet. "Good night." She shut herself in her room.

What the hell just happened? Was I destined to let down the women in my life?

Chapter Eight

Poppy

Jensen and I were seated across from Clover and Elijah in a booth at Rattler's. Clover's boyfriend was *a choice*. Of what, I wasn't certain. He was handsome enough. Very good-looking with his short, styled hair and business-casual clothing. He reminded me of the finance bro I told Jensen about. I might just be irritated with Elijah because I hadn't gotten my sister to myself since she'd arrived. I might be protective of my barely younger-than-me sister, but I hadn't felt this way about Lily and Eliot or Violet and Evander. Yet I had a similar emotion when it came to them and their exes.

Dread pooled in my stomach, but I put on a smile as Clover gushed about the food to an unimpressed Elijah.

"Afraid this place is more my brother's speed," he said in what I expected was a practiced, cultured voice. "I'm more of a sushi and sashimi guy." His mouth turned up. "You know the difference between them?"

I snuck a glance at Clover, but her adoring stare was on her new boyfriend. "Yes," was all I said.

"I'm sure I've had both," Jensen said congenially. "Sashiu—" The rest of the word got garbled. "Sash-sh—" He winced. "Sorry. Tongue-tied."

Elijah's laugh dripped with obnoxiousness. "It's not a hard word, my man."

"He just got tripped up, my man," I said in a sweet voice. Jensen's snort was quiet.

Clover's startled gaze landed on me. She was lucky I didn't launch into a diatribe about how dyslexia affected speech and it was more than just flipping sounds around like aminals instead of animals. Sometimes it was remembering the correct word, knowing it but not being able to say it, but that wasn't my issue to discuss. Could I say "dyslexia" really quietly around Elijah's phone so he could be served all sorts of ads for learning programs?

Wait, my feeds weren't full of ads for it, and I talked about dyslexia all day.

I could run ads when I opened my center. But I'd wait until then. I should have at least the key to the house first.

Jensen laughed. "Sometimes my tongue doesn't cooperate. Sashimi," he said deliberately, "isn't something I eat a lot."

"Not landlocked like you are." Elijah's grin rubbed my last nerve.

"Omaha is quite the coastal Mecca." My sarcasm came out stronger than I intended, and I earned a sharp glare from Elijah.

Clover shot a warning look my way. I'd try to rein it in.

"I've lived other places. Sacramento, Miami, a

summer overseas." Elijah snapped his cuffs back and rolled his sleeves up.

"Remington is the chef here," Jensen said, his tone light, but I caught the competitive glint in his eyes. "He says he'd offer more choices beyond walleye, but the resort on the lake is superb, and he doesn't want to compete with their seafood and sushi menu."

"The population cannot handle both." Elijah had a rich man's laugh. "And there is a snake on the logo, so I shouldn't have gotten my hopes up."

Elijah couldn't handle not getting in the last word.

Clover rubbed Elijah's arm. "I'm sure you'll find something you like. Everything I've had here has been great."

Jensen nudged me with his knee under the table. We were mere inches from each other. "What's your favorite Rattler's special?"

"Ribeye. It's the only place that can compete with Dad's grilling."

I ignored Elijah's dubious expression. Clover was leaning over him, studying his menu.

"One of my top choices too." Jensen searched my gaze as if to ask if I was okay. I peeked at my sister and her boyfriend, then rolled my eyes toward Jensen.

He smirked and covered it up a second later. "Go ahead and get a drink. I'll drive."

"You sure?" I asked. Auggie was at Jensen's mom's place, and I could be a driver.

"Completely," he said. "Go ahead. They have some of Reservoir Barrel's beer on tap."

Well, when he put it that way. They had the same pale ale I drank with Jensen the other night. I didn't drink away my problems, but between the mindfuck of Jensen offering to compliment me only for me to run off scared and then not being able to talk to Clover, I just wanted to relax a little.

Winding down at Jensen's was getting harder. He was home, for one. I had to see those wide shoulders. I stared out the window way too much when he swaggered from the shop to the house.

I kept waiting for the other shoe to drop. For the inevitable Hassie comparison. It had sat wrong with me as a kid. Funny at first and then more proof that I'd never live up to Rodeo Barbie. Life after that had only proved that I didn't need Hassie to fall short, but this was like returning to the scene of the crime. I'd be holding my hands out and asking for my knuckles to be slapped.

Two years with Dillon had made me even more sensitive. My figurative knuckles were permanently bruised, and Jensen's absurd level of hotness didn't help. It'd only sting worse.

And now, I couldn't tear my bestie away from her new man long enough to talk to her. I could turn to Lily and Violet, but they had lives. They had husbands and kids, and I just wanted to bend a friend's ear with my drama. Besides, being so close in age, Clover knew Hassie. She'd commented so many times that Hassie was a know-it-all and not fun to play with.

When we ordered, Elijah had to ask the poor teenage server a zillion questions about the cut of meat, quality, freezer time. I had no idea there was so much to know about asparagus.

"He has allergies," Clover whispered across the table when he'd started on the type of oil used for cooking.

I respected allergies, but Elijah was probably more allergic to not being the center of attention.

Jensen leaned back and stretched an arm around me. My heart skipped a beat and I stiffened.

"Linda, twelve o'clock," he said under his breath.

Sure enough, Linda and Darren had entered and wandered into the bar section. Disappointment filled me. I'd gotten a thrill for nothing.

Clover saw how Jensen was sitting, then followed our gazes. "Oh my god. Good catch." She rubbed Elijah's leg. He had finally finished ordering. "Remember? I told you about the houses."

She'd told him? Was she trying to claim her property? I didn't want her to have to put up with Elijah for a whole year.

"Family, am I right?" he said, smirking.

Jensen let out a good-natured chuckle. "More like wills and trusts."

Elijah shrugged him off. "I'd be screwed. My grandma keeps mixing up my name with Sully's."

"Van," Clover said. "Doesn't your brother like to be called Van?"

"Probably." Elijah made a *whaddya do?* face. "Sullivan. Sully. If he leaves my parents' basement, he can call himself whatever he wants."

"Is it just the two of you?" Jensen asked like he was trying to move the conversation beyond insulting relatives.

The time between ordering and getting our food felt like an eternity. When the plates showed up, Jensen removed his arm, and I spied on my aunt and uncle. The movement caught Uncle Darren's eye, and Jensen tossed him a wave. I did as well. Linda spotted us, and while her smile was faint, it was wide for her.

Tonight did double duty. I met one of my date obligations, and we looked like a real couple to my aunt and uncle. The drawback was that I missed the heat of Jensen sitting so close. Each time we had to pretend to be a couple, I liked it more.

●●●

"Insufferable," I mocked after we returned home. The night was cool, and I wasn't ready to go in yet. I aimed for the porch, and Jensen kept pace with me. "'It's not a hard word, my man.'"

"Calm down, tiger. I'm used to stumbling over words around people."

"It doesn't matter." I whipped my head toward him. He should not have to be used to getting called out for a simple error. "Mr. And That Summer Overseas can learn some manners. Maybe his brother's in the basement to keep from dealing with people like him. I can't believe that guy. Clover must be dickmatized."

"That'll do it."

"Ugh. Do you think she's going to ask him to marry her so she can get her home?"

Clover could not be that desperate. We still had time before the terms of the trust ran out. "He took one look at the motel and insisted on going to Bismarck to get a room."

"Was it the 'don't clean fowl in the shower' sign that scared him off?" He shook his head. "I'm surprised, honestly. I remember Clover as precocious. She knew her own mind, and then to show up with...him."

"I wonder if it's all of us," I mused and took a seat on the porch swing. Clover hadn't had more luck than me, but Elijah was the most blatantly obvious cocksucker.

"Lily's the youngest, and she's been married twice. Violet was almost married twice. I don't think she and Willis would've lasted long." I had to think Violet would've eventually seen what we all had. "Even Alder married twice. Now you and me." That was odd. Talking about our impending nuptials so casually. *Hey, we're getting married. How 'bout a beer?*

"She's feeling the pressure?"

"Only from herself. But..." I debated telling him what was on my mind. He was waiting for me to continue. This guy listened. Actually, he always had. He had listened when we were on the playground, and that was why he had always amped me up, goading me to push myself harder and go farther faster. He thought I could do it. "When we were kids, we'd talk, you know. Little-girl stuff about our weddings and what our husbands would be like."

"And you mentioned an outdoor wedding at your aunt's old place?" The corner of his mouth lifted, but he wasn't teasing.

"Yes. Small, almost intimate. Clover had said she wanted something similar with the lake as a backdrop."

"Which lake? Nelson?"

Laughter bubbled out of me. "Why, yes. With the power plant as a backdrop?" Nelson Lake was a cooling reservoir for the plant, making it a warm body of water that drew a crowd all year. It was pretty, but maybe not a wedding setting unless the theme was rural industrial.

"Sakakawea, then?"

"Yep. At the resort by Twelve Mile Bay."

I toed the floorboards to rock the swing. He gazed at the property, leaning his elbows on the railing. I got a front-row view of his ass, and it was amazing. Round and firm, I just wanted to walk by and swat it. My hand would probably sting and—

He looked at me over his shoulder, and I jerked my gaze up.

"What else do you want for the wedding?"

I swallowed hard. The guy I was marrying was asking me what I wanted for my wedding. Quivers ran through my belly worse than when we'd had the audience of my dad, aunt, and uncle. "Umm... What about you?"

"Like I said, I've been through it once already."

And he didn't want to think about the perfection he'd had? Or...was there something else? He'd thought the sun rose and set only to make Hassie even prettier than she already was. "You already got your dream wedding?"

He chuffed and gazed back out across the drive to the shop and the rolling hills behind it. "At the time, I might've thought so."

"Was a horse a bridesmaid?" Oops. I hadn't meant for the cattiness to slip out.

"Close. There was a horse-drawn carriage. A friend of hers had drafts, and that's how we rolled." His tone was back to neutral. His wedding had to be the happiest day of his life, second only to Auggie's birth, but no one would know from the sound of it.

"Sounds fun. Country chic style?"

"Yep. Auggie likes to look through the pictures. Maybe he'll show you sometime."

Maybe, but hopefully he wouldn't. I didn't need to see how blissed-out Jensen was over his real bride. I didn't care to witness the hearts in his eyes cemented for eternity in photos, and definitely not right before our wedding or when he was married to me.

Still, I didn't want him to have to grit through our day. "It's like a party we're throwing together. What's something you want?"

He pushed off the railing, and I lost the sight that would taunt me at night when I also remembered how solid he was next to me with his arm around my shoulders.

He draped a hand around the back of his neck. "I said I don't need—"

"Neither of us needs anything other than to get married. Might as well make it fun. What do you want?"

I tried not to squirm under his stare. I couldn't read his expression. "You don't want to wear a tux. What else?"

"I get two decisions?" he asked lightly, but I heard the surprise.

"It's the dog, isn't it? You want her to be the ring bearer."

Luna panted from her spot in the fading sun at the end of the deck.

His eyes crinkled at the corners when he laughed. Jensen had no business getting that much sexier as an adult. "Now that you mention it, I don't want a fleet of attendants."

"One or none?"

"You'd really be okay with none?"

The swing hinges squeaked lightly as I rocked. "It's either all the sisters or none of them, honestly. None makes it easier."

His expression turned contemplative. "I always envisioned just a bride and a groom. Simple. Elegant. But not fancy."

"What was your wedding like?" I almost said first

one, but it felt wrong. Technically correct, but he wasn't mine. He wouldn't be, even as my husband.

He crossed his arms and stared into the distance, giving me his profile. "Big. I swear everyone we ever met was invited. There were horses, a decked-out horse trailer to haul us around instead of a limo. That's what the horses pulled."

"Wasn't that dangerous?"

"They went slow." He worked his jaw. "It was...an event. Epic. People talked about it for years."

"Wow." Should I plan more? Our wedding would look like a kiddie rehearsal. It wasn't a competition, but did he want more?

His gaze pierced me. "It was chaotic, Poppy."

"You got more than you bargained for?"

"You could say that." He scuffed the toe of his boot against the porch boards. It was the only western item he wore, but he'd done that in school. He was a ranch kid, only it hadn't been his identity. Perhaps that was why we'd found ourselves doing so many of the sports together, forming our own competition. "But no to the dog being a ring bearer. I love the girl, but she'd eat it."

"Ha! True. I'm highly suspicious she ate cow shit the other day."

"She one hundred percent did."

I giggled and he grinned, open and unjaded. My heart flipped right over.

I might have a crush on my fiancé.

Alarm spurred me inside. I could not have those thoughts around him. It'd seem more...pathetic. "I should probably get to bed. Night." I darted into the house.

"Poppy." He was right behind me. "You okay? Was it something I said?"

"No," I said lightly.

"You're lying."

I frowned, irritated that he called me out on my shit. I stopped before I got to the hallway nook. "No, I'm not."

"What'd I do?"

Fine. If he wanted to push it... "You've been flirting."

His brow creased. "I didn't mean to."

Oh. Ouch. The tangle of my conflicted emotions pushed against my chest walls. "Of course you didn't."

His brow furrowed. "Poppy, talk to me. Do you *want* me to flirt with you?"

"No, that's absurd."

You know who'd look even better in a dress? Hassie.

You know who has the prettiest eye color in the world? Hassie.

You know which woman I'd rather be married to?

He'd never said that last one, but I could extrapolate. I needed to get away from him and his broad shoulders and those searching, caring eyes. I was mistaking his feelings for genuine affection. We were friends. We had never been more than friends, and we never would be, wedding vows or not.

I made another attempt for the bedroom, but he rushed to block me, standing in the opening. "Can you talk to me?"

"There's nothing to say." I backed up. I'd sleep in the office upstairs if he pushed me. "It's getting late."

"Bullshit."

I glared at him and tried ducking around him. "Jensen."

"Poppy." He scooted over and blocked me.

He wouldn't let me out of this... A smile played along his lips like he was just waiting for me to take the bait and race him around the island.

"Not everything's a game, Jensen."

Finally, his smile broke out, and my stupid belly flipped. "No, that's absurd." He echoed my earlier answer. "But if I catch you, you have to be honest."

"Do not."

His eyes lit. Damn. I would race him and he knew it.

Then I'd better not let him catch me. I sprinted to my left, going for the island. Laughter broke out of him and he raced around the other side. He was fast, and he was toying with me. I spun just as he rounded the end and dashed in the other direction. I slowed, pretending like I was doing it so I didn't slide and crash into the oven and fridge. He was almost on me when I whirled again and put on my thrusters.

My heart was in my throat, but I was almost free of the island when Jensen leaped over it, hip sliding on it like it was a race car. He landed in front of me, and I ran smack into his hard chest. He wrapped his strong arms around me.

"That's cheating!" I sounded like I was ten again, but I didn't care. His body was solid and warm and his face was inches from mine.

"Was not." The words came out a rasp, and we both stilled. His gaze dipped to my lips. "You never could stand it when I came out on top."

"It's not that. You were a dick about it."

"Probably," he murmured. "I'm not anymore, but I do like being on top."

Awareness of every inch that was smashed against him crept in. The band of his arms. The way his chest pressed against me with every breath. I wanted to drink him in. I couldn't. "I like to be on top too," I murmured.

A lazy grin spread across his face. "Now I know you're telling the truth."

His smile faded, and his attention was back on my lips. He dipped his head. My heart stopped. His warm lips brushed against mine. My knees wobbled, and I might've gone down if he wasn't holding me.

He deepened the kiss, opening slightly. I answered, and when he gently licked his tongue out, tasting me, I invited him in. Flattening my hands on his chest, I felt the vibration of his small groan. I was caught between wanting to rub my palms all over his head, stuff them in his hair, or hook them around his neck and hang. This guy could kiss. He was stroking and sensual and he'd learned—

He'd learned from his ex. His high school sweetheart. The woman he married.

I jerked back. His eyelids slid open, confusion ripe in his blue-gray irises.

"We can't do this." I backed up a step and his hold loosened, letting me go. "You're not..." My type? Into me? Over your ex?

The disturbing conclusion was that he was my type. I liked him. I wanted him. If we didn't have a five-foot, bleached-blonde piece of baggage between us who was the mother of his kid, I'd be all over this. I'd be hauling him to bed instead of trying to outrun him in his own home.

"I'm not what?" he asked. I was going to retreat another step, but his gaze was searching. "Talk to me, Poppy. Please."

The please did me in. "I've known you most of my

life." When he nodded, I nodded. He was listening, and I'd forge ahead, hoping he didn't want to break the deal when I was done. "That whole time, Jensen, you were all about Hassie. You compared me to her in a way that made me feel like she was better, she was prettier, she was more desirable. Then you married her—and if I was still around, I would've been happy for you. Of all people, I knew how much you were into her. And I know you're not married anymore, but the thing is, I've never known you not to be into her. Where there was Jensen Hollis, there was his obsession with Hassie Heart."

Color leached from his face. "I'm not that guy anymore."

I didn't know that. I poked my chest with a finger. "But this girl? Remembers. The competitive part of me remembers that there was one game I'd never win and that was the comparison game with Hassie. You made sure I knew I'd never live up to her. I'd never be as pretty, and you'd never like me like you liked her. We might've been just kids, but that shit stuck with me. For years, Jensen, you compared me to her, and I lost every single time. It was a game I couldn't win, and it's one I've quit playing."

With that, I walked around him. No running. No sprinting. He wanted the truth and he got it. I should feel lighter, but I didn't. Sadness perched on my shoulders.

Just before I shut the bedroom door, his words reached me. "I lost that game too."

Chapter Nine

Jensen

Poppy's words kept me up all night. How the hell did I come back from that? The destroyed look in her eyes gutted me. But damn, it answered so many questions. Why she would get skittish around me. Why she was guarded and kept her distance. Why she hadn't been honest.

There was one thing she couldn't lie about, and it was that kiss. The way she'd opened up and let me in. The way she'd responded. I wasn't imagining the connection between us, but just because it was there didn't mean she wanted it.

...you compared me to her, and I lost every single time.

Ouch. I was the biggest asshole alive. Was I why she put up with men like Dillon? Would she take an Elijah over a nice guy who admired her powerful body, her sharp brain, and who couldn't quit daydreaming about her wet T-shirt?

I had been an obnoxious kid, and now I wasn't, but she'd had to live with the impact of it. No wonder she hadn't been thrilled to see me on the other end of the computer. While I'd been nostalgic and eager to learn who today's Poppy was, she'd been waiting for me to demean her in some way.

Shit.

I rolled out of bed and scrubbed my hands down my face. I had some sanding to get done before Mom dropped off Auggie. When I went to the bathroom, Poppy's bedroom door was closed. I didn't expect her to be awake with a smile, but that damn panel of wood only served as a reminder. It remained shut when I was done cleaning up. I made some coffee, grabbed some breakfast, and went to the shop.

After working for a few hours, I lost track of how often I peeked out the door to see if I could spy movement in the house. Even Luna quit getting up to follow me to the window.

I finished some doors I was sanding and staining for one of Mom's friends and picked up my tools. I had some computer work to do that I'd been putting off. Time to see if I could pay bills this month or not. Each year, my expenses got higher. My work should be able to speak for itself, but if I couldn't speak for it, how did I expect others to?

I had two queries. One asking for an estimate and the other telling me they loved my work in a home I'd done eighteen months ago. They wanted to hire me. I couldn't fuck this up.

I texted Poppy before I could ask myself if she really wanted to hear from me.

Jensen: Hey got a potential client don't want to fuck up. Can you come to the shop

I was getting warnings about my punctuation but I let it go. I wasn't beneath using my lack of punctuation to lure Poppy out of hiding.

Poppy: Just a minute.

Triumph and relief left me grinning at the dog. "Fuck yeah, Luna. It worked."

She lifted her head, looked around, and went back to sleep.

I couldn't focus on a thing until I heard her footsteps crunching across the gravel a few minutes later.

She slowly leaned in through the open door, her expression impassive.

"Wasn't sure you'd help," I said. I wasn't teasing. It was time for more honesty and less competition. But I still had to be careful. She was skittish and it was my fault.

"We have a deal." Her face was expressionless as she crossed the shop. Her hair was pulled back and she was dressed in leggings and a snug, zipped-up top, curves on display. I drank her in as discreetly as I could. The only thing that prompted a smile was the dog's thumping tail. She was all business when her attention returned to me.

I shifted the laptop so she could see the screen. "I wrote a reply email. And I followed the prompts of that program you installed, but I have to make sure this is right. This job could be a sure thing."

She leaned in, but I got up so she could have the chair. She didn't sit but tapped a few keys. I steadfastly kept my gaze on the screen. I couldn't make her uncomfortable.

"There. That should do it." She swiveled the computer back to me.

"Hold on," I said before she could scurry off. "I have one more to respond to."

I pulled up the email asking for the estimate and banged out a reply. Then I kicked the chair out of the way so she could proof it.

Her mouth twisted when she concentrated, but she nodded and leaned back. "Looks good."

Pride ran through me, and I hit "send." The feeling diminished as soon as she turned to leave. "I'm sorry."

She folded her arms, almost like she was hugging herself. "It's fine. We were kids."

"That's no excuse." I scratched the back of my neck. "I've been thinking about why I did that, and again, not an excuse, but maybe I was trying to convince myself I was more deserving if I put her above everything, including others' feelings."

Her features were still neutral. "I get it."

"Maybe I thought you were a threat to how I felt. Like if I let myself admire your freckles or your legs, then I must not be genuine and it'd be a betrayal. My dad was so into my mom. She used to joke that he had eyes only for her, and I wanted to be like Dad." I hadn't thought about how much losing Dad affected me when it came to relationships until now. When I had married Hassie, I had hoped he'd be proud of me. He wouldn't have been proud of how I'd made Poppy feel, and I wasn't either.

"I understand, Jensen." Her tone was softer but still distant.

I moved a little closer. Only a few inches. "I really am sorry. You were a spectacular fucking kid and you're an even more amazing woman. You won't ever catch me making a comparison like that again."

She laughed. "Okay. Sure."

"I like you."

Her smile died. "Like I said last night, we shouldn't. We've got to keep clear boundaries."

"I agree." I didn't want to, but she was right. Our families were in on this, and we couldn't let each other down and, in turn, them. "For once, it's nice to know my role in a relationship."

Curiosity filled her face and her attention was fully on me. Just how I liked it. "How do you mean?"

"Me and Hassie...it wasn't a fair union. She had all the power, and I was eager to please. But that life, the one she wanted, wasn't for me. I like horses as much as the next ranch kid, but I also wanted balance. I wanted balance in my career, in how I lived, how I raised our kid." In the relationship itself. Everything was what Hassie wanted and how she wanted it, and in the end, I didn't know if I was a part of either equation. "When I wasn't sure if Auggie factored into how she balanced everything, I had to leave."

"I'm sorry your marriage didn't work out."

Me too. I was sorry about a lot.

"Is it hard?" she asked. "Planning another wedding?"

Maybe if I thought about it. I tried to tuck all my feelings about Hassie and how things played out in the back of my mind. I couldn't have it affecting my son. "No. It's different." I ducked my head. "Not better or worse. Just different."

It was a fuck ton better, but if I said that, she probably wouldn't believe me. I had to earn her trust.

She nodded, but her gaze skated away.

I nudged her chin up with a couple of knuckles. When did I get this close? "I promise that I'm never going to make you feel bad again. I'm only going to show you how amazing you are."

She rolled her eyes. "You don't need to placate me."

"There'll be no placating when all I can think about in bed at night is you in that soaked shirt."

"It wasn't soaked," she croaked.

"It was wet in all the right places." I stroked my thumb over her plump bottom lip. "And you in those leggings with the seam that goes between your butt cheeks. I want to know how my hands would look framing that ass. But what really takes up more mental space than I could've ever imagined is your legs. That power. That muscle. Wondering how wild a guy would have to drive you to find out just how crushing the power is around his head. How hard do you clamp down when you come with a man's face between your legs?" I had just agreed with her that we needed boundaries, but dammit, she kept thinking I couldn't be serious about how she affected me, and I couldn't have that. She wasn't trying to brush me off, she was brushing herself off.

Her lips parted, and her pupils dilated. Only a squeak left her. I continued stroking the lip I got to taste last night. She'd been sweet, like the beer we'd had. Refreshing. Addicting.

"You're trying to get into my head," she whispered.

"I very much am not. I meant every word."

The sound of an engine approaching had her stiffening. She'd run if the table wasn't right behind her. "I'm not the same kid you knew. I've grown. I've matured. So have you. And I've found myself living under the same roof with a very attractive, very sexy woman with freckles I want to count with my tongue while I see how far down your body they go."

Her eyes shone, and her breath came in pants.

"Dad!" Auggie's shout came from outside the shop.

I pulled away from her, gave her one last intense look to make sure she knew I meant every single goddamn word, and went outside to meet my son.

●●●

Poppy

Jensen: Do you have break in sessions I'm overhauling my site with a coming soon page for the Perez house

He hated using the keyboard, even with the app I installed, but it shouldn't be missing this much punctuation. I focused on his message. At least one word was missing.

Poppy: I'm done in forty. Then I'm off the rest of the day.

I still hadn't worked on building my own client base. Vacations were starting, and Debbie was throwing more fill-in jobs my way. It was giving me a reprieve from worrying about building my own list. No keys, no client base. That was my mantra.

I finished with Caden, an active six-year-old who couldn't concentrate for the whole half hour. I didn't blame him, but the policy is a minimum of ninety minutes a week. So his mom arranged for two sets of fifteen minutes three times a week. This was our second set of fifteen minutes.

I pressed my hand to my stomach. I'd go downstairs to meet with Jensen about his website, and like I'd been trying to do for the last week, I'd try forgetting that he wanted to trace my freckles with his tongue. I'd attempt to quit considering how serious he was. We'd acted like roommates since that day in the shop, and I'd started to wonder if I'd imagined it.

He claimed to be a different guy, and honestly, I'd made some prick moves as a kid. I'd said things I regretted and I had behaved abominably at times. All kids did. I shouldn't be holding it against him. But his words had burrowed in and molded into my personality, and I couldn't reverse that.

His tongue might be able to.

No, Poppy.

I made a few notes about my sessions, emailed Debbie an update, and closed my laptop. The spare room upstairs was sparse, but it was quiet. A perfect office, minus the view. I couldn't wait to get into the Perez house.

Anxiety clamped down on the sandwich I'd had for lunch. Even if this marriage worked and the house was mine, I'd need a job to live there and to keep the house maintained. I had some money socked away for the renovations Jensen would be undertaking but beyond that... My learning center needed a name. It needed to be launched. But the renters had only just parked a moving van on the sidewalk. So that could wait.

It was time to face Jensen and forget about how his calloused fingertips had felt on my skin.

He was sitting at the island when I reached the kitchen. The laptop was open in front of him, and he was deep in a plate of chips and queso.

"Hey," he said around a mouthful. "Want some?"

"I'll grab my own bowl if you promise not to tell

Auggie when he gets home from school that I'm ruining my supper."

"Why do you think I'm eating it?"

"If you don't like the chicken you threw in the Crock-Pot, why did you make it?"

"Because I didn't know how busy I'd be with the estimate. Some clients talk an extra hour, and I'm not in a place to tell them I have to go." He shoved a chip full of queso in his mouth. "Mom's picking Auggie up."

Disappointment heated the back of my neck, and I retrieved my own bowl. Did he think of asking me? "I could've helped out with that."

"I was hoping you'd go to the estimate with me."

"Oh." He had plans for me? I liked that thought. At least one of us did something that wasn't impulsive. I sat at the island next to him, stole some of his queso, and grabbed a handful of chips. "Why?"

"Can you make sure I get their names right? It's Germy and Kate."

"Jehr-eh-me."

Frustration flickered in his eyes. "What am I saying?"

I spun to face him. "You're saying germy." I walked through each sound of Jeremy and how it should feel for him. He didn't shrink away, but he couldn't smother his embarrassment.

"Jehr-eh-me. Jeremy." Concentration filled his eyes. "Jeremy. I shouldn't fuck up Kate."

"Since we're working on it, mind if I ask how the keyboard app is working?"

"Fine. I've been using voice-to-text more."

A lot of my students who were old enough to have phones often used voice-to-text. "Remember punctuation though."

He flashed me a grin. "I will when I'm not texting you. Nice to not have to worry about it."

Pleasure filled me. I was his exception. "You don't have to impress me."

"I very much want to impress you, Poppy, but in this, I know I can't win, and you know why. There's a comfort there. I can just be my miswired self."

I put my fingers on his forearm. "You're not miswired. Just wired differently."

"And that's why it's nice not to worry about it with you." He put his hand over mine, blanketing my hand with his. "You understand. Not many do. I get shit as an adult for stumbling over words."

"Well, the Elijahs of the world suck."

His smile was tight. "I worry about it with Auggie, but people like you get him and teach him how to live in this world. How to be easy with himself when he has trouble spelling *what* as an adult."

"The curse of the sight words."

"Lifelong," he agreed. "At least it's not all the time. Just every once in a while I get stuck knowing that the word I'm writing is wrong, but I can't fix it for the life of me. Or that I'll know what I'm trying to say, but I can't summon the word for it." He brushed his fingers along the back of mine. A light shiver traced down my spine. "I really do appreciate what you're doing for Auggie."

"I'm just a sub." Any other tutor would do the same.

"You're so much more." He leaned closer, sparking a glow inside of my chest. "He asked about a soccer team this morning. Said he told his teacher that his friend plays and 'she's real good.'"

I laughed. "Is that a quote?"

"Direct. She actually wants to talk to you about starting a summer travel team."

My good feeling took a nosedive. "I don't have anything to tell her."

He gave me that look, the one that said he knew I was brushing him off without explaining. "Are you sure about that?"

"I can be impulsive with my planning and things fall through, so yes. I'm sure." Saying it out loud was a release. He had his own business and he was doing well. He didn't think so, but he hadn't moved towns when his plans and hard work tanked—twice.

"Wanna tell me about it?"

No. "It was humiliating." But if he could relax and be himself with me, maybe I could give a little something in return. Wasn't that how we worked? "After graduation, I played soccer for a school in South Dakota."

His hand was still on mine. He continued with his slow caresses, and I soaked up the comfort.

If he kept that up, I'd let him find out how many freckles covered my body. I didn't stop him, but soccer was a safe subject. "After, I was all soccer all the time. I coached it, and I even reffed."

"Yeah? Gettin' after those parents."

I grinned. "Sometimes, but I mostly got in trouble for taking too much time when I corrected the kids in the middle of the games."

"Coaching is in your blood."

"It was. Then I was recruited to start a league. Parents were disenchanted with the bigger club in town and the preferential treatment of some kids. I said I'd do it. It wasn't like I was reinventing the wheel, right?"

He hooked his fingers through mine. "Didn't go well?"

I couldn't bring myself to pull away. "It was a dumpster fire. The bigger club dominated the town. They got all the field times, blamed us for any damage to the grass or fence line, and the one weekend I planned a small tournament, the Parks and Rec board rented the fields out for a cornhole tournament. 'Oops, we double-booked.'" I mimicked the snide voice of the Parks and Rec lady, who I learned later was the wife of the club's president. Old emotions tumbled back until the utter failure hung like cement blocks off my shoulders. "I was on the hook for it all. The club went broke. Coaches were irate. Refs who thought they had a weekend gig were pissed. A couple of teams traveled, paid for hotels, and no games. I took all the blame."

"You were sabotaged."

I shrugged. "The buck stopped at me."

"You were what? Twenty-three?"

"By then, yes."

"But they'd been jerking you around earlier. And let me guess—the older adults who recruited you to run everything knew how everyone was, knew the politics, and left you out to dry."

Feeling moderately better about my role in the ordeal, I nodded. "I moved and started grad school and never played again." No matter how much I missed the movement and the kids.

"That's wrong." He stroked his thumb along the side of my hand. "Is that why you don't even have a name for your center yet? You're too afraid the town is going to sabotage you?"

"No one owes me anything." And no one would look out for me.

"Let's come up with a name."

"What? Now?" My pulse jackknifed. It was just a name. Why was worry clawing through my gut? I could come up with something and change it at any time. Yet my mind blanked. "Don't you have the meeting?"

"We have a half hour before we leave."

"The website?"

"Can also wait. I just want to add a Coming Soon page where I tease the Perez house remodel." He pivoted until he was facing me, our knees interconnected, and let go of my hand in the process. "Names."

Nothing came out of my mouth.

He placed his hands on my thighs, one on each leg, and my pulse sped up for a different reason. His ponderings about my thighs streamed clearly through my head.

"Little Minds?" He winced. "Shit, that will be taken the wrong way."

"I'm sure something like Duke's Dyslexia Center will work." It was just a name, so I hadn't given it thought. That was all.

"As much as I love the way DDC rolls off the tongue, you didn't put any thought into it."

"Hollis Cabinets?" I pointed out.

"Branding. My name's in the title, so they don't have to look hard. I'm well known enough in the area, so if someone says, 'Hey, is there a cabinet guy?' then Hollis jumps to mind." He gave me a gotcha grin. "Poppy's Pupils."

I laughed. "People will think I'm an eye doctor or something."

"Poppy's Field of Dreams Center." He grinned,

rubbing his hands up my thighs. "Poppy's Dream of Fields Center."

I let out a scandalized gasp.

He continued stroking my legs, stoking a thrum between my thighs. "No kidding, Poppy, I would pronounce it that way at least once."

I chewed on my bottom lip. "I want a title that will inspire kids but also make them feel like they're not standing out when they say it. DDC does that."

"You want a title that means something. DDC doesn't do that." He looked down at his hands and his fingers tensed over my jeans, but he didn't lift them off me. "I have no doubt you'll come up with something perfect."

"I have all the doubt."

"I might've said some stupid shit when we were kids, but I never doubted you. Ever." He stood up and pulled me to my feet. "Can I give Auggie's teacher your number?"

Oh. No. Not soccer. I liked kicking the ball around, but coaching again? Being in charge? "I'm homeless, and I work out of a spare room. I shouldn't be in charge of a team of kids."

"Yes, you should. I don't know anyone better."

I rolled my eyes. "Now you're overcorrecting."

He tugged me closer, wrapped an arm around my waist, and feathered the backs of his knuckles down my cheek. I turned my face into his touch.

What was happening? Why was I letting it happen?

Because it felt good. I liked it. And I didn't want him to stop.

"You're scared," he murmured. "Don't mistake that for a lack of ability. Part of our deal is that I'll help you get the house ready for you and for tutoring. That means helping you with Poppy's Peep Into Your Mind."

"Oh my god, that's awful."

His gaze lingered on my lips. "I really want to kiss you right now."

Yes, please. No. Boundaries. Those were important. I couldn't remember why. "You shouldn't."

"You keep saying that, yet nothing changes. I still want to kiss you."

I wanted him to, but then what? We had to navigate even more complicated boundaries. Because once he kissed me, I didn't think I'd want him to stop. "We have to look at your website and get to your estimate."

"Yeah." He didn't move. "I shouldn't go there with an erection."

"You do not have—" I dropped my attention down. Oh. The bulge in his jeans was impressive. And it was for me. "That would be bad for business."

"So far, you've only been good for business." He released me and adjusted himself. "But I'd better not test it. It'll be bad enough watching you wander around in those tight fucking jeans."

● ● ●

The house he'd been asked to do an estimate for was several miles out of town but wasn't far from his place. Jensen was amazing with clients. His issue wasn't his typos—there weren't many at all. I checked on our way over. Nor was it the few times he might mispronounce something. His issue had been one woman being catty.

If I had a dollar for all the stories I'd heard from my students about getting teased for mispronouncing words and names, for asking how to spell words others found simple, or for missing punctuation or some other grammar rule that made people feel superior knowing, I wouldn't have to marry to afford office space.

His main obstacle was population. The community was small. He'd have to travel to get more clients, and it was hard when he had a son to care for. He'd said his mom had started going south in the winter, and that left him with even fewer hands to help.

We wrapped up at the house. He'd practiced saying Jeremy and Kate all the way there and I didn't hear one "Germy."

"Want me to drop you off before going to Mom's?" he asked.

"Only if it's better I'm not there."

"It's never better," he said easily.

I wanted to roll my eyes again, but the warm spark ignited in my chest every time he said something like that.

Could I trust his intentions? He claimed he wasn't placating me, but how did I know? He was a single guy and he said he didn't date. I was a single woman who he was supposed to marry. I was convenient, and I'd been convenient before.

He opened the door for me and gave me a wink when he closed me in. My cheeks grew hot. Was I blushing?

Never in my life would I have thought Jensen Hollis would make me flush with more than anger that he beat me at something or that he had goaded me into another competition.

He got behind the wheel and drove to his mom's place. We flew by familiar pastures. I used to sit on the bus with my head on the glass and watch it all pass by. Then I'd watch a scrawny Jensen make his way down his drive, massive backpack on his shoulders. "Remember our bus driver?"

"Bonita Franks? She's in the same retirement community Mom stays in down in Arizona. She doesn't tell me to sit down anymore."

"You were always standing on the bus. You couldn't sit still."

"I still can't. Auggie's the same. Drove his mom crazy." He cleared his throat. "Sorry."

"I didn't say you can't talk about her." A mix of emotions battled behind my ribs. I wanted to hear about Auggie's mom, but then I'd remember who she was. "I was friends with Rodeo Barbie."

He cocked a brow at me as he turned onto the highway that'd lead to town. "I believe she'd say she was Barrel Racer Barbie and probably list all her winnings."

I chuckled. He had to be proud of her. He'd supported her through it all to get to where she was. "I have to admit that I have a hard time reconciling Hassie and Auggie's mom as the same person."

"She does too."

I blinked at him, but he didn't elaborate, turning off the highway to his mom's house. He'd made cryptic comments before, but if she'd been that bad, would Auggie still cling to a magazine she was in? Or have his room cowboyed up?

Auggie was playing in the yard, kicking a soccer ball around. When it came down to it, I didn't know him that well, or his history, and it wasn't my business, no matter what wishful thoughts went through my head.

I tapped the passenger window. "He's seriously taking to it."

"It's something he can do. He had a hard time around

the horses. A high-energy kid who didn't want to be held back. High-strung horses. It wasn't the best combo." As if Auggie heard our conversation, he sprinted over. "Poppy! My teacher wants to talk to you!"

Oh. I should be elated. I had dedicated so much of my life to the sport. I had lived for playing. Like Auggie, I hadn't gotten in trouble when I raced around the field. Dribbling the ball and kicking it off the wall kept me busy at home until Mom chased me out of the kitchen because the noise got to her.

If it wasn't for what happened after my college graduation, I would've jumped at the opportunity. I probably would've been coaching.

"What'd you tell her?" I asked.

Auggie beamed. "I said you'll take me to school on Monday and talk to her."

"Augs," Jensen groaned. "You've got to ask first."

The sweet boy blinked, oblivious to the tide of panic he started. "Well, you're supposed to be my new mom."

The word "mom" referring to me was trippy, yet I wouldn't mind hearing it again. Should I be bothered by that? Boundaries and all? Jensen's eyes went wide, his gaze flying to me.

"Riiiight." New mom. I wasn't going to reject the idea and hurt his feelings. He was a great kid, and he tugged at those strings in my heart, the ones that were getting shorter the older I got. They'd be tied up for good. I wasn't old, but my closest shot at getting married was striking a bargain with an old friend who'd never been interested in me. "I'll give you a ride, no probs."

He grinned. "Really?"

"Any time, as long as I don't have a client." I'd change my schedule if he asked, but I didn't want to overstep his dad. "I'm not sure if I can coach though. Starting a business and all."

His expression fell, yanking my heart down with it. "Okay. I was going to be on a team if she got one started this summer."

If there was a Most Wanted List for breaker of kids' hearts, I was on it. Not a good feeling. "I mean, I'm around all summer, so I'm sure I can do something with your team."

"Yeah!" He jumped up and down. "Grandma!" He raced off.

Jensen crossed an arm over his chest and stroked his chin with his other hand. His eyes were dancing. "He took you down that easy? Weak, Duke. Weak."

He wanted to play that game? "Auggie! Your dad said he'd coach too!"

Jensen made a choking sound, and I dissolved into laughter.

"You think that's funny?" He lunged for me, a wicked glint in his eyes.

I took off. I didn't know what he planned to do, but I was mostly afraid he'd wrap those big arms around me and I wouldn't struggle. Terrified a moan would leave me. My nipples would get hard and poke into him.

I sprinted to the garage, and dammit, he let me win. There was no way I'd gotten faster than him in the last twenty years.

Erin watched us charge in, an indulgent smile on her face. Auggie was probably telling her everything about soccer, but her grin only grew. "Sounds like it's going to be an interesting summer."

Chapter Ten

Jensen

I waited at the kitchen table while Auggie finished getting ready for school. Poppy was supposed to take him again. It'd been two weeks since she'd first driven him so she could talk to Miss Whitfield. She'd been roped into coaching one team and being a consultant. Since Auggie had heard her shout that I'd coach, too, I might also be involved. Miss Whitfield made Poppy the head coach of what would become Auggie's team, and Poppy had also helped by designing age-appropriate drills. There was more official paperwork to do, but Miss Whitfield was on it.

Since then, Auggie had been asking Poppy to take him to school more often. I gently tried discouraging him. She was basically our guest. We weren't married yet.

Dread mixed with excitement. I couldn't look forward to marrying Poppy. The marriage was literally designed to be fake. But I liked being with her. The thought of spending the next year with someone I enjoyed being with...

No. I couldn't go there.

I checked the time on my phone. Was she even awake?

Miss Whitfield had asked the principal to meet with Poppy this morning. He was working with Miss Whitfield to get the soccer team set up through Parks and Rec and had some questions.

"Poppy?" I called.

No answer.

Auggie wasn't downstairs yet, but he'd be ready to go. If I didn't make sure Poppy was awake, he'd charge into her room.

I went to her door and knocked lightly. "Poppy? You up?"

Still no answer. Shit.

I knocked louder. Was she okay? I cracked open the door. Light poured in through her open blinds. How could she sleep with the sun shining on her— A laugh punched out of me just as my dick took notice of how she slept.

She was passed out on her back, covers tossed off. Her shorts rode up her thighs to gather at her crotch, leaving acres of long, golden legs on display. Her shirt was my best and worst nightmare. Twisted across her torso, it was plastered to her chest, leaving almost nothing to the imagination. I could trace her areolas if I wanted to.

Jerking my attention to her face, another smile played over my lips. The blinds were open because she wore a sleeping mask. A bonnet contained her curls and over that were a pair of headphones. No wonder she didn't hear the knocks.

"Poppy." I got closer to the bed, afraid I wouldn't be

strong enough to keep my lecherous gaze off her legs, stomach, and tits. She was like a gift, waiting for me to finish unwrapping her. "Hey, four-ten," I called louder.

She twitched, and a sultry little groan slipped from her.

Whoa.

"Poppy." My voice was gruffer. "Wake up." *Put me out of my misery.*

"Jensen." A sexy moan resonated from her, and she scissored her legs. "Yes."

Fuck me. An erection was going to rise faster than the morning sun if I didn't wake her. I pulled one side of the headphones away from her ear. "Poppy, wake up," I barked.

She gasped and sat up, cracking her head on my chin. I reeled back, grateful for the pain shooting through my skull. My blood got distracted from filling my dick.

"Wha— Jensen?" She clawed at her head to get everything off, but the sleep mask got tangled in the headphones, and her bonnet pulled sideways.

"Last time you said my name, you moaned it."

"What?" She ripped everything off in one tangled heap. She scooted backward on the bed, putting her hand over her mouth. "Ohmigod. Don't get closer. I need to brush my teeth."

"Honey, morning breath isn't going to scare me away with your shirt and shorts all knotted up like that."

Her hair pressed against her head. She glanced down and yelped. "Ohmigod." She tried to cover her boobs, then her crotch, back to her boobs, before giving up and yanking a blanket over her. "What are you doing in here?"

"You're meeting Miss Whitfield at the school today."

Another gasp echoed through the room and she shot out of bed. "Sorry!"

I turned to leave, but the lonely creep in me snuck one more glance at her skull-crushing legs. "I'll leave you to it."

"Jensen."

I didn't turn around. I'd violated enough of her privacy, and I wanted to do it again. "Yeah?"

"You were kidding, right? I didn't moan your name in my sleep?"

I should be a standup guy and spare her, but Poppy was one of the only people I could actually be myself around. "No, Poppy." Before I closed the door behind me, I said, "You moaned *after* you said it."

●●●

Poppy

My blood pressure hadn't returned to normal levels after my meeting with Miss Whitfield. There hadn't been much more new information. The city was willing to work with our little ragtag group, and Aspen—Miss Whitfield—had flyers already printed to recruit kids. It was coming along, and as long as she was in charge, my anxiety was kept at bay.

I moaned Jensen's name in my sleep? That part didn't surprise me. That he heard was a total embarrassment. What were the odds that one of the dreams plaguing me, where he peeled a wet shirt off me, happened exactly when I had overslept and he walked in?

Why else was I slumbering too long? I hadn't wanted to wake up from that wet dream.

But I had, and he'd seen me in all my *bonnet, sleep mask, and headphones* glory. And I'd had a wedgie from hell after writhing around.

We loaded back up in his pickup. I couldn't look at him. He hadn't minded the wedgie.

"So what's with the sleep routine?" He pointed to his head.

"My hair's so fine that it tangles like a nightmare. Mom got tired of fighting me to brush it, so she ordered a bonnet. I've been wearing them since. The sleep mask happened when a college roommate used to study all night and her light shone in my face." My phone vibrated, but I wanted to finish the explanation to save some face after the morning debacle. "Sometimes I wake up too early and I can't get to sleep if I'm not listening to a podcast or something."

"Makes sense. It was cute."

"You don't have to try to make me feel better."

"I'm trying not to make you uncomfortable, or I would've said it tied with the sexiest thing I've ever seen. I'll have to see you in that wet T-shirt again to decide between the two because, with all that leg on display, it's a tough choice."

He did not mean that. He'd been married to Hassie Heart of all people. She had more sexiness in her little finger than I'd possessed in my entire life. My phone buzzed again.

I took the distraction and pulled it out of my pocket. "It's Aunt Linda." I answered.

"Oh, Poppy." Her light voice came through the line. "Sorry if I woke you."

"No, I've been up for a while." I had to twist away from Jensen, or he'd see me blush. Sexiest thing, my ass.

Apparently, it wasn't my ass but my boobs and my legs.

"The tenant—former tenant—called. Their house closed early, and they said they'd be moved out by the end of the weekend. I didn't want to tell you if it ended up falling through, but they gave me the keys this morning. Usually, Darren replaces the locks right away, but I thought I'd wait. You might want something else."

"Yes, I can take care of that." Excitement swelled inside of me. It was happening. The worry sparked right behind it. I was at the beginning of a long road. "Do you mind if I come by and get the keys?"

"Not at all. I have to warn you, I don't know the state the house is in. There's always some sort of mess left behind."

"It's fine. I'll take care of that too." It sounded like she was sick of dealing with renters. My benefit, otherwise she wouldn't let me in so Jensen could get to work.

"I'm in town now, and I can meet you in a few minutes."

"See you in five." I hung up and spun in my seat. "The house is open."

Jensen turned at the end of the block without asking. Going straight would've taken us to the highway to get to his house.

I pressed a hand to my stomach. "I'm nervous."

"It's normal. Doesn't mean you can't do it. In no time, Poppy's House of Dyslexia will be open."

"That's really bad, Jensen." Yet I was grinning.

"Poppy's Brain Time."

"Nope."

Linda waited outside of her car. She didn't stop for small talk but thanked us in her pleasant way and drove away.

I clutched the cool metal keys. This felt like such a monumental moment, even though the house wouldn't be officially mine for a year after the wedding, which was in a month. What if all the floors needed to be replaced? The roof? The closets. Did closets get replaced? What if the house was that bad?

Jensen waited next to me while I gazed at the house.

"It'll need a paint job." I stuffed my thumb through the key ring. "A couple of shutters need to be replaced."

"The deck looks solid," he said. "I'll check it out before we leave, but all in all, it looks good. Shingles are in decent shape, drain spouts are straight, and the fascia and soffits are strong."

Relief flooded me. Without Jensen, I wouldn't have known any of that. I could call Dad. He'd be here in a heartbeat, but he and Mom had bailed me out of the mess in South Dakota. They'd given me money to move for my master's degree. I hadn't told them about the Wyoming debacle. Alder was a CEO. Violet was a chemist. Jasper used to work some high-paying IT job and now he was ranch manager for Knight's Cattle Company. Lily had a good job and was raising a family. Clover was a geologist. I wasn't going to be the first Duke to be a failure to our parents.

He placed his hand on the small of my back. "Ready?"

He couldn't have known I needed his strength, but I soaked it up from his warm touch. "Ready."

Nerves exploded in my stomach as I opened the door. This whole place was my responsibility. Linda trusted me with it. The Perez house was a community treasure. And now it was in my care.

Pushing inside, I waited to be impressed. It didn't happen. "It's...normal."

Jensen lightly touched my hips as he skirted around me. I almost leaned into him. He wandered to the stairs across from the front door. They were plain oak stairs. Whatever had originally been installed had been replaced with the look of the time, and the time looked to be—

"Poor thing is stuck in the nineties," Jensen said while doing a spin. To our left was a kitchen with a similar style of cabinets, and to our right was a living area with a bay window and the white wispy curtains I could see from outside. "And not the 1890s."

That would've been more ideal. "It's underwhelming."

He ran his hand over the square banister. "Most of it's cosmetic. When you start profiting, you can redo the stairs, replace the banister, put some crown molding back in place."

"It would look beautiful with crown molding."

"Eliot has a brother and sister-in-law who restore old homes. She's an interior designer and they do consulting." He tested the floor's squeakiness, pressing his foot in different places as he worked his way to the kitchen.

I followed him. "Lily's Eliot?"

"Yeah. I've done some work for them, but they do a lot themselves, and they've slowed down a little since their kids are younger." He ran a hand over the end of the counter. "Might be worth giving her a call."

"How much is she?"

"I can write it off as a business expense. We'll do the remodel in phases. Cabinets first. Painting and cosmetic stuff. Then, after you're in, we can update the look of the stairs and, I'm guessing, the bathrooms."

"No." I crowded close to him. "You're already giving up time for something that may not earn you money. I can't have you incurring more time and expense." Yet I couldn't afford a consult from specialists on old houses, and we should have one before he started. "We don't need one anyway. I trust your knowledge."

He straightened to his full height, towering over me, which wasn't hard to do—and I liked it.

I ran my tongue over my lower lip. His gaze tracked the movement. "You can't stop me from calling."

"Can too."

"Try it."

He was putting me up in his house, refurbishing this place, and marrying me so I could own it. "You're getting way less out of the deal."

"Yeah." His attention dropped to my lips. "I am."

His tone suggested we weren't talking about the same thing. Desire unfurled in my belly. "I've barely touched your website."

"I know exactly what you haven't touched." Did his head drop lower? "And I know exactly what I'd like you to touch. What *I'd* like to," he murmured.

His lips were so close to mine. So achingly close. If I just rose a little...like this...

Our lips touched and time froze. He was warm and real and this wasn't enough. As if he read my thoughts, he snaked an arm around my waist and increased the pressure of his kiss.

Yes. I wrapped my arms around his neck and stood on my tiptoes. If I could crawl into him, I would. He was a wall of muscle, so damn strong, and he was here with me.

A growl ripped from deep in his chest and he lifted me. My ass hit the edge of the counter. He adjusted until I was firmly in place. I automatically twined my legs around his hips, my lust building.

He invaded my mouth and I let him, tilting my head so he could delve deeper. The man knew what he was doing, licking and stroking his tongue against mine, sending tingles straight down my spine until they exploded between my legs in a pulsating cloud.

I moaned and cinched my hold tighter. A hard ridge pressed against me. Oh god, why did he have to be impressive in everything? My curiosity rose. Did he fuck like he kissed? Could I find out?

He swept his warm hands up my shirt. I whimpered. His rough fingertips whispered against my skin as he skimmed upward. I took his hat off and flung it on the counter, not caring where it went. Then I ran my hands over his head, letting his trimmed hair prickle against my palms.

He reached my breasts and covered them with his big hands. My hard nipples poked through the fabric like they were trying to reach him. He hooked his fingertips over the bra's edges and dragged them down. Thank fuck I didn't wear a sports bra today.

A distant voice in my head said we should stop, but it wasn't coming up with a good reason why.

He left my mouth to kiss his way down my neck. I tipped my head back while thrusting my chest into his hot hands. Cool air wafted across my exposed nipples. My shirt was pushed high, exposing me for him. He cupped my breasts and licked across one nipple before sucking the pearled tip into his mouth.

The cry I let out was so full of need I would've been embarrassed any other time.

"You know how fucking wild these have been driving me?" Hot breath gusted over my wet flesh. He switched to the other side. "So fucking perfect."

He claimed that nipple, and the wet heat of his mouth was all-consuming. I had to brace myself on the counter while he indulged himself. I didn't realize I was rocking into him until the energy inside me started coiling and concentrating between my legs. The sensation grew stronger and more demanding. I shamelessly rubbed myself against him to steal all the pleasure he was building inside me with each stroke of his tongue.

"Jensen?" I sounded like I was begging, and maybe I was.

"You're needy, aren't you?" He was still playing with my greedy nipples, but he slid a hand up my thigh. I widened my legs for him.

He put an inch of space between us. I whined from the loss of friction, but then his calloused fingertips hit my inner thigh. I rocked into his touch.

"Poppy." He lifted his head, and the picture he made would forever be the one to get me off when I was in bed by myself with my toys. His chiseled face was framed by each of my breasts and my thighs bracketed his body. "I need to hear you come."

"I need to come." I squirmed, trying to get closer to him. I hadn't been able to do anything, too afraid he'd hear and I'd die of embarrassment. Now here I was, ready to detonate, and he was still inches away from my pussy.

"I could use my finger." He licked across my nipple, making me shudder. He dipped his hand into my shorts and stroked me over my underwear.

Waves of muted pleasure rolled over me. Why, oh why, did I wear panties today? I did every day, but that didn't matter right now.

"Or I could use my mouth." His hand was gone. I wiggled my ass like I could find where he took those talented fingers.

Then he tugged my shorts down, and I was in the perfect position to lift my hips only slightly for them to slip off. My underwear stayed frustratingly in place.

"Fuck, Poppy." He ran his hands all over my legs, pushing my knees wide. "I've been dreaming about getting my head between these thighs." He took me in. "Ah, baby. You're wet for me."

I should be embarrassed, but I wasn't. I nodded. "I need…"

"I know what you need, honey. And I'm going to give it to you."

My breasts were still jutting out of my top, my skin feverish. The bottom flap of my shirt had fallen but didn't cover them entirely. My lower half was almost bare, but Jensen didn't let that stop him. He hooked his arms under my thighs and tugged me close to him. My ass was at the very edge of the island and I was open to him, yet I wasn't self-conscious. I needed this too much.

He used a thumb to hold the crotch of my underwear to the side. "Fuck, Poppy," he groaned. "You look even better than I imagined. And I thought of this a lot."

He couldn't be seriou—

He licked through my slit with a quick flash of his tongue, landing on my clit. Electricity snapped over my skin. I bucked into him, and he growled, his strong grip holding me in place. He worked me like he thought this would all stop in a heartbeat. It couldn't stop. I would implode if I couldn't explode. The combustion had already started, and I needed to finish.

I tangled the fingers of one hand in his short hair. My abs were clenched, holding my knees up and out to the sides.

"Yes, Jensen. Yes, yes, yes." In a faraway part of my brain, astonishment swirled and coalesced. At no time in my life did I think I would be in this position with this man. Not only that, I was more comfortable with him than anyone I'd been with. Broad daylight shone through the windows. Thankfully, the kitchen faced the empty field that would be mine a year after I married this man.

Married. My desire swelled and a flush of heat hit my center. "I'm so—" I wasn't close. I was there. "Jensen!"

My voice echoed through the room as I came, my body shaking. I was no longer yelling, but all I was saying was gibberish. Murmuring my thanks, my amazement, my utter appreciation for the best orgasm of my life.

"Christ, that was beautiful." He put my underwear back in place and kissed the inside of my thigh. "When can I do it again?"

Reality crashed into me. He was rising, his gaze on my exposed chest. I wrestled my shirt down, and disappointment filled his expression. My shorts were...somewhere. Now what? We weren't supposed to fuck around during this arrangement.

There were no rules against oral sex. Should I add some?

My body still hummed, and the satisfied thrum between my legs would be happy for all this to happen again.

"Um, we probably shouldn't—"

He cupped the side of my face with a big hand. "You're getting scared away."

"I'm not scared, and you don't have to make everything into a competition."

Confusion darkened his eyes, but I jumped off the counter and searched for my shorts. They'd landed in the sink.

"It was an observation," he said quietly. "I'd never coerce you to do anything like this with me."

I exhaled, clutching my shorts in my hands. My back was to him. I didn't mean to accuse him of that, but that was exactly what I had done. "I know. I just wasn't expecting this. Between us. It makes getting married so much more complicated."

His dry chuckle lacked humor, and yeah, I knew how that sounded. That sort of chemistry with marriage vows? I'd want fifty years to go by before we remembered we were supposed to divorce. But I got a year, and I didn't want to come out of this three hundred and sixty-five days later wishing for forty-nine more years while he was signing the divorce papers.

"It doesn't have to be hard," Jensen said.

I turned around, wishing I'd put my shorts on, but it would be distracting now. Except the way his attention kept dropping to my legs was doing the same. His reaction made me want to walk around without pants all the time.

"We're adults," he continued. He adjusted the big ridge behind the fly of his jeans. Even after the way I reacted, he was still hard? "We can fool around and be mature about it."

"Feelings happen."

He tilted his head. "And you don't want them to?"

"I don't want to get hurt." I was more exposed than I had been minutes ago. "I like you, and you make me feel good, and I'm not even counting what you just did to me. That was...well done."

Smugness filled his eyes, and to prove how hopeless I was getting, I found it sexy. "You liked it?"

My cheeks burned. "Did you not hear me holler your name?"

"Your thighs were around my ears."

I was going to ignite. He twisted me up inside and out, and the result was that I wanted more. "Just because I liked it"—a lot—"doesn't mean it's a good idea."

He crossed his arms and leaned against the island, seemingly oblivious to the monster erection he still had. "I'm going to do whatever you're comfortable with. You tell me never to touch you again, and I won't. I can't promise that the next time I jack off I won't be seeing your sweet pink pussy in my head."

His words were a hot breath on my smoldering kindling.

"You don't think you're helping me, but you are, Poppy. Before you showed up in town, I was coasting through life, knowing my path was veering off the road. I was afraid I'd have to move me and Auggie or that I'd have to get a job that would keep my mom from going to Arizona where she has some beau who's making her giddy again." He swallowed, his expression turning solemn. "I was an empty shell, wondering if I'd ever feel again. Then you showed up with that wet shirt and those legs, and I'm very much a man. Your part of our bargain has already paid off. Just having you understand me and what's going on? I don't feel like I'm a wannabe who can't do what the professionals can. Not only that, you're trusting me with a gem the whole town adores right after I lost a job because I spelled my name wrong. That's priceless."

Humbled, I tightened my hold on my shorts. I didn't do all that for him. He did it all for himself. His work should've spoken for itself. It wasn't his fault people didn't bother to look below the surface.

He made me feel good, and I did the same for him. Could it be as simple as that?

"I need to think about it," I said. We each had our end of the deal, and I couldn't risk that for either of us.

"Take all the time you need." He pushed off the island and adjusted himself. "I need to walk this off before we grab some lunch. Then we can make a plan of attack for the house."

I watched him leave the kitchen before I scrambled into my shorts. My nipples remained tight peaks. My body thought his offer made so much sense. We were adults. He didn't say I was convenient, but the idea plucked at my insecurity. I should tell him no. We couldn't do this at all. But as I straightened my clothes to make sure I didn't look like I was half stripped down, I was glad I didn't tell him to quit touching me.

Chapter Eleven

Jensen

My erection was going to kill me. At what point did I have to call a doctor? Technically, the damn thing had gone away, but it roared back with nothing but a thought. It hadn't helped that I'd spent the whole day with her. I was taking refuge in my shop, but not much work was getting done. I had to pick up Auggie in a little over an hour.

She tried to hold back, but the more we talked, the more excited I got. I would be able to get in at the start. Instead of trying to match cabinets to the flooring and countertops, I would get to help pick the materials that would tie them all together.

An hour ago, Poppy had to run into the house for a tutoring session, so I pulled all sorts of examples. Tomorrow, we could go look at samples, but this way, she'd go in informed. Until then, my hormones could cool the hell down.

I was finally erection-free when she strolled back into the shop. She had two cans of sparkling water, but all I could see were her creamy tits with the rich pink nipples and the way she glistened for me.

A blush graced her cheeks. My expression must be absolutely feral. I dropped my gaze. This would be harder than I thought. I didn't want to make her uncomfortable.

I stayed sitting in my chair. "How'd it go?"

"A little rocky, but that's working with kids. They have good days and bad days." She approached the desk, and I gave up trying to keep my lecherous stare off her. The sway of her hips mesmerized me. "Whatcha got?"

I moved to get out of the chair, but she set her hand on my shoulder.

"Stay." She spun me while sitting and patted my lap. "Can I sit?"

Lust punched me low. "I might beg you to."

She was almost shy when she perched on my lap. I rested a hand at her hip and maneuvered through the tabs I kept open.

"I can get the hardwood looking...hard." My concentration was obliterated. My erection raged back stronger than ever, and I was starting to sweat. The way her ass wiggled on me when she leaned over gave me all sorts of ideas about leaning her over the desk.

She did it again when she looked back at me. "How hard?"

"Christ, Poppy, I'm so fucking hard."

She slid off my lap to her knees in front of me. I was dreaming. She went inside for her session, and I fell asleep at my desk. This wet dream was going to be amazing. But when she reached for my fly, cool clarity rushed in.

"What are you doing?" I knew what she looked like

she intended to do. I knew what I wanted her to do. But this couldn't be real. I'd been prepared to have a very abstinent marriage full of one-sided yearning.

"Making us even." She reached for my crotch.

I put my hands on hers. "Christ, Poppy. You don't have to do that. Don't get me wrong, that tops my list of things I'd like to happen, but I don't want you to do it out of obligation. I can behave myself."

"You can behave yourself because you didn't have the most powerful orgasm in your life. I can't think, Jensen. It hasn't been that long, but I could barely pay attention to my students. It's not fair. You should have your brains scrambled too."

Fuck, yes, I should. Scrambled so hard I didn't recognize myself. That was a problem. I wasn't thinking straight around her as it was. All the blood my brain needed was gone, filling my dick until I had no heartbeat but the one behind my zipper.

"Then we'd be even?" I should be shutting this down. I would've if she hadn't laid out what her release had done to her. I didn't need an eye for an eye. Pleasuring her had been enough while never being enough.

"Even Stephen."

"Best orgasm I've ever had?"

Vulnerability traced through her features, but before I could dissect the reason it was there, she flipped the fly of my jeans open and the tips of her fingers grazed my erection through the fabric of my boxers.

"Fuck," I groaned.

"I haven't even touched you yet."

"It's not going to take much." I gripped the armrests as need slammed into me.

She slid the boxers over the crown of my dick, and it

popped free like it'd been suffocating for months. More like years.

I lifted my gaze from the way I was straining for the ceiling with her tanned hand wrapped around the base to the interested way she was studying my package. Her eyes were bright and there was an anticipation there. She wanted to do this. She wanted to wrap those full pink lips around the tip of the crown and take me inside her mouth as far as I'd go.

I didn't know what I did to deserve this, but I'd keep doing it. Forever. I had a beautiful woman on her knees in front of me and she wanted to pleasure me. She didn't act like it was a chore. She claimed it was to get even, but that look on her face said differently.

Then she licked her lips.

Just as she was leaning in, I grasped her chin. "You're pretty goddamn amazing, you know that?"

"Because I'm going to suck your dick?"

Well, yes. "Because you look at me like you want to."

"Because I do." She tightened her grip and gave me a pump. *Fuuuuck.* I rolled my hips into her exquisite touch. She rubbed her cheek against my palm. "You make me want to give you the same pleasure you gave me or die trying."

"You're already giving me more than I've ever had."

A flash of confusion preceded her disbelief. "I'm already on my knees. Are you going to let me suck you off or not?"

"Yes. Very much yes." I peeled my finger and thumb from her chin.

She gave my shaft another stroke and then dropped her head. All air froze in my lungs when her lips wrapped around my crown.

"Fuck, Poppy." A tentative lick had me gripping the armrests of my office chair.

She moaned and sucked me in as far as I could go. I jerked against the chair, and she clung to my hip with her free hand.

I sucked in marginal amounts of air as the sensations she caused overpowered me. I was but one giant aroused nerve. I charged toward my peak, unable to hold off the orgasm so I could enjoy this a little bit longer. But I'd be reliving it every night in bed. During every shower. I'd have my hand wrapped around my cock, and I'd strive to replicate the bold licks of her tongue.

"Poppy, your mouth feels like heaven. I'm going to come."

She moaned in response. It was my undoing.

I tangled my hand in her curls. "I can't hold back." It was a warning. She needed to save herself before I unloaded like I never had before.

She didn't back off. I flipped over the edge, tumbling head over heels as I orgasmed. She licked and sucked, and instead of a quick climax, I came and came and came. The chair's wheels scraped against the floor, and I nearly yanked the armrests off.

Shudders racked my body when she finally released me. My dick popped free of her mouth and cool air wafted over my glistening shaft. All I wanted to do was curl up with her, but she wiped her mouth and sat back on her heels. No, that wouldn't do. I gathered her into my arms and onto my lap. I buried my face into the crook of her neck. "That was fucking amazing."

"Good." She settled against me. We fit perfectly. "It's a bad idea. Right?"

"You giving me head before school pickup is a great idea."

She giggled and poked my shoulder. "No. Fooling around. But orgasms before the school run do sound like a good deal."

She wasn't ready to sleep with me and she might never be. We'd be married, but I'd have months to get to know her. To show her that this wasn't a bad idea. That maybe we weren't a mistake. What crackled between us wasn't a fluke. It wasn't something we should just ignore. Already, this arrangement was working better than what I'd experienced before.

She'd moved to Coal Haven just when I was resigning myself to a long single life. I was marrying this woman. It might be a business deal, but...what if it wasn't? What if we fanned these flames and made a fire that wouldn't burn out from disinterest and a lack of priorities?

She hadn't indicated she wanted more, and I wasn't going to ask. The days of begging for a woman's affection were over. But if she wanted to explore our chemistry? I was there for it.

Chapter Twelve

Poppy

What was I doing? I snapped back to focus on my laptop. Jensen had run to pick up Auggie from school. My body hummed from the minutes before he left. The way that man could twist me up should be illegal.

I could barely concentrate during my daily sessions. For the last four days, I stared at the clock, and an hour before school pickup, I went to the shop and got an orgasm and then I gave one—in that order. Each. Day.

I wanted more. Having his fingers in me or his tongue on me wasn't enough. I wanted him inside of me. I wanted to feel him moving in me. But if we had sex... I had always been left disappointed with my previous partners. Would Jensen feel the same about me? He'd been married to every man's dream. Hassie hadn't needed him to help coach her through a business. Hassie probably hadn't needed to do much to blow his mind with a climax. Just seeing her naked probably rocked his world more than I ever could.

I scrubbed my hands down my face. I wasn't this insecure. Okay, I was, but not about me.

Maybe a little.

I could sit and spiral, or I could talk to someone. I picked up my phone and tapped into the text thread with my sisters.

Poppy: Can anyone meet me for a drink tonight?

I didn't have to wait long.

Violet: Evander's going to throw me out of the house if I say no, so yes. I need a night out.

Lily: I'm in. Where?

Clover: You guys are making me jealous. I'm two states away, but I'll have a drink in solidarity for whatever Poppy's going through when I'm out with Elijah tonight.

My lips curled into a sneer when I read her boyfriend's name. Ugh. My appreciation crowded out my disgust. Clover could tell something was going on, and I hadn't said a word.

Lily: OMG, what's wrong? I'm so clueless.

Poppy: I need you to talk sense into me.

Clover: Bone him.

I laughed out loud, the sound bouncing off the walls.

Poppy: NO. I said talk sense into me.

Violet: I have to admit I agree with Clover.

Poppy: Then just let me get drunk and tell you why I shouldn't. Meet me at 7, downtown, where Lily plays darts.

Violet: Deal.

Clover: To keep me in the loop—this is Daddy Jensen, right?

Poppy: Gross, Clover.

Clover: Bet that's not what you said when his tongue was down your throat.

My cheeks heated, and I slid my phone across the desk. Jensen and Auggie would be back soon, and Jensen said he'd grill hot dogs and brats tonight. I was stupidly excited about something so simple.

My phone buzzed. I wasn't going to look at it, but the all caps made it irresistible.

Clover: OHMYGOD HIS TONGUE'S BEEN DOWN YOUR THROAT!!!!

I groaned. I'd busted myself. Might as well not try and hide it since that was what I needed to talk to my sisters about.

Poppy: That's not the only place it's been.

Poppy: I owe you for that bet. He doesn't have a tattoo of Hassie.

My phone exploded with replies filled with emojis— at least ten of them were eggplants.

Just when I thought it died down, there was one more buzz.

Daisy: I know I'm late to the party, but I can't miss this.

The drone of Jensen's pickup reached me. I finished scheduling my calendar for next month so I could send the new summer schedules to the families I was working with. How many would be willing to come to in-person tutoring and switch from Debbie's place? I didn't want to poach her patients, but she was practically throwing them at me. Being overbooked was a good problem to have and even more beneficial for me. But the pressure grew with each client who indicated they would like to continue with me when I opened my doors.

I had the keys in my hands, but putting names on my list didn't seem prudent until the work in the house was done. Then I could take on full-time clients.

Flutters erupted in my stomach. From the thought of my tutoring center actually happening, or because I'd get to see Jensen in a few minutes? We'd pretend we hadn't just been half-naked in the shop getting each other off.

I shut down my computer. The weekend officially started.

I found Jensen at the grill. The garage door was open, so he could go use the table he had set up inside for his supplies. When he spotted me, his gaze heated and the corner of his mouth kicked up. Just from that, I could strip down again.

"Poppy! Come play with me!" Auggie yelled from the yard, where he dribbled a soccer ball around the trees.

I was on a trajectory to give Jensen a hello kiss like I hadn't seen him all day. Like we were a real couple. We weren't. We couldn't be. Now was not the time to risk my heart and my personal life.

"I'll be right there," I called to Auggie. I stopped far enough away from Jensen that I wouldn't beeline straight for his arms. "I'm going to meet my sisters for a drink after dinner." I almost said *if that's okay,* but we weren't a real couple. A few more repetitions might convince my body to behave.

"Sounds fun. Call me if you need a ride."

"I joked I was getting drunk, but I'm not." I just needed the girl talk. The reality check. Clover wouldn't be there, so I might actually get one.

"Have fun." His eyes twinkled.

After a couple of seconds, I caught myself staring at

him. I jolted. "Excuse me, I have some passes to teach your son."

I jogged to the yard where Auggie was, but really, I was running from Jensen and everything I wanted to do to him.

●●●

The bass of the band at the bar acted like a privacy wall. Sure, I had to practically yell to tell my sisters a PG13-rated version of what I was doing with Jensen, but they could barely make out what I was saying.

Finally, the band took a break, and the sound lowered to a dull roar.

"What are you afraid of?" Daisy asked, twirling her glass. Other than her, we'd all had our one drink and were sipping on our Blue Dolphins—water. "Falling for him and he doesn't feel the same way? Or that he'll fall for you and you won't feel the same?"

That he wouldn't fall as far as me. "Yes to both." Close enough. "I mean, he married Hassie."

She blinked at me like she couldn't determine how that was critical.

"He also divorced Hassie." Violet rested her chin in her hand. "If he was obsessed with her, he would've done everything to make it work."

"Unless she refused to. I don't really know what happened between them, but she's still Auggie's mom. She's still in his life—and Jensen's. What if he's just waiting for his moment? For her to say, 'Okay, now I'm ready to love you more than horses.'"

Lily snorted, digging her cherry out of her empty Shirley Temple. "From what little I remember, people like her don't love men more than their horse—because the animal is the extension of self."

That shouldn't have made me feel so much better, but a part of me lifted. "Think so?"

Violet pursed her lips. "It doesn't matter what we think. Have you talked to him about whether it'll be just sex to him?"

I crossed my arms. "I told him I wasn't looking for a relationship. Can you imagine how awkward that would be if he thought I was looking for a love match and he just wants a good time until Hassie gets bored of barrel racing?"

"Hate to sound like a broken record," Lily said, "but Hassie's not going to get tired of barrel racing."

"I want all or nothing." I shook my head. I couldn't give Jensen all of me and then have her swoop in. If a few comments when we were kids had stuck with me so long, what would that do? I had a career to get off the ground. "Which is too bad because I really do want him." His appetizers were amazing. What would the full course be like? I'd hunger for nothing but him.

Violet's face was screwed up like she was thinking hard. "What if...what if you had rules?"

I perked up. I knew surrounding myself with smart ladies would help. "What do you mean?"

"Not in his bedroom," Violet said. "Or yours."

"Or not in *a* bed," Daisy added. "Since there are ways to have sex in a bedroom but not in bed."

"I really have a hard time when it's my brother you're talking about." Lily shook herself. "But I'm also happy it's you with my brother you're talking about. What a mindfuck."

"Totally," Violet said. "I might need another drink."

"We had a roommate agreement when we first married." A blush darkened Daisy's cheeks. "Admittedly, we broke the rules pretty quickly."

"I'd ask what rules," I said, "but also it's our brother." I thought for a moment. Rules were boundaries and that was what I had thought we needed. We still did. "The idea has promise."

"Like after Auggie's in bed." Lily ticked a finger. "No beds. No cuddling after." She continued ticking off fingers. "Um, no candlelight dinners."

"Straight fucking." I sucked in a deep breath. Could I do that? He'd said he was willing. Would he mind a roommate agreement? A fake marriage arrangement? Since we weren't married yet, it'd be an engagement agreement. Semantics, but I clung to the fine line. Because I'd be dancing on it as soon as I got home.

Chapter Thirteen

Jensen

Auggie was asleep, and I reclined on the couch, watching one of my favorite episodes of *Brooklyn Nine-Nine*. Poppy wouldn't be home late. She and her sisters weren't like that, but on the off chance she was, I had the urge to wait up for her. I wanted to make sure she made it home safely.

An anxious tangle formed in my gut. I didn't like the sense of waiting, of wondering. Of having to nurse a hungover wife who'd partied with clients and fellow cowboys. Of wondering if this time she'd smell like someone else's cologne. Or when she'd rush right into the shower. Back then, I'd known it was a matter of time. My ex had a code of honor, but I was never sure how long it'd protect me.

Headlights swung by the window and a knot in my stomach eased. It was barely after ten, and she was already home. She'd joked about getting wasted. I hoped if she did, she caught a ride.

My phone pinged. Frowning, I glanced at it.

Poppy: Can you meet me outside?

I was out the door in a minute. All I had on was a white T-shirt and a pair of pajama pants full of brightly wrapped presents that my mom had helped Auggie pick out for Christmas.

Poppy was waiting by my pickup, shifting from foot to foot like she was doing some ankle warm-up drill from her soccer days. The sky wasn't fully dark. I could see her pretty clearly, standing between our vehicles. She had worn the same thing to the bar that I had taken off her in the shop this afternoon. That had also been like a balm to the scars inside me. She hadn't dressed to the nines like she wanted to be the center of male attention—because being the center of mine wasn't enough.

"What's up?" I asked, shoving my hands into my pockets. The pants dragged a little lower on my hips, but the other option was to squat and run my hands down those muscular legs that drove me wild.

She started pacing. "I'm sorry that I had to talk to my sisters about us."

Lead lined my stomach. What'd they say? I'd been the topic of "girl talk" before and it was about how much I'd been a downer. "It's fine. You needed to talk."

She stopped abruptly in front of me. I drank her in— the fading light on her soft curls and the sparkle in the yellow flecks of her eyes. "They had some, uh, good ideas." When I lifted a brow, she nodded and her cheeks flushed bright. "Like an engagement agreement."

"Don't we already have one?"

"For sex."

My dick immediately came to attention. If this kept up, all she had to do was think about sex, and I would get hard.

"We don't do it in a bed," she continued and licked her lips. Fuck. "We only do it when Auggie's asleep, and no cuddling or that'd invite emotion, and we haven't even started our official time together." She wrung her hands. "Mostly, I don't want to mess this up. I like you and I like our arrangement. I know the sex will be good, probably *amazing*, and if we catch feelings, then...we risk messing up our bargain."

Mulling over her words, I also enjoyed the nervous buzz of energy coming off her. I didn't smell alcohol, just her normal sunshine-and-peaches scent. She was serious. So serious, she'd had a Duke sisters meeting about it, about us.

She'd thought it out. I didn't have to ponder for long. "Auggie's asleep and we're nowhere near a bed."

Her lips parted and a soft inhale resounded between us.

I wrapped a hand around her waist and caught those puffy lips. She plastered herself against me. Her sweet tongue was in my mouth. I met her stroke for stroke, tasting the syrup in whatever drink she'd had tonight. I'd been wanting this woman since I'd first seen her on the laptop screen. I fumbled behind me, searching for the door handle of my pickup.

After getting the door open, my ass hit the seat. The dome lights stayed on and we made our own private cove. I swiped my hands up her shirt, landing on that soft, velvety skin I felt in my dreams. It was getting darker, but

I didn't want to risk stripping her down entirely. Ditching her stomach, I hooked my thumbs in her pants and started to tug down.

Clarity hit me. We were adults, and we had to be smart about this. I broke the kiss. If only I could see her puffy lips and dazed eyes, but this was important. "Sorry. I don't have a condom with me."

"Oh." She twined her hands around my head and kissed me. "I mean, if we're going to be it for each other for a while, and I'm on the pill..."

The thrill I got from thinking of sinking into her wet heat with nothing between us should concern me. I was near feral for Poppy Duke. "I want that, baby, but you've gotta be sure. I haven't been with anyone for a long time."

"Me either, and I get checked at every physical."

"I had to. After..." I did not want to think about that part of my history right now. "You're okay with it?"

Her shadowed smile was sexy. "It's more efficient, right? Since we'll probably have to seize the moment a lot?"

"I like how you think." I dragged her pants down. "Now kick those fucking pants off and climb on top of me."

She got them off and stepped out of her shoes at the same time. My butt slammed on the seat, and she was scrambling in with me.

I yanked my pants down and her hands were there too, freeing me from the confines of the fabric. I hissed when she gripped my erection.

"You're going to feel so good," I said through gritted teeth.

She tried to straddle me. One of her knees hit the metal frame and her other bumped the console, but that didn't stop her. Desire must be coursing as hot through her blood as it was through mine. I helped her lift her leg between the front and passenger seats and I raised her other until it draped over my shoulder and the seat.

"I'm really exposed," she said breathlessly.

I held her with her pussy hovering right above the tip of my cock. "My favorite is when you're exposed. And I have all the control."

I lowered her and notched inside an inch. Tight, wet heat gripped the tip of my cock. If this was only the beginning, tonight would be seared into my memory forever.

"Jensen." She dug her fingers into my shoulders, and her ass muscles flexed as she tried to wiggle her hips.

"I need to make sure you're wet enough." I lifted her and lost some of that drugging warmth. We didn't have much room, but I dragged her back and forth across my crown. She coated me. "Fucking dripping."

Her whimper got lost in the night. "I need…" She was breathing hard, her legs tense and her body taut. I supported her, but her position wasn't a natural one.

"Tell me what you need, Poppy."

"I need you to fuck me." She clamped her legs around me as much as possible, and I lowered her. So fucking close to heaven.

She had no idea how much that got to me. My control nearly snapped. "Say please." I needed to hear that she needed me just as much.

"I need you to fuck me, please." She said it without hesitation. The push-pull we normally had was absent. Desire swelled larger in me, pulsating and demanding. I carefully lowered her as I thrust up.

Tight, wet heat enveloped me, all-consuming. "Fuck," I said against her mouth. "You feel so good."

She wriggled until she'd fully settled on me. "You're so big."

"You're just right." She was. A perfect fit. We were in an uncomfortable position, but we clicked together.

Some of the stiffness had left her. By the time I was done with her, she'd be completely pliant. I took over, pumping my hips as much as possible and lifting her. My pleasure skyrocketed. I gritted my teeth to keep control. She squeezed me as we both chased a high that came closer with each stroke.

The way we were crushed together provided the friction she needed. Her walls rippled, on the brink of her climax, gripping me tight, pushing me ever closer to the edge.

"Jensen?" She said my name like another plea.

I couldn't get enough. "Let yourself go, Poppy. Let me feel you come."

She fought to go faster than I was letting her, but I kept the pace steady. She whined and rolled her hips. She was ready to release, but I couldn't have her hitting her peak before me.

She sank onto me, over and over, with nothing between us. My arms started shaking, but it wasn't from her. I fought to keep my climax at bay, until finally she barked out a cry, her shining gaze flying to mine.

"That's it," I said. "Take it all."

She dropped her head back and came—hard. That was all I could take. I exploded as a freight train of an orgasm hit me. She chanted my name in my ear and that only made me come harder. I'd never experienced anything like this. The power, the closeness. I couldn't tell where I ended and where she began.

Fear dampened some of my desire. This was consuming. She was consuming. I wanted to give her everything, and I knew how that turned out last time.

I held her as she collapsed against me. She was pliant like I'd wanted her to be despite our awkward position. No beds.

That was right. We had rules. An engagement agreement. And I'd need those to keep from turning into the stupid, smitten man I'd been for most of my life.

●●●

Poppy

I woke the next morning with a delicious sensation between my legs and the question of when it would happen again in my head. Jensen had carried me in after helping me back into my pants. I had cradled my shoes. Then he'd brought me to my bedroom door, gave me a sweet kiss, and disappeared into his own room.

I'd never had that strong of an orgasm. Had it been the position? The suddenness? The lack of protection?

How soon could I test those factors?

I rubbed my hands down my thighs. It was Saturday, and I was going to work on the house. Jensen had supplies ordered, and he was already working on the cabinets. I could clean and paint.

After I dressed, I went to the kitchen. Auggie was at the table, a soccer ball at his feet that he was rolling around while he watched a show on his tablet. "Morning, Poppy."

"Morning, kiddo."

Jensen came out of the shower, towel-drying his hair. The gray shirt he had on hugged his powerful torso. My mouth went dry, and I forgot what I was doing.

"Morning, Poppy."

The way he purred my name sent a shiver right down my spine. "Morning, Jensen."

So proper. Last night, when I was split over him, we were so not.

He ruffled Auggie's hair. "Did you take your clothes to the laundry room?"

"Not yet."

Jensen's lips flattened. "Unload the dishwasher?"

"Oh. No." Auggie put the tablet down.

"Feed Luna?"

"Not yet."

"Auggie." Jensen blew out a breath. "You were supposed to do that after breakfast. Before you watched your show."

"Sorry." Auggie popped up.

"Be right back." I jogged upstairs and grabbed one of the write-and-wipe boards, along with some markers, out of my tub of supplies. I scribbled the three things Jensen told him on it before I raced downstairs and put the board and marker on the island. "You have anything else for him?"

Jensen shook his head and propped his hands on his hips. "Mom called and offered to have him sleep over."

"Yay! I'll go pack." Auggie darted for the stairs.

"Not so fast, quicksilver," I said. "You have to finish your duties first."

Auggie's little shoulders slumped.

I added *pack* to the list and pushed the board to the edge of the counter. "Here you go, Auggie. Check off each item when you get it done."

He peeked at the list, gave one determined nod, and ran up the stairs. I was just happy he was willing to try it.

Jensen wandered over and checked the board. "Think that'll work?"

"I've been told by parents that it helps the kids who get verbal lists jumbled in their head. Some parents swear by it."

"Hmm." He studied my writing. "If it's as simple as that, I'll take it." He leaned over the counter. "And if he was asleep, I'd also take you right on this island."

I let out a little gasp, but my gaze dropped to the counter as my belly tingled.

A rough growl left him. "Tell me, four-ten, do those rules account for when Auggie's having a sleepover?"

I licked my lips, and he tracked the move. "I think that gives us a lot more flexibility."

"And the Perez house? What rules are there?"

Oh god. So many options. I had to squeeze my legs together. "There's an island there." His pupils widened. "And no beds."

"Fuck, Poppy." He came around the island, but footsteps pounded down the stairs. He reared back and turned away from the stairs. The bulge in his jeans was clear. I'd never tire of his reaction to me.

"I got my clothes, Dad." Auggie went in the opposite direction to the laundry room.

Jensen looked over his shoulder. "Thanks, bud."

"The coast is clear," I whispered.

He scowled playfully. "It's never going to be clear with you. You going to the house?"

"Yes."

"I'll come by after I drop Auggie off."

A thrill coursed through my veins. We were definitely going to test at least one surface in that house. "Okay."

"And remember—it's date night."

Chapter Fourteen

Poppy

I was upstairs in the Perez house when I heard the front door open and close.

"You should keep this locked when you're here alone."

I wiped my hands off on a rag and screwed the lid on the paint I'd picked up this morning. I left my future office and stood at the top of the stairs. "It's Coal Haven."

Jensen gazed up at me from the base of the stairs. He was wearing work jeans that were already spattered with paint and a different gray shirt than he had on this morning. "Sorry I'm late."

"It's just painting and cleaning." He'd called and said a potential client had gotten a hold of him. Since Auggie was with Erin, Jensen said he could look at the project and prepare an estimate. That way, he wouldn't have to email. "How'd it go?"

He shrugged. "Good. They want new cabinets in the

kitchen and laundry room—all brand new, and then asked me to install the old ones in the garage for a workspace."

"Doable?"

"Of course." He took the stairs two at a time.

"I'm covered in paint."

"It'll wash off." He planted a kiss on me. My back hit the wall. I giggled into his mouth.

"Don't forget what night it is," he said against my lips.

"Saturday night."

"Date night."

Dates and sex. Either/or was one thing. Was both at the same time smart? I went still and he pulled back, concern in his eyes.

"What'd I say wrong?" he asked, suddenly serious.

"I don't know if date night and fucking should go together."

Realization dawned in his eyes, chased by disappointment. Then his gaze went neutral.

"I'm sorry," I whispered.

He stroked the backs of his fingers down my cheek. "For what?"

"I keep pushing you away." What if, someday, he kept that distance between us? "I just don't want to confuse myself."

I had trash taste in men, but Jensen didn't fit in that category. So if he let me go after our year of marriage was up? I'd be devastated. Everything I had was getting invested into this house and this business. I wouldn't be able to pick up and move. I'd just be crushed and have to see the crusher around town.

"I understand." He kissed my forehead and stepped

away, his movements stiff. "How about we add another rule to our agreement?"

My nod was jerky. "What?"

"You make the first move."

"Oh." Why did that bother me? He was giving me all the power.

"That way, you're not going out of your comfort zone."

That made sense, but there was something off. His shuttered expression didn't match his tone. Just then, a text made my phone vibrate. I didn't make a move for it.

"Go ahead," he said softly. "Answer it."

Since I didn't know what else to do, I retrieved the phone from my pocket.

Clover: When are we going dress shopping?

Oh. The dress. The wedding. I hadn't started planning much. Rattler's was catering. Alder said he'd round up the tables and chairs. That left one main thing. "Clover wants to go dress shopping."

"Sounds fun. Can't wait to see you in a dress."

Old memories crowded into my brain. "Really?"

"One hundred and ten percent. One giant leg tease. I'll be hard all day."

The comparison game demanded to be played. Me in a wedding dress versus Hassie in a wedding dress. But all the comments about my legs slowly erased what he'd said when we were younger. I was tired of comparing myself to her. She was someone I hadn't seen in twenty years, and I may not see her for twenty more.

●●●

Jensen

. . .

I pulled the potatoes out of the oven. Auggie hated baked potatoes and the texture, so when he was gone, I made them for myself. Poppy was in the bathroom taking a shower and cleaning the paint off herself. She'd been distant since I told her to start making the first move, but I couldn't be that guy again, begging for his wife's attention and getting turned away.

Didn't mean I didn't want Poppy with every breath I took. It did mean I was at her beck and call, should she choose to come calling, and that was an easier place to be. Supposedly.

I tugged at the collar of my shirt like it was slowly tightening around my neck and finished getting the rest of the meal ready.

"Smells delicious." She came out of the bathroom, squeezing the ends of her hair with one of my blue towels. She wore my favorite leggings and an oversized black shirt. The sight of her being so domestic in my home never failed to clench all those knots in my chest. The instinctual *I want this* came right after. Now that we'd had sex, the sensation only got stronger.

"Auggie fails to see the potential in the toppings." I gestured to the crispy chicken, bacon, shredded cheese, olives, tomatoes, onions, lettuce, sour cream, salsa, and I even added diced ham and sliced cucumbers to give her more options.

She studied the selections lined up on the island. "So the potatoes are a vehicle for a bacon salad?"

"Basically."

"Auggie's a smart kid. He'll see it eventually."

I went still. "It means a lot that you say that."

"That he's smart?" Surprise resonated in her voice.

"It's something I never got. And when I talk to Mom, all she remembers are the teachers who treated her like crap and made her feel small." In Coal Haven, many of them had been my teachers too.

"It's nice to be in a time when we understand more." She slid onto a stool and grabbed a plate. "And we can do something about it. Someday, I hope to be out of a job."

"Yeah?"

"I know how expensive it is to get tutoring. Debbie's had so many families have to drop out because they couldn't afford it, and that's with the cost offset by fundraising. One family who graduated out told me that she estimated spending forty grand on tutoring over the ten years she had kids in it."

"Fuck me. I hadn't calculated how much I'm in for already. He needs it. I'll make it happen." I enjoyed watching her pick through the selections and load up on the same things I would, except for the onions.

"Right? Debbie said they wiped out savings and racked up credit card debt. It shouldn't be like that. Debbie asked me to help her with the next legislative session."

"You should be mandatory in all the schools."

"I don't always get along with the administration." She popped a piece of bacon in her mouth.

"Is that the real reason why you left Wyoming?"

She stiffened and her gaze darted around, but she kept chewing. "No, the timing was right." The way she cut open her potato was stabbing it and ripping it apart. Was she hungry or pissed off? She sighed and put her knife down. "I argued too much."

"Poppy, I don't believe it." When she playfully

scowled at me, I chuckled. I wanted to keep the tone light, mostly to keep her talking. "I know you're in the right without asking."

"I dunno. I should've played ball more."

I slid my plate next to hers and sat down. We could be closer than when we sat at the island. "Poppy, one hundred percent if you thought something was wrong, it was."

"The caseload was too high. Over and over. So many kids needed help, but the school system would hire another administrator instead of another therapist. I tried to come up with ideas to help, but...they didn't pan out."

"Why?"

She gave me a tight smile. "No support. I got to be the scapegoat. Design a new schedule, they said. Because apparently, I knew better. Then, our load got worse, more therapists quit, and my coworkers blamed me. Anyway, that's why I should be my own boss."

She made it sound like that was her only choice. "You don't want to be?"

She pivoted to face me. "Dad was coming from a good place, but he gently suggested that I gave up too early."

"Harsh." Poppy adored her dad. That had to be akin to being told she was a failure by a guy who'd held the same job for over half her life.

"But true." She lifted a shoulder.

"There's nothing wrong with wanting something better." It sucked to be the one left behind because they weren't enough, but Poppy hadn't left anyone behind. Just a trail of men who didn't deserve her.

We ate our meal, chatting about the food and different

recipes, then cleaned up. When the dishes were done and the counter wiped, I hovered by the island. Was she going to retreat to her room for the night? Tell me she wanted to have sex? My arousal was instant and choking, but I'd kicked the ball to her. She had to decide what to do with it.

She wandered to the front window. "It's beautiful out. I might have a beer outside. Wanna join me?"

Abso-fucking-lutely. "Sure."

I grabbed a couple of bottles and met her on the porch. She sprawled on the porch swing and accepted the longneck bottle. "I never dreamed of a place like this. Not since we moved."

Her leg muscles flexed as she pushed against the porch boards to rock back and forth. I took one of the Adirondack chairs but cocked it to face her. "What did you dream of?"

"I missed our old house. I hear it has excellent new cabinets now."

She was teasing, but that didn't douse the spark of pride I got from working on that job and for a guy I had respected growing up. "I hear the Perez house is getting some nice ones."

"Mm. I've heard the same rumor." She took a drink. "Dad is beside himself to see the work you're doing. He wants me to send pictures as you go."

The young kid who lost his dad rose up inside me, ready for his approval. "He can be the first to see the portfolio."

"You don't mind?" She gently swung as she watched me. "My dad getting into your business?"

Her dad had to sign off on us, so no. It was smart to have him involved. But excitement to show off to him grew in my chest. "Sometimes I wish I could show my dad what I've done."

She straightened from her reclining position. "Oh, Jensen."

I waved off her concern. "I don't mean to get serious." It'd been a long time, but the loss was there. I missed a man I had too few memories of. "No, it's an honor to have a dad take interest. Mom's proud, but you know, it's not the same. Dad was always the one out in the shop."

"How much of your skills did you get from him?"

"Most of the basics and all of his tools."

"I think Jasper gets dibs on Dad's tools. If he ever moves to his own place. Terminal bachelor right there."

"Takes us all by surprise."

She chuckled, but then she contemplated me. "You're not going to be a bachelor for long."

"Another year to be a married man." This time would be different. I knew what I was getting myself into.

"What was it like?" she asked softly. "To be married when it's not fake."

I held back a bitter laugh. I wasn't sure how much of my marriage had been real. "I don't know if I'm the one to ask. Hassie and I weren't on the same page, and that made it harder. Mom said marriage shouldn't be that difficult."

"Right person, wrong time?"

I wasn't sure about that either. The right person would have never made me feel that way. "Something like that."

She chewed on her lower lip and stared into the distance.

Like always, I hated talking about my ex to Poppy.

She was light, funny, and full of energy. The opposite of my marriage. "What would your Prince Charming be like? You know, if you were able to marry for love instead of a house."

"The house is a really good deal, and it's coming with awesome cabinets and some free handiwork."

I laughed. "Got it."

She fell quiet for a moment. "Well...I'd want what my parents have. A ride or die. Someone who always supports me. When Mom first started writing, she was told that she could never make a living off of kids' books. I strongly suspect she outearns Dad."

"No kidding?"

"It'd be close. She had to put in a lot of years to get there, but Dad never doubted her. He carries her business cards, not his."

She picked at the label on the bottle, her focus too intense for a lifted corner. "It's the way he looks at her. Pure obsession. Sometimes she'll just be typing away and he'll have this adoring look. Then she'll see, roll her eyes, he'll smirk, and they go back to what they're doing." She gave up on her peeling efforts. "I guess I've been surrounded by guys giving those adoring looks to their women, and I want it for myself. Dad with Mom. Alder with Daisy. You with Hassie."

The name was a cold splash and unwelcome on this warm night with a beautiful woman. "Jesus, that was a long time ago. I wouldn't put me and Hassie anywhere near your ideal relationship."

"You used to stare at her all lovelorn." She sounded only half teasing.

"Did not." I so did. If I could go back, I'd give myself a reality check.

"Did too." She put her beer down and gave me a starry-eyed look, then added heart hands.

I fought a smile. "Exaggerating isn't cool, Poppy. You should watch yourself."

She barked out her laughter. "'I can get that for you, Hassie. What do you need? Do you want half my sandwich?'"

Not a lie was told, but I refused to let her win. "I clearly recall giving you my pudding cup."

"Because she's lactose intolerant."

I spread my hands. "You still got it. Every time. And the ice cream cup."

She put her hands in a heart shape in front of her sternum and batted her eyes. "I didn't get this."

I start to push myself out of my chair. "Oh, I'll give it to you."

"You'll spill my beer!" She held up her hand. "Fine, fine. You win. You weren't all heart eyes because I got the pudding cup." She returned to rocking the swing with her toes. "You don't like being reminded of how you were as a kid."

My humor vanished. "No. I was over the top." Not only had it been pointless, but I had hurt Poppy and hadn't known it.

"We all were. I thought I was a super soccer stud."

"You were. And you still are. Next week, you're going to show the town what those legs can do."

"And what can they do?" She dropped her voice, making it sound more like an invitation.

Heat sunk down low in my gut and my cock stirred. "It's up to you to show me. Remember?"

Chapter Fifteen

Poppy

My back hit the cushions of the couch. I yanked Jensen down on top of me. My mouth was fused with his, but we had to come up for air so he could take my top off.

He'd thrown out the challenge, and the sex-starved goddess inside me had reared up to snatch it.

"I need you naked this time," he growled against my lips.

My shirt came off. I wrestled with my bra while he grabbed the back of his shirt and dragged it over his head.

"Wait."

He paused, and I flattened my hands on his chest.

"You're so hard." I felt up his pecs and scraped my palms down his abdomen to bump over his abs. His stomach muscles tensed and his breaths were shallow.

"You have no idea."

"Oh, I do." I unbuttoned his jeans. He was holding himself over me, with one hand on the back of the couch and one gripping the edge. His arms shook, but I continued, wrapping my hand around his hot length and pulling him out.

A drop of precum wet his tip and I spread it around. "I want to play with this."

"Too bad. I want to taste you." He pushed off and peeled my pants down my legs before shedding his own.

I didn't have a stitch on, and fading sunlight poured through the window. I had the urge to duck and hide, but he was also gloriously naked. His erection jutted out, and I got the full view.

I cocked a leg up and propped myself on an elbow. "I mean, there is one way we can do both."

His dick twitched. "Fuck me, Poppy. Are you suggesting a sixty-nine?" He raked his gaze down my body, and it should've been impossible, but his erection swelled more.

"Is that what the kids call it?" My face burned and I wanted to roll into the blanket I was sprawled on. Yet, I didn't. Knowing we had an end date and that he wasn't going to search for someone else until then made me so comfortable.

"Call it what you want, I'm in," he said gruffly.

A sixty-nine would be the epitome of exposed. I wasn't trained to look hot while contorting into sexual positions. Last night it'd been dark, and this time, I would be pushed into the couch. I wasn't as insecure as usual around him, but my ass in his face in full light would do it.

He took my hands and pulled me up.

Startled, I landed against his chest. "I can't do a handstand."

"No, four-ten. My balls don't hang that low. You're going to sit on my face."

Panic seized my chest. "N-no. I can't do that."

He lay down and rubbed his chest, his gaze eating up my body. "You can." He stroked his fingers down to his erection and gave it a pump. "Get on. If you want to."

He wasn't issuing a challenge, or I might've launched myself onto his dick. My body hummed, wanting everything he had to offer. His tongue. Those fingers. His cock.

But sitting on his face?

He stroked himself again, his gaze roaming from my breasts to my crotch.

"Do guys really—"

"Yes. Whatever you're asking, yes."

"How can you breathe?"

"Smother me."

A nervous laugh left me. Between his ravenous gaze, his pulsing erection, and the throb between my thighs, I wasn't quitting now. "Okay, then."

I shut my brain off and concentrated on his cock. It worked until his hot breath wafted over my pussy while my ass was in the air. My urge to flee kicked in, but his hands were wrapped around my thighs. The first stroke of his tongue and the following groan immediately settled me.

Arousal centered me. There was nothing but the two of us and the ecstasy we could give each other. I concentrated on my task and matched his pace. We fell into a mirror rhythm, and as my pleasure ramped up, I worked him faster. He twitched more, his hips rolled up, and his abs clenched and unclenched. I'd never experienced this level of connectedness and synchronicity before.

My climax grew fast and hit with little warning. I couldn't cry out because my mouth was full, but a sound ripped from my chest. Just as I spasmed, so did he. I clamped on tight and rode out my orgasm while taking all of his.

I had to pull away from him, gasping for breath. My butt was still exposed, and dammit, I should've closed the curtains, but my brain wasn't exactly online right now. Jensen helped spin me around and he gathered me into his chest.

I didn't want to move. He was warm and hard and we were both naked and messy.

"Oh, shit, sorry." He scooted up with me in his arms. "This is cuddling, but I wanted to make sure you're okay."

He released me, and I didn't want to go. This was why I didn't want to cuddle. I could sink into him and never come out. Just like now. I didn't move. A couple of minutes wouldn't hurt. "I'm okay. Trust me."

"Me too," he murmured. "You and that mouth are going to kill me."

I giggled, tempted to trace through the fine hair sprinkling his chest. "I thought I was literally going to kill you when I sat on your face."

"I would've lived and died well."

I laughed and pushed at him. "I would not crush your head."

He slid his hand down my body and squeezed my ass. "I want you to. Your legs drive me nuts."

"What else drives you nuts?" The panic from earlier surged. Was I going to regret this?

"A lot," he said, his voice low. "The way you challenge

me or rise up to my challenges. You always engage, and that means a lot."

There was something more in his meaning, but I couldn't say what. Just another time I felt like he wasn't saying everything. He was a guy who put it all out there while also keeping a lot inside, but all I had was a gut feeling.

"I like how you take everything with Auggie in stride," he continued, "and I love seeing you charge ahead when something scares you. It's sexy."

Just like I found him calling me sexy so damn attractive. "I charge ahead just fine. It's sticking it out that's been my issue."

"You'll stick it out." He said it with so much confidence that I almost nodded.

"I don't have anywhere else to go."

"You do, and that's why you're not going anywhere. You want to be here. You want to be with your sisters, and you want to be here when Clover finds her way to claim her property with that douche canoe."

I giggled. "I especially want to be here if she marries that ass."

"That laugh drives me wild." He ran a hand up and down my back. "I hope you're ready to go again."

"You're hard already?" He was. I moved like I was going to straddle him again.

"On your back." He flipped us around so fast my legs flew up. "I'm going to drive into you over and over and over again until we're both out of our minds."

"Watch me rise up to that challenge."

Chapter Sixteen

Jensen

The last week had been one of the best of my life. I got another job, and the clients didn't want me to start until July. That would be after the wedding and when I would be done with the house. The couple was older and didn't like email, so I wasn't bugging Poppy with proofreading.

She had combed through my website and made a few changes. She also polished up the look. Each page was shinier and more refined. She also set me up with an email signature so I wouldn't fuck up my name again. I didn't struggle with technology, but it was all shit I never thought of and would've never thought of.

The write-and-wipe board had saved my sanity more than once. Auggie didn't love it, but he liked referring back to it and crossing off what he'd already done.

I entered the house. It was Auggie's last day of school, and while Poppy and I had been finding a nonbed spot to have sex in before school pickup, she had a session today.

Clover was coming to town Friday, so she readjusted her schedule to get the afternoon off.

I was getting a drink of water when she came down the stairs laughing. Auggie and I did fine on our own, but the sound of a happy woman under the same roof as me was a nice treat. The running leggings and fitted athletic shirts were a welcome bonus.

I lifted a brow at her and took a long pull.

She grinned. "My student said she hates crossword puzzles sometimes because, with her dyslexia, 'I dunno, it could be Vermont or Virginia.'"

I chuckled. "She gets them mixed up?"

"I really don't know what she meant, but she's a funny girl. Tiny package, big attitude. Crosswords don't scare her off that much because she made one of her own for slang. She said she got the descriptions for each slang word." Poppy bit her lip, fighting back a smile. "She goes, 'Something about BDE made me think I shouldn't include it.'"

"Did you have to tell her what it meant?"

"Nope, and I'm not going to. The 'big dick energy' privilege goes to her parents." She glanced at the clock on the oven. "Can I ride with you to the school? Aspen wants to talk about the club. I can drive if you don't want to wait around."

"We'll wait. Auggie likes to play for a while." There wasn't a lot that would get me to quit waiting for Poppy. Except my first marriage. Every time I thought of how that went, my urge to linger was cured.

"Oh, about our date night tomorrow night—"

"Don't worry about it. Clover's in town, and you'll want to be with your sisters."

"I thought maybe we could do it Sunday, but with Auggie?"

Surprise flitted through me. I'd been ready to write off the date altogether. I looked forward to them, but not if they were an obligation. "You want him to crash our date?"

She shrugged. "Why not? I mean, it would help fit the narrative that we're marrying for real. But I'm sure he'd like to go out with us."

"He'd love to, I just thought... I know you like him, but you don't have to entertain him for show." I held my hope back. For my son's sake, I had to make sure her offer was genuine.

She frowned and crossed to me. "Do you think what I'm doing is performative?"

"No, not at all. Just that you're not obliged to spend time with him."

She recoiled. "I never feel obliged with him. He's a great kid, and he's not just a student. None of the kids I work with are." Hurt crossed her features. "I'm sorry if you thought that. I really didn't mean to—"

"His mom never wanted him around." It sounded so much worse when I said it out loud. Damn, I hated talking to Poppy about this. I hated to have her see what I'd been willing to put up with. "I was always asking Hassie to spend time with him, but he was scared of horses."

"She didn't want to hang out with her own kid?" Genuine confusion mingled with the disbelief in her eyes.

What did I tell her? I couldn't just brush her off, and surprisingly, I wanted to share. "Once I realized Hassie's priority would always be her horses and competition, it was easier to understand."

"But it's not right."

"No. It's not."

Her puffy lower lip stuck out. "Poor Auggie."

Her concern was genuine, so had her offer to have a date Sunday with him. Affection swelled so big in my chest it turned into something different, something deeper, richer. An emotion I wasn't ready to face just yet. "It'd mean a lot to him to go out with us."

"Let's make it a date day."

As much as I wanted to frolic with them, I had promised her to get the house ready. "I was going to sand the cabinets."

She shook her head. "We have a whole year after we say our vows. Let's go to Twelve Mile Bay, grill some hot dogs, throw a frisbee, skip some rocks. It's supposed to be beautiful."

"What about Clover?"

"She's going to leave Saturday, and besides, there are three other sisters in town. It's you, me, and Auggie. To be honest, she'd probably love to hang out with him for a while too, but I'm kind of looking forward to a day out with just us now."

Auggie didn't have aunts or uncles. He still talked about the gathering we had to meet her parents. "Change grilling to going out to eat after and it's a date."

The corner of her mouth lifted. "A family date."

●●●

Poppy

· · ·

My hands were getting sweaty. I could not touch this dress. I'd leave stains. A faint tremble traveled through me as I gazed in the mirror. I'd never worn something so fancy. "What do you think?"

Clover rolled her eyes and snapped some pictures with her phone. "What do *you* think?"

I stared back at myself. Sleek, silky fabric hugged my body all the way to the floor. The dress had a deep V-neck and it gave me va-va-voom curves. "It's glamorous."

"Glamorous isn't what you wanted?" Lily gave me an intent look. She had Cali perched on her lap.

"You look like a Barbie," Cali said.

"Ohmigoodness." I almost smoothed my hand down the bodice, but I held my arms out like I needed the air circulation. There could be no pitting out on the expensive dresses. Soccer Barbies didn't get armpit stains on dresses. "You're my favorite niece."

"Not fair," Violet said in a scandalous tone. "Your others can't talk yet."

I grinned and turned to the side. "I'll try another," I said to the young attendant, Hadley. She'd grabbed at least ten gowns when she'd first led me to the dressing room. She'd asked my style and then seemed to pick her favorite dresses. She was so excited about them, I hadn't had the heart to ask for different ones. I'd wait for the next round.

Clover lowered her phone. "Can you get her a looser, less formal one?"

"Of course." When she turned her back, Clover pointed toward a row of dresses and mouthed, *I got you.*

Relieved, I picked up the hem of my skirt and scurried after the attendant. By the time Hadley helped me out of my dress, someone was knocking on the door.

"I found some I like," Clover called. "Indulge me and try them on next."

I smiled. Clover was trying to keep the process going smoothly by taking the blame. Hadley blinked at me like a little doe in front of a semi.

"It's fine," I said.

"Oh. Okay." She inched open the door of the changing room and accepted three dresses. As she shut the door and hung up the dresses, she frowned at the choices. "These are...cute."

I bit the inside of my cheek and gestured to one that didn't look like I'd have to be poured into it. "Let's try that one."

"Sure." She took the clear plastic sleeve off and helped slip it over my head.

The flurry of changing gave my hands time to dry. I ran them over my hips and swung from side to side. The skirt was loose, with the empire waist tucked under my boobs. The skirt swished. I liked it better already.

"Want to try another?" Hadley asked.

"Um, let me see it in the mirrors. This is more of what I'm looking for." When her lips formed a troubled line, I nodded so she knew I meant it. If I had to mold myself into another formfitting dress, I'd opt for a pantsuit.

"It's a backyard, outdoor wedding. And it fits over my butt and thighs better." I patted my ass. "Too many years of soccer. All my muscle is here."

Her brown eyes lit up. "You played soccer?"

"For a long time." I stepped out of the dressing room. My sisters watched me approach. I didn't have to hold the skirt up and there was no train. The hem brushed the tops of my feet. Violet's mouth twisted. Lily was the same. Clover was shaking her head.

"You look like a princess," Cali said, beaming.

"Thank you." I stood on the little platform. I agreed with my sisters' dubious expressions. It was too *Pride and Prejudice*. "It's gorgeous but not as *chill summer* as I was hoping. Let me try another of your other choices, Clover."

"I used to play," Hadley said on our way back to the changing room.

"Yeah? What position?"

"Goalkeeper." We entered the room, and she helped me change. "We drove to Mandan for a long time, and then a few years ago, I just quit. It was a lot with everything else." She hung up the dress and pulled out a plain cream one that was more the style I was looking for but too plain.

Still, I let her help me into it. My head popped out, and I blew a chunk of hair out of my face. "What if there was a team in town?"

"A team to play on? Or to coach?"

Ooh—a coach. "Both."

She thought for a moment. "I think coaching would be fun. In sixth grade, I would get so mad at my coach because she would tell me to go against what I learned in my goalkeeper practices."

"What about playing?" I didn't have to look at the dress to know I wouldn't pick it, but I'd take the same style with less sleeve and more decoration. "This is a little too mother of the bride. I'll just try the other one right away."

Relief crossed her face. "Of course." Her nose

scrunched the tiniest bit when she took in the modest bodice of my last choice.

At least it was easy to slip off. She hung it up and slipped the next one free.

A little gasp left me. "I love it."

She held it up and cocked her head. "Yeah, I guess it has a simple beauty."

"It's a simple ceremony."

"There's nothing wrong with that." She bunched it up so I could duck into it.

Soft fabric whispered over my skin. The skirt twirled when it fell to its full length and brushed the tips of my toes. The beading along the A-line bodice framed my cleavage and stopped at a line that rimmed around the torso. From there, the chiffon skirt draped in light layers that didn't puff out.

I squealed. "This is it."

She smiled and opened the door. "I wasn't sure at first, but I really like it."

I rushed out to the mirrors. Cali's gasp was the loudest, but the sounds came from more than one sister.

"Is that it, Aunt Poppy?" Cali jumped up and down, clapping.

Clover grinned like she knew exactly what I'd pick.

"Stunning," Violet said. She dabbed at the corner of an eye. "Oh my god, why do I cry so easily now?"

"Well, it's not—" I caught myself before I said *real*. I liked Hadley—not her taste in wedding dresses—but I couldn't let just anyone know.

"Doesn't matter," Violet declared as if she guessed what I'd been about to say. "You're my sister and you're in a wedding dress and now I want to cry."

"You're going to make me cry," Lily said, "and I know my hormones can't take it."

I stepped on the platform and analyzed my reflection in the three-way mirror. I could see the elegant taper in the back, but my eyes captivated me. Happiness shone in them. The wispy sleeves made my biceps look cut, and the lift the layers gave the skirt made my hourglass figure pop. I could wear my hair however I wanted and it'd work.

My excitement grew until I was nearly vibrating. I had the dress. My family all planned to be there. The wedding I hadn't dared to dream of was happening. And the groom was phenomenal at sex. I was getting it all. For one year.

Chapter Seventeen

Jensen

Auggie helped me finish folding the towels. "She really wants me to go on your date night?"

"Why wouldn't she want you, bud?" I played it cool and started on the shirts, but I willed Poppy to wake up soon. She had said we'd head out by eleven and it was after ten. She'd stayed out late with Clover last night.

He shrugged and put a haphazardly folded towel on the pile. "Dunno. Mom said dates are for two people."

I paused midfold of a washcloth. "When did you talk to your mom about dating?"

I hadn't told Hassie about the marriage yet. I honestly didn't know if I could trust her, but I didn't want Auggie to feel like he had to lie to her—in the event she actually called. It'd been months since we'd heard from her. Part of me hoped that she'd stay away for a little over a year and then I wouldn't have to worry about it. Her parents had moved after we married, and she only had some casual friends left.

"She was going on a date the last time she called," he said. "I asked to go along."

That Hassie was dating wasn't a surprise. I had barely moved my things out of our house when she posted a photo of her and some bronc rider she'd been partying with for years.

The old tug of hurt and flare of anger were weaker than normal.

Auggie grabbed another towel. "You said you weren't really dating Poppy. It's part of a deal."

"We're not and it is." We're not really doing a lot of stuff we're doing, and I didn't want to quit. "I haven't talked to your mom yet about Poppy."

His expression perked up. "You talked to Mom?"

"No, bud. She hasn't called for a while."

His little shoulders fell. "Oh."

Goddamn, how much would getting let down by some important adults in his life affect him?

The door to Poppy's bedroom opened and she burst out, her hair as wild as her eyes. "Sorry! I just need to brush my teeth and then it's lake time."

The disappointment was wiped out of his expression. "Can we bring the pail and shovel?"

"Absolutely," she said before shutting the door behind her.

I glanced at the time and relief puffed inside of me. She was cutting it close, but she was up and we would be leaving.

Poppy wasn't in the bathroom long, and she flew into the kitchen. "So I didn't pack snacks last night because I didn't want to wake you up, and I wanted to ask— Are we going to eat lunch first or wait and have an early dinner?" She looked between me and Auggie.

"Lake first," Auggie said, grinning.

"You got it, my dude." She ping-ponged through the kitchen, loading a lunch bag with pouches of snacks, fruits, and veggies. Then she filled water bottles and stole from my stash of juice boxes. I had to hide them, or Auggie would drown himself in juice. Auggie and I finished folding.

"Whew," she said. "We have time to put laundry away and then it's eleven. Right on the dot."

"Yeah!" Auggie grabbed an armload of towels and sprinted upstairs.

"I'm so sorry," Poppy whispered loudly. "I had an alarm set, but it was for evening, not morning."

"I thought you were sleeping one off." I should've given her the benefit of the doubt, but old habits died hard.

She frowned. "I didn't have more than one drink. My sisters are not a wild crowd."

I held my hands up. "Sorry. It's just...history." I gathered towels for my downstairs bathroom. The weight of her gaze was on me. When I came out of the bathroom, she was in the same spot in the kitchen, her lips in a troubled line.

"Did she sleep one off a lot when Auggie was waiting on her?" she asked.

"Does a horse have four legs?" The tension from earlier threatened to form again. I made sure Auggie hadn't returned before I continued. "We divorced when he was five. But I left six months before that. He needed constant vigilance, and that infringed on her time. Then the first few years after our divorce, she'd try taking him for a weekend, but by then he was walking. And running. And...yeah. He was stood up a lot by his mother."

Her lips parted and sympathy filled her face. I'd allow it. For Auggie. But I wouldn't tell her how many times I'd waited, the pathetic husband hoping for some scraps of attention from his wife.

Small footsteps pounded down the stairs.

"I'm ready!" Auggie was in shorts and his feet were bare.

Poppy's fraught expression vanished. She aimed a bright smile toward him. "I am, too, but your dad's not in shorts." She blinked innocently at me. "Do you have sandals for wading?"

It wasn't even June. "The water's going to be frigid."

She laughed. "We're not skinny-dipping."

"What's that?" Auggie asked, curiosity filling his voice.

I cocked a brow and bit back a shit-eating grin. "Yeah, Poppy. What is it?"

"I—uh..." She gulped. "I'm not the parent, so I shouldn't—"

"No, really." I stifled a laugh and pretended to think. "Skinny-dipping? Not sure I know what that is."

She narrowed her eyes at me before sliding her gaze to Auggie. "It's when you go swimming with no clothes on."

"Naked?" Auggie asked, scandalized but also interested.

Poppy nodded. "Nothing on."

"Yeah, that'd be cold. I'll be in the car!" He sprinted outside, forgetting his shoes. I'd grab them when I left.

She shot me a dirty look. "Thanks for throwing me under the bus."

I let my laughter free. "The look on your face was worth it."

"I almost told him that I can't be getting naked around his dad."

I closed the distance between us. She tipped her head back to look up at me. I liked having her attention on me, just like I could get used to the security of her keeping her word. "You can get naked around me all you want." I dropped my head farther. Our lips were inches apart. "Just remember the rules and that Auggie's bedtime is nine in the summer."

I got even closer. A puff of her minty breath hit my chin. I could claim her mouth so easily. A quick kiss, or hell, a long one. Auggie wouldn't be back inside. But I'd been thinking about her naked and sprawled on the couch. How her mouth had dropped open as I plowed into her. The way she took me and called my name.

Her pupils widened. Good. She was thinking the same thing.

Just as she swayed forward, I grabbed the insulated cooler she packed. "Last one to the pickup is a rotten egg." I raced outside.

"You play dirty, Hollis!"

With Poppy, I couldn't help myself. If that was what it took to get that hot look in her eyes, then I'd do it every day.

* * *

I hadn't dated since my divorce. The loneliness sucked, and so did jacking off by myself when I just wanted to go to the bar and find someone to fuck. But I refused to leave Auggie with some stranger and then I hadn't wanted him to think I was more interested in my social life than him.

Now, seeing Poppy and my son splashing around in the water, giggling and screeching about the temperature, was reassuring. I'd made the right decision for me and Auggie. I had to wait until I was comfortable enough with someone, and it had helped that there were no expectations. To Auggie, she was my friend.

They high-kneed out of the water, their feet bare.

"Ouch, ouch, ouch." Poppy stopped at her sandals and stuffed her feet in. "Those rocks are sharp."

Auggie had brought his water shoes, but he'd taken them off for solidarity.

He picked up the frisbee. "Go long, Dad."

I jogged away, and he tossed the neon yellow disc. It curved right back into the water.

"Oh no." Poppy had a teasing note in her voice. "It's your turn to get it."

"Yeah, Dad. It's your turn." Auggie propped his hands on his hips like my mom would when she expected me to do something.

Poppy grinned like she thought I wouldn't get my feet wet with cold water.

I held eye contact while I shucked each shoe and peeled my socks off. She was practically vibrating with energy by the time I trotted to the shoreline. The frisbee was rocking on the gentle waves and getting carried farther out.

Frigid water licked at my feet, then my shins. It was refreshing, but since Poppy was watching, I refused to give her the satisfaction of a squeal. She'd been frolicking in the waves a couple of times already.

"Go, Dad!" Auggie jumped up and down.

I spun and let the frisbee fly, purposely overshooting him. He jumped for it, then spun and ran. That was when I picked up my pace.

"Whoa," Poppy said, turning toward me. "A little long—" She screeched as I charged her.

Rocks bit into my feet, but gleeful laughter burst out of me. She hadn't seen me in time, and I wrapped my arms around her waist. I swung her into the air and curved around to head for the water.

She started wiggling, half laughing and half screaming. "No— No! Jensen, you can't. We're supposed to go out to eat." She kicked her legs.

I ran into the water until the chilly line licked my knees. "We can run home so you can change."

"Don't you dare!"

What was it about her issuing challenges? She made me want to play. I pretended to drop her.

She cried out and clung to me, laughing. "You're so mean."

I turned toward the shore. Auggie was jogging back with the frisbee in his hands, a big smile on his face.

"What do you think, bud?" I lifted her up and down, more as an excuse for her to cling to me tighter. "Should I dunk her?"

"Tell him no, Auggie." Her body shook with her laughter. "Tell him he'd be really mean if he dunked me."

"Tell her that she deserves it," I said.

He grinned and danced back and forth, enjoying the show but torn on how to answer.

"She's naughty." I tilted my head toward her.

"You like when I'm naughty," she said only loud enough for me to hear.

"Don't fucking stop," I growled back at her.

Auggie giggled. "Don't do it, Dad."

"Maybe you need a dunk," she joked. She still had her hands clasped around my neck.

I waded for the shore. "If I keep holding you, I will."

I set her down so her feet were out of the water.

She turned to me and ran her lower lip between her teeth. "You're always getting me wet, Hollis."

The lust could've choked me. We were out in the open, and my son was watching. "I can dry you off again. With my tongue."

A blush tinged her cheeks. I was rewarded with a sultry smile before she turned away. "My turn to catch the frisbee."

She ran off. I stayed where I was, both to watch her ass and because my son's skill with a frisbee would land me in the bay again.

Chapter Eighteen

Poppy

"How's this?" I concentrated on making an airplane out of the paper napkin holder at the restaurant.

The din of the restaurant surrounded us, but my world was focused on the booth holding me, Jensen, and Auggie. Sun kissed our skin, and mine felt tight and like I needed to blast the dust off my body. Next time, we'd remember the sunscreen, and maybe I'd shower before we went out to eat.

"Hmm." Jensen's deep rumble came across the table and right into my belly. "I think mine's going to fly farther than yours?"

"Oh, you're on." I held my tiny plane in the air. "This is going to fly so good the US Army is going to call and ask what my secret is."

He tipped his head back, and his Adam's apple jumped up and down with his laughter. "Sure, four-ten. You'll be on speed dial."

"What about this?" Auggie brandished his attempt and damn. It was really good.

"I don't know if I want to compete against you." I set my plane down. "The general will be phoning you."

The way he beamed melted my heart. He put his plane by mine after marking them with the crayons left at the table. Auggie didn't color, but he drew ten different tic-tac-toe boards around the unadorned picture. He scooted the red crayon toward me.

I grinned. We started to play.

"I can't wait for soccer," he said, drawing a line through his win.

Dang, he was good. "Next week." Nerves crushed against my ribs, and I lifted my gaze to Jensen.

He gave me an encouraging smile and eased some of the pressure.

"Aspen said she'd procure all the balls and practice pinnies." I was growing more excited than I wanted to be. I loved working with kids. One-on-one tutoring fit me well, and so did running them around the pitch. I would coach all day, every day. Aspen was rooking me into helping her run the club and not just coach, and that made my stomach churn. I didn't need to be involved in planning games or, worse, tournaments.

"Who?" Auggie asked.

"Miss Whitfield," Jensen said. "Though you might call her Coach Aspen this summer."

Auggie's wide gaze landed on me. "Will you be Coach Poppy?"

Hearing Coach Poppy was like getting wrapped in an old, familiar blanket. I hadn't heard that for years. "I answer to anything as long as it's respectful."

"I like Coach Poppy, but I get to call you just Poppy."

My heart dripped into a puddle at my feet. "I'll always be just Poppy for you."

His grin took over his face, and he started another game of tic-tac-toe.

Thank you, Jensen mouthed. His expression warmed, and a smile played over his lips. He gave Auggie a half hug and got ignored.

I lifted a shoulder. Auggie would always be a special kid to me.

Just like I'd never forget his dad, the man who swung me in his arms to run on the beach.

●●●

I was on one end of the couch. Jensen was on the other, and we were watching a show while Auggie took a shower. By the time we had left the restaurant, it was raining. A steady patter hit the house, and as much as I loved to be outside, this cozy evening sunk into my bones. I was more relaxed than if I had gone to a spa.

Beach time. Dining out. And now I was reclining with a hot guy in a nice house.

Auggie sounded like a baby elephant trampling down the stairs. Jensen winced at the way his son's hands whispered along the wall.

He went straight for the fridge. "Can I have a snack?"

"Yeah, but nothing big before bedtime," Jensen said. He'd kicked his feet out.

I still had to shower, but Jensen had sat on the couch, and I hadn't wanted to leave him. I also hoped that he'd hop into the shower with me again after Auggie was asleep.

Auggie grabbed a banana and went to the table.

Jensen's phone rang. He tugged it out of his pocket without taking his gaze off the TV.

"Who is it?" Auggie asked.

Jensen frowned. "Your mom."

A chill worked its way over my skin. Hassie?

"Mom!" Auggie jumped off the chair.

"Hello?" Jensen answered, his brows drawn together.

I shrank into the corner of the couch even more.

Auggie bounced in front of Jensen as he went through a greeting, his tone cautious. Was it hard to talk to her? I wanted to throw up my chicken and pasta.

"Here he is." Before Jensen was done, Auggie snatched the phone out of his hand.

"Hi, Mom." He skipped back to the table.

Jensen's mouth was tight and his stony gaze was on the TV.

"Guess what we did today?" Auggie asked his mom.

Jensen popped his head up, alarm flaring in his eyes. I wanted to be one of those cats that could disappear into the cushions.

"Went to the lake with Poppy," Auggie proudly announced. "You remember her? She said she knows you."

I wanted to groan. Something about that line made me sound needy or something. Like a fangirl who wanted to take over Hassie's life.

Auggie kicked his legs on the chair. "She's staying here. Her and Dad are getting married."

"Shit," Jensen said under his breath.

It'd been a month, and he hadn't said anything? He had mentioned she hadn't called, but he also hadn't reached out to inform her of something this significant. Had he avoided telling her?

"Yep. They're getting married," Auggie announced proudly. Jensen dropped his head and squeezed his eyes shut. "But it's not real."

A snort slipped out of me, and I pressed my hand to my mouth. Jensen cracked an eye open and looked at me.

Sorry, I mouthed.

An amused grimace twisted his lips.

"Dad," Auggie said, "Mom wants to talk to you."

His expression went blank, and he glanced away. Our brief moment of connection was gone. As he stood, I was taken over by the urge to run, to go for a long drive, or even check into the motel in town. I was the interloper, and my presence was going to cause tension. I also didn't want to be around when he appeased Hassie. Old feelings tumbled back. Would he tell her that we were sleeping together? That I was better at soccer than her and that was it?

I couldn't go outside while it was dark and raining, but I had to leave.

"I'll give you some space," I whispered and scurried to my room before I could see if he was relieved or not.

I sat on the edge of my bed, thumping the backs of my legs against the mattress. Jensen's deep voice rumbled through the walls, but I couldn't make out any words. Panic clogged my throat just thinking that I might.

That's a pretty dress. I bet Hassie would be prettier in it.

He'd been an impulsive eleven-year-old when he'd said that, but my brain was replaying it like it was yesterday. Hassie had been prettier in a dress back then and she probably still was.

I pulled up Clover's number and hit send.

She answered on the tail end of a giggle. "Hey. Everything okay?"

No. "Why wouldn't it be?"

"Because it's a Sunday night, and I just saw you."

I called Clover for a reason. I could let my anxiety chew through my stomach or talk to her. "Hassie called, and Auggie told her that Jensen and I are getting married."

"He hadn't told her yet?"

"No, she hasn't called since I've been here. But he also didn't call her."

Clothing rustled, and she murmured something to someone, probably that arrogant prick who'd likely end up as my brother-in-law. "So, you've been there a month and this is the first time she's talked to him? She hasn't talked to her kid for a month?"

"I dunno. It's been longer than that, I think?"

"Geez, seriously? So is she pissed?"

"She asked to talk to Jensen right away, but Auggie also told her it wasn't real." I probed my forehead. The throb of a headache was starting. Would a pretend marriage be better or worse to Hassie? I was living with her ex and her son.

"What'd he say to her?"

"I don't know. I'm hiding in my bedroom."

She made a strangled sound. "You aren't eavesdropping? Poppy, I thought I taught you better."

I chuckled, grateful for her levity. "I can't risk hearing him tell her how much we're fake."

"He wouldn't do that, would he?"

"For Rodeo Barbie?"

"You're hot too."

Jensen's voice resonated into the room, talking

rapidly. I lay back and stared at the ceiling. "I'm not a badass like her."

"Poppy, this isn't like you." My usually teasing sister, who couldn't seem to take life seriously, turned frank. "What's really going on?"

I let out a sigh. "Remember what he used to be like with her? He adored her. She was the center of his world, and he made sure everyone knew it." I didn't reiterate some of the comparisons Jensen had made when we were kids. Clover knew them. She might not remember, but she'd been the one to tell me it wasn't okay.

"Does he still do that?" she asked. "I'll drive there and kick his ass."

"You're not going back to that place," Elijah complained on the other end.

I rolled my eyes. I wouldn't want Clover to make another trip, but now I wanted to tell her that yes, I did need her and to ditch that prick and come back.

"No, baby, not tonight," she said in a simpering tone. So not like her. "Has he?" she practically barked into the phone.

I got no simpering from her. "No, but I haven't seen or heard them together."

"What does he say about her?"

I chewed my bottom lip. I couldn't spill all of Jensen's private life. "Not a lot. He's made some comments that maybe she wasn't around a lot, and he seemed really disappointed with how everything turned out. He doesn't rage about his shitty ex or anything, and he wouldn't around Auggie anyway."

"Okay, so you panicked and ran, but he could be telling her all about the fake wedding and to keep her trap shut and that he changed his mind and you look prettier in a dress."

Another small laugh burst out of me. "Theoretically, he could be."

"Then think about those theoretics until you know for sure. And if he talks shit about you, we'll both kick his ass. But, Poppy?"

I didn't know if I'd like what she had to say. "Yeah?"

"The way that man looks at you isn't how a guy stares at the second-best-looking girl he's seen."

* * *

Jensen

I tucked Auggie in. The stress of the phone call hung over me, along with the self-recrimination. I should've called Hassie earlier, but for a woman who'd been occupied with everything but her husband and kid, she was a little salty about the thought of her ex getting married. I didn't appreciate her sudden demands to know the situation, but for Auggie's sake, I had played nice.

"Night, Dad." Auggie rolled over and his breathing evened out almost immediately. Today had been a full day, followed by an exciting night. If he sensed some of the tension between me and his mom, he didn't let on. He'd been so damn happy to hear from her. She had that effect on people.

He didn't move when I got up and left his room. I should talk to Poppy. She'd have to be curious since Hassie's reaction could affect her. When I got downstairs, I stopped to listen. Nothing.

Was Poppy asleep? I hadn't seen her since she also sensed the potential conflict of the phone call. I hated that she felt like she'd had to flee.

She deserved an update. And maybe I wanted to have someone to talk to after dealing with my ex. I knocked lightly on her bedroom door. The slightest movement came through the wood before she cracked the door open a few inches.

"Hey." I scratched the back of my neck and took in her curvy legs. She was wearing her pajama shorts and a loose shirt. I didn't look close enough to see if she was wearing a bra. My brain would go offline if I did. "Can we talk?"

Worry filled her eyes. "Sure."

I wanted to smooth the divot from between her brows. She opened the door wider, her expression expectant.

"In the living room?" she asked.

Oh. Yes. She was in pajamas, and if I entered her bedroom, I'd want to spread her out on the bed and forget both the "no bed" rule and the one dark cloud in the day. "Sure."

We sat in our same corners on the couch, only she faced me, one leg curled under her. Her shoulders were hunched. No bra. Warmth spread through my gut and headed lower. I would never not be turned on around her.

"If we need to refigure this deal," she said, "that's fine."

"What? No." Did Poppy think I'd put a stop to everything over a Hassie hissy fit? I wiped a hand down my face. Hassie might feel better about canceling the arrangement, but I wouldn't. I looked forward to the next year, and after Poppy had returned from dress shopping, her face glowing, I was eager for the wedding. I wanted to see her in that dress, her smile aimed at me. "I made sure Hassie knew the marriage is a deal between us and that discretion is key."

"Okay." She drew the word out. "She was good with that?"

"I don't care."

Surprise lifted her brows. "You don't?"

"I've had my own life for five years, and she's been involved in very little of it." I shrugged. Hassie's insistent questions had been irritating, and I'd patiently answered them all. Beyond that, I owed her little else. "I also stressed that her son lives here, and if it got out that we were faking a marriage to get the house, it could hurt his reputation at school and negatively impact my business."

"Dang... I didn't think this through. I can't risk you and Auggie—"

"No." I grabbed her foot. She straightened her leg until her heel rested on my lap. I worked my thumb up her arch. Her eyelids fluttered, and she moaned. My erection was going to push right into her sole, but I didn't move her foot off me. "We're doing this, and my ex can figure out how to handle it. She's probably forgotten it already."

She giggled and then looked guilty for doing so. "Auggie was so excited to talk to her."

"I know. Breaks my heart."

"Did you—" She shook her head. "Never mind."

"Ask me."

"No, it's not my business."

I feathered a fingertip up the bottom of her foot. She jerked, but I held her ankle.

"You're mean." She tried to tug her leg away, but I refused to let go.

"Talk, woman."

She sighed and quit fighting me. "Fine. Did you think she'd be like this when you married?"

My grip on her foot loosened. I hated thinking about the Jensen from back then. The wildly oblivious man who forged ahead when he should've stopped for a moment and thought really hard about his future. "I thought it would be different once we were married."

She sucked in a sympathetic breath. "I've heard that from some divorced women I know."

I stroked her foot under the guise of a massage. Having my hands on her grounded me. "I think she thought the same. I dunno. It's probably giving her too much of the benefit of the doubt to even say she thought that much about it. I was nothing but blind adoration, and whether I turned into a rodeo cowboy or not, I'm sure she assumed I'd follow her anywhere."

"I'm surprised you didn't," she said softly. "You were all about her."

I beckoned for her other foot. A little blush stained her cheeks, but she gave me that one too.

"She was safe, in a way," I said.

She blinked. "You did not act like she was *only* safe."

I was going somewhere I never talked about, and I'd rather haul her on my lap to talk about it. Amazingly, I didn't shove the words back down my throat. I never talked about my dad, but other than Mom, there was no one to talk to about him. "Dad knew her. He'd heard me talk about her. Everyone did," I said bitterly. My face burned at the memory of how I used to be. "So when I was going into high school and getting used to life without Dad, without telling him about my day or who I talked to, it was easier to stay in Hassie's orbit than to adjust to another change in life."

Her lips parted. "That's understandable."

"When I thought about who I was marrying, it hurt to think about meeting someone he didn't know. He was already missing everything, and he'd miss being a grandpa." I let out a long breath. At some level, I'd known why I made the decisions I had, but I had still been too close to the loss.

"Oh, Jensen." She scooted closer, bending her legs until she was sitting at the edge of my lap. "That makes so much sense."

I ran my hands up her legs. "It was immaturity."

"It was also really sweet and innocent."

"Well, she wasn't."

Poppy didn't reply. Her steady gaze remained on me as if she was waiting for me to elaborate. "Did she cheat on you?" she asked when I didn't say anything.

"She says she didn't." I was probably a dumbass to have believed her. I could leave it at that, but Poppy had opened up about her dating life. "Who knows? I went for a full physical after I moved out, and I was honestly a little surprised it came back clear. Every little itch was making me paranoid."

"Why did you think she cheated?"

"You left before she got really popular."

"She got even more popular?"

I gave her a pointed look. "When all grades merged into one for high school, and then she got noticed by upperclassmen? You bet. We didn't date until senior year was almost done."

She held up a hand. "Wait. You and Hassie weren't high school sweethearts?"

Surprised, I shook my head. She'd been gone. Had she assumed I'd been tied at Hassie's hip until the divorce? "She dated other rodeo guys and Trey, the quarterback."

"He played football?"

"Puberty loved him. He grew like a foot the year after you left."

She laughed. "Ohmigoodness. I missed it all."

"You missed awkward high school dances where all the kids cleared out early to party in a pasture?"

"There was some of that in Billings."

"I could've challenged you to a dance-off." It would've made those nights more fun. Having Poppy around during those days might've changed everything.

She chuckled. "So how did you two start dating?"

I dragged in a deep breath. I'd been so fucking stupid. "I'd gone out a little here and there, but no one stuck, probably because of my Hassie infatuation. But she was with some guy from Dickinson. So I asked Becky Lee to prom. Remember her?" She pursed her lips and tipped her head back and forth. "Well, she was nice and she liked me, so I asked her to prom and we started dating."

Her eyes flew wide. "And you being with some other girl made Hassie jealous?"

"I liked to think she finally saw my potential and realized what an ideal mate I was," I said wryly.

"Sure." Her reply was light, but her eyes were guarded. "That's what happened."

"Whatever the reason, I fell for it. She laid it on thick at prom, and by the next day, I broke up with Becky and went all in with Hassie. I followed her to Texas, then to Colorado, and when she got injured, I took care of her. I was a dutiful husband, taking freelance jobs around her schedule until all her partying took a toll on us. When Auggie started to ask where his mom was and why she didn't want to play with him, I decided that was it."

"I'm sorry," she murmured.

"Not your fault." But it helped to have someone understand. Mom did, but I hadn't let her in on everything that had happened. I skimmed my hands up Poppy's legs. "Unless I blame you for moving away."

She laughed. "What? Like, you would've asked me out?"

I gave her a steady stare.

Curiosity filled her gaze. "You really think we would've been something? At least, until the first prom when Hassie said, 'not on my watch.'"

"I can't promise I would've been in my right mind. I needed each day until my prefrontal cortex matured."

She giggled. "Perhaps I did too. I needed to date more Dillons to know that being single is better than that."

"But the house?"

A sexy smile spread across her face. "The house is worth marrying a talented cabinetmaker struggling to get by as a single dad. He doesn't know how sexy he is, and my job is to show him that not only is he good with his hands, but he's good with his tongue."

The lust that had been kindling the whole evening—hell, the whole day—roared to a fully stoked fire. "Auggie was asleep before I left his room."

Interest lined her face. "Oh? I haven't showered yet."

"Neither have I."

She leaned forward, stopping when she was close to my mouth. "Race you."

Chapter Nineteen

Poppy

The week after Hassie's call turned into one of the best weeks of summer I'd ever had. I'd done my lessons with Auggie. Then more tutoring, went to the house to paint and clean, or snuck into the shop for a quickie with Jensen. Some days, we weren't so quick. But with Auggie at his grandma's for certain hours of the day, it was like we were kids at home alone and ready to party—but with each other.

Jensen had gotten two more queries this week. He'd had me proof his replies, and while the editing programs had caught some minor issues, it had let a few slip through. I would have to look through some other programs, ones that he could input what he wanted to say and have it clean up his grammar. I had another parent ask me about what others did, those who'd slipped and slid through the school system, adapting and learning by brute force that hurt their brain, only to have a few lingering issues as adults. I'd have to make some resources for adults, too, who came to me.

I finished typing up my notes for my last client and made a few reminders for me for next time, then answered a few emails. Just as I hit send, I sensed Jensen's heat before I saw him.

"Hey," I said.

"Hey." The corner of his mouth tipped up. "Mom's texted me twice on Auggie's behalf. He's excited for tonight."

I groaned, but a smile still played over my lips. "I'm only nervous when I think about it."

"And that's every second?" When I nodded, he chuckled and walked toward me. "I'm excited to see you out there, Coach, being bossy and showing those legs off."

"Who am I showing my legs off to?"

"Trust me. Dads and a few moms I know are going to be looking."

I tapped my chin. "Hmm...what if I'm checking out their legs?"

He sucked a breath through his teeth. "I'm going to have to put my shorts on so you're only looking at mine."

"What's my incentive to check you out?" He had nice ones. Muscled with dainty ankles that I admired. I'd always had sturdy legs and was more self-conscious in dresses because of them. Then there had been Hassie and Jensen's dress comment. That hadn't helped. But each time Jensen ran his hand over my skin rewrote history.

"You can check out anyone you want, as long as these legs are wrapped around me in the shower tonight."

Arousal kindled in my gut, always on a low burn

around him. "You're getting bold, Hollis. You think I'm a sure thing?"

"If you're not, I'm doing something wrong." He knelt and slid his arms around me, tucking them between my back and the chair.

I took his hat off and stuffed my hands into his short hair, letting the soft strands float through my fingers. "What if no one shows up?"

The soccer club was Aspen's show, not mine. Technically. I was involved, and the closer we got, the more emails she'd sent me, and she'd called a few times. Whatever I felt could be considered nerves by proxy, but the first practice was only a couple of hours away.

Jensen buried his face in my lap. "At least one kid is showing up, and I know Auggie will shout to the world that he loves it."

"I can see that he enjoys playing. I'm not worried about working with him. What if kids have changed since I coached? Or they get there and think it's lame?" I lived for the sport, but it wasn't my identity. However, coaching had been my personality once. I'd loved it, I'd loved mentoring, and I got a thrill out of watching skills develop and grow.

Jensen lifted his head. He rubbed my back with his thumbs, relaxing more than the knots he worked through. "Then coach for Auggie. Every kid out there is an Auggie. A sponge who loves it."

I pushed my hands over his scalp and skimmed them around his head to frame his face. I appreciated him for more than his rugged good looks. He boosted me up. Even when we were kids, he challenged me because I was the only one he'd seen as real competition. I was the only one he'd cared about.

The deal between us...what if it grew into more? What if...

"Dad!" The front door slammed and footsteps pounded up the stairs.

Jensen pushed back, and my hands dropped away. He jumped up, adjusting himself as he half turned his back to the door. The bulge behind his jeans was noticeable, but Auggie wouldn't be able to see from the doorway. He definitely wouldn't get a glimpse with the lightning-fast way Jensen put distance between us.

I was the one who made the rules. Of course, I respected that he didn't want to confuse his son by telling him that our marriage wouldn't be real and then him see us making out. Yet hurt echoed through my chest, plucking at each rib until tears pricked the backs of my eyes.

I was being unreasonable. I was stressed. Tonight was basically a replication of the worst debacle of my life, an old professional humiliation that could occur again right here in this town where I hadn't even started over yet.

No pressure.

That was why I was feeling so emotional. Had to be. Otherwise, I was in for over a year of watching Jensen drive away from me.

● ● ●

I pushed my sunglasses up my nose. Fifteen kids were in a file, kicking the ball around the fresh lines that Aspen had arranged with the city to paint. Her blonde hair was piled on her head, and she wore aviator shades that were infinitely cooler than my gas station pair.

She was working with another fifteen kids. The age

ranges varied, but from the forms they turned in, we could actually make a couple of teams. Then there was Hadley with a group of her friends. They were laughing and joking as they kicked around a few balls. She said she'd work with the younger kids, but this was an intro and a couple more older girls showed up. There could be one team with her age group alone.

"All right, that's time." I waved my group in. "Dribble your balls here."

I dropped to my butt in the cool grass. They formed a half circle around me and dutifully sat. One kid leaned back and pushed the ball back and forth with his heels, touching each side and rolling it back and forth. He was going to have killer footwork if he kept that up.

"You guys did good. I'm really excited for this year and glad that you joined me."

"My mom said you played pro," one boy announced.

A group of wide eyes swiveled toward me.

"Uh, not pro, no," I said.

"The Olympics?"

I chuckled. "No. I played through college." Sage nods were the only response I got. "So, after we learn some more skills, there's an app I want to let your parents know about."

"For games?"

"No, for skills, but it's only if you want to use it." My answer was met with disappointment. I stuffed back a smile. "Am I going to see you all on Monday?" Our practices were Mondays and Thursdays. They nodded and half waved their hands in the air. No questions, just an enthusiastic response. "See you all then. I can't wait."

Aspen let her group of girls go, and I met her by one of the goals.

"How'd it go?" She grinned, her amber eyes twinkling.

"Great. I think I'll even see them all back." I hoped so. I pressed a hand to my stomach. I'd never been this worried before, but the nerves threatened to come back.

She bounced on her heels. "That's awesome. I'm so glad the first night turned out. I've even got some emails from parents in Crocus Valley and a few other towns asking about getting their kids on the team."

"We'll need more coaches."

Her gaze landed over my shoulder. "Any chance your fiancé is harboring a lifelong passion for coaching kids' soccer?"

My fiancé? Oh—Jensen. Yes. I was engaged. I twirled the ring on my finger. Moments like this felt like I had a foot in two worlds. "I can ask him."

"You two make such a cute couple. He's a fan favorite with a lot of the single moms, but I think they all thought his wife was just out of town with the way he wasn't interested in anyone."

"He keeps his feelings close to the chest." Except he didn't, while at the same time, he did. I shouldn't want everything from him, but the more he gave me, the more I wanted.

She laughed. "No, after seeing him with you, I really think he wasn't interested." She hitched a netted ball bag over her shoulder. "Have a good weekend. See ya Monday."

"Enjoy summer vacation."

"I get this week and then summer school starts," she called as she walked off.

Smiling, I turned. My heart somersaulted. Auggie was giggling and trying to steal the ball from Jensen. For a guy who'd never played soccer outside of gym class, he had hidden skills. He'd always been good at whatever he'd tried. Looking back, I could see how he'd been making up for his struggles in the classroom, trying to earn respect and recognition outside of his academic attempts.

He glanced up and kicked the ball to Auggie. "Hey. You were a rock star out there."

Auggie veered off, dribbling the ball down the line. "Thanks. It was fun."

Jensen's attention went deeper. "Yeah?"

Was he worried about me? When the soccer debacle had happened in South Dakota, I'd been alone. Now I had Jensen. "Yeah. I'm only fifty percent terrified this will be an epic failure that I'm at the center of."

"Not every endeavor is a raging success. Doesn't mean you shouldn't keep trying."

"I like being on top though."

His eyes heated. "I know."

My arousal flared. Auggie would be asleep in a few hours and then I would be in Jensen's arms. We started for the gravel parking lot outside of the pitch.

"What are we doing for our date tomorrow night?" he asked.

"You keep making me suffer the punishment of Saturday night dates."

"It's awful, I know." His eyes flashed when he grinned, and my stomach was the one to flip this time.

"Horrible. I don't recommend it. But I hear Bishop's is open."

His eyes lit with interest. "Bishop's. They have good seafood for being right smack between two oceans."

"We used to go there before we moved. I was delighted to hear it's still open."

"Then we'll go."

He put a hand on the small of my back as we walked across the plush grass. "Mom's coming over to watch Auggie, and I told her if she falls asleep on the couch again, I'm not waking her up to drive home in the dark all groggy."

"Fair."

He tipped his mouth close to my ear. "But that means I won't wait until we get home to get inside of you."

I shot him a sly look, but my body tingled in all the right places. "There are a lot of secluded spots by the lake."

"A lot. And since I've been out there doing some estimates in the last couple of weeks, I've learned about more."

A shiver traced down my spine. "It's a date."

"It's going to be."

Chapter Twenty

Jensen

The large windows making up a wall of Bishop's overlooked the lake. Built on the higher side of Lake Sakakawea, the restaurant looked like a sprawling shack from the outside and a small-town bar on the inside. Poker and pull-tab machines filled a room to the right after we entered, and various booths and tables lined the space around a square bar. Dishes clanked and sizzles were muted from the kitchen on the far side of the place.

We were seated at a cozy table by the windows. A giant canoe was mounted on the wall above our heads and the paddles were crossed and secured directly across from us. When I was with Poppy, I didn't feel like an accessory. She was with me. Jensen Hollis. A dad who didn't write the best but could make gorgeous cabinets. I didn't have to be anything more than Jensen with her.

Poppy pushed her plate away and rested a hand on her belly. "Ohmigosh, that was so good."

"We're going to have to come every night so I can hear you moan like that." When she'd put that first piece of shrimp in her mouth and groaned, rolling her eyes closed, I'd been ready to haul her out over my shoulder.

Pink tinted her cheeks. "I wasn't that bad."

"It's not bad. It's too good." I loved her moans. She didn't have to make a sound for me to know that she liked something. She clenched around me, gripped my shoulders, swiveled her hips. The sexy sounds were the cherry on top to complete the sensory overload she gave me.

She took a drink of her raspberry lemonade. "I was afraid the food quality had gotten worse over the years, but it's better than I remembered."

"I haven't been out here since I moved back."

"Thanks for coming."

"Anytime." I meant it. Whenever she wanted to eat at Bishop's, I'd take her.

"Think Auggie would like seafood?"

"Maybe. I don't usually cook it." A warmth flooded my chest. She was always thinking of him, involving him. The first night of soccer practice had hit me in the feels. I'd watched her coach my son and build him up. She'd done that with all the kids in her short time with them. She was a natural, and it wasn't for show. I'd never be able to tell her how much that meant. There were no words strong enough. Nor could I describe what it did to me. I'd have to show her.

I started to see a different future for myself, one that wasn't full of me hustling to earn a living to keep me and my son in our house. I could picture more days like the last few weeks. I'd work in my shop, meet with potential customers, book steady work, and talk to Poppy about it all. We'd spend time together, the three of us, and then when Auggie was in bed, she'd be all mine.

The only thing that'd make it better would be to wake up to her.

My skin grew tight. In a couple of weeks, this wedding was supposed to be for show, but it was getting harder to deny that I wanted it to be very much real.

What did Poppy want? She seemed happy. She seemed content. But she'd admitted to being a girl who left when the going got tough, yet she'd also been alone. Would I be worth sticking around for? I wasn't begging to be loved ever again.

Would I have to beg with Poppy?

The teen server came by. "Can I interest you in any dessert?"

I lifted a brow at Poppy. She had a sweet tooth, and if she wanted to moan over some cheesecake, I wasn't stopping her.

"Uh…" Poppy's gaze landed on the dessert placard, and she drank in the slice of cookie dough cheesecake front and center of the options. "…nah. I'd better not."

"I'll share it with you." I'd rather feed her a bite and then sample the flavor off her lips. Actually, that was a good idea. "A slice of the cheesecake, please. Can you pack it to go?"

The girl smiled. "Absolutely."

Poppy shook her head, an amused smile dancing over her lips. "To go?"

"Yeah, I want to take a drive with you."

Her grin deepened. "Is that all you want to do?"

"No, it's only the beginning."

● ● ●

Poppy

The dessert container lay open and empty in the front seat. I was in the back, racing toward my orgasm with my head wedged between the seat and the window. A copse of trees hid us from the dirt road that we'd followed to get here.

Jensen drove into me, his shorts around his ankles and his shirt pushed up because I couldn't get enough of touching him. I raked my fingernails down his torso as he plunged in and out. I arched into him as best I could.

"Fuck, Poppy." His biceps strained against the sleeves of his shirt as he gripped the seat backs on either side of me. "I can't get enough of you."

When he came undone like this, I believed everything he said. It wasn't a put-on to get me in bed. I was already under him. He had no reason to boost my pride.

He grabbed the back of my head, his weight pressing harder into me, and devoured my mouth. His hand took the brunt of the force of his pounding.

I exploded suddenly and with barely any warning. He'd told me he couldn't get enough, and he held me like it. That, more than the physical ecstasy, pushed me over the edge with the force of a cyclone.

I cried into him, and he caught all the sound. With one more thrust, he buried himself in me as far as our position would allow and shuddered, coming inside of me.

Waves of pleasure crashed over me and through me. I hugged him to me as I rode through the climax. Then we both went still, our breaths filling the cabin. The windows were fogging and it was finally dark. The whisper of the wind through the trees surrounded us. This moment was ours.

"I wish I could take you home and carry you right to bed," he murmured and instantly went stiff. "Sorry."

"No, don't be." I didn't want him to apologize. I wanted to know how he felt about me. We were engaged and we were friends, but we went on dates that were more amazing than any others I'd been on. We had frenzied sex like this when we couldn't get enough of each other. The cheesecake had taken two minutes to eat, and then he was licking the crumbs off my lips and boom. We were in the back seat and my shorts were on the console. "I'd like it too."

My pulse cranked up a notch.

He placed a sweet kiss on my lips as he pulled out. Shit. Did I make this awkward? Did he say something he regretted and I ran with it?

My heartbeat thudded through my body as he helped me get dressed and got himself zipped back into place. But he didn't open the door and shuffle me into the front seat. He sat facing me as much as possible and threw his arm across the seat back.

"I like you, Poppy."

A pulse stopped my pounding heart for a moment. I waited for the *but*. "Okay?"

He worked his jaw back and forth a few times before speaking. "I think we have something here."

A pleasant bubble of surprise popped in my head. "You do?"

His gaze was earnest. "Do you think so?"

"I think..." I fiddled with my fingers, twisting and twining them in my lap. We hadn't even said *I do* yet and feelings were involved. Didn't friends with benefits last longer than a few weeks before they grew feelings that threatened their plans? I didn't want to lose the benefits or the friends. The vulnerability shining from his eyes knocked down my guards. "I think so too."

He let out a long exhale. "Good. So now what?"

"You mean, how are we going to get married when we're fucking and supposed to be only pretending to be married?" I grimaced. "We messed up."

"No, we didn't." He caressed my face. "I'm having fun again, and goddamn, I didn't think life could be like this."

His words sunk in, and instead of calming me, I wanted to run. That would mean leaving him, so I'd be honest. "I'm scared."

"I know," he whispered. "We'll take it slow. I know a wedding in a couple of weeks doesn't scream slow, but that's not about us."

I wanted it to be. When I saw myself in my wedding dress, my first thought was what Jensen would think when he saw me. I wanted him to see when normally I might hide. But he made me comfortable. He might've created some of the wounds inside of me, but he was slowly smoothing over the scar tissue so they didn't tug and pull at my insecurities anymore.

"This is us." He placed a sweet kiss on my lips. "You and me, right here. We like to go out on mandatory date nights. I'm obsessed with your legs, and you love my ass."

I laughed. "I never said that, but I do love your ass."

He sat back and pulled me with him. I curled up on his lap and rested my head on his shoulder.

"We're cuddling," I said.

"Yeah. I'm one hundred percent sure Mom is passed out on the couch, or I'd take you to bed."

My anticipation leaped, but I reined it in. Going to sleep in Jensen's arms was becoming a fantasy, so was waking up to him. "What about Auggie?"

"He's understood a lot so far. We would just talk to him." He dragged in a steady breath and blew it out. "We shouldn't get caught until I do. If we feel like we're speeding through this and we know what we've been doing, he's going to have a hard time understanding."

My disappointment was understandable but present regardless. We were in a complicated situation, but I also wanted him to toss caution to the wind and claim me. Ultimately, like him, I'd never disrupt Auggie's life for my selfish wants.

His heartbeat thumped under my hand. We stayed like this until little pricks of light appeared and disappeared in the distance.

"Fireflies," I said, pushing up. "I haven't seen them in years."

"I used to when—sorry. Never mind." He sat up and opened the door.

"You can tell me." We were sharing our bodies, and we'd shared a lot of ourselves, but this moment was proof that he held back.

I didn't think he would, but he paused with the door halfway open. "I used to wait up for Hassie when she'd be out partying after an event. I'd sit outside the trailer, fucking miserable and getting eaten alive by mosquitoes, and sometimes fireflies would be out."

"You didn't party?"

"Not after a while. It was just a bunch of rodeo people talking rodeo. I grew up ranching, yet I was the impostor."

"Because you never rode a bull?" I said lightly.

"Not intentionally. And the barrels I raced were to get to a calf and get it tagged and vaccinated and get outta there before mama cow body-slammed me." He squeezed the bridge of his nose. "But I didn't do rodeo and I didn't live and breathe horses, so I didn't fit in. It's like they thought my time helping Dad on our ranch was cosplay."

"Just so happens I like former cowboys turned carpenters who are raising their kids and encouraging homeless women to start their own business."

He laughed. "You weren't homeless."

"I had no address."

"Now it's the same as mine."

"Yeah," I said softly.

He squeezed my hand and ushered me into the passenger seat. He leaned in and gave me a lingering kiss before shutting the door and jogging around the hood of the pickup.

We wouldn't be going to the same bed tonight, but we were going home together. We'd cuddled, and I looked forward to much more of that in our future.

The drive back to his place was quiet. Was he wondering if we were making a dumb decision to explore this chemistry between us? Were we foolish to think we could fan these flames and not explode while we were still married? I didn't know and only time would tell, but with Jensen, I wasn't as worried. He was calm and logical, and he looked out for me.

He turned down his drive. When he got closer to the house, a big silver Dodge dually sitting in front of his garage glinted in his headlights. He jolted like he'd gotten shocked.

"Who's that?" I asked, frowning at his reaction and

the large vehicle. If it looked this expensive in the dark, how fancy was it in the daylight?

He didn't have to answer. The front of his house opened and a tiny woman sauntered out, legs as long as her shorts were short. Her blonde hair fell in waves down her back, and she stuffed her hands into the teeny pockets of her denim shorts. The porch light acted as a spotlight for her.

The shrewd but uncaring expression on her face made all sorts of memories tumble back. Recollections of a little girl who used to be my best friend until time and her superior attitude had put distance between us. Thoughts of a girl who hadn't been sad when I moved, and she hadn't said goodbye. Jensen's ex-wife. Hassie.

Chapter Twenty-One

Jensen

My stomach bottomed out and the postcoital glow and optimism from minutes ago vanished. What the hell was she doing here?

Hassie watched me coast to where I normally parked, but her dually was blocking my spot. I gave her a little wave to try to keep the peace. Her returning smile was tight.

"Well, Hassie's here." My mom's car was still parked by the shop. My ex must've just arrived, or Mom would've texted. Mom might've also made Hassie wait every minute of our date night to keep from bothering us. I'd have to apologize to her for the unexpected guest later. I hadn't known my ex-wife would surprise us with a visit.

I swung around and parked by the shop too. Poppy was quiet. I killed the engine.

"I didn't know." I also didn't want to get out of this vehicle. I had no desire to face Hassie or to figure out where Poppy and I were now after we'd just talked about where we were going.

Poppy wasn't looking at me, but she also wasn't looking toward Hassie. "It's fine." Her gaze stayed on her hands on her lap. "She's Auggie's mom."

"She should still call first."

Poppy finally lifted her tentative attention to meet mine. "Feels a little awkward."

"That's one word for it. Look, I don't know why she suddenly showed up, but it's suspicious that she finds out I'm getting married, and now she's on my doorstep." If this had been five years ago, I'd have been flattered. I might've even stayed married. Some efforts came too late.

"She must care about you."

Only when it was convenient. Rather, in most cases, inconvenient. We were being watched, and I wanted to shield Poppy from any backlash. "We should go in. See if there's a reason for her to be here."

Poppy dropped her focus to her hands again. I hopped out. I was running around to open her door, but she beat me to it. She stuffed her hands in her pockets, but I took one last look at the legs that had been wrapped around me earlier. I suppressed my sigh. Things couldn't be fucked up between us. Not this soon.

"Hey," Hassie drawled. The slight southern accent she'd picked up over the years didn't grate on my nerves as much as it used to. I had once viewed it as a sign that we were growing further apart and that she'd been getting closer to others in a way that had torn through me. Now, it only highlighted the distance that had always been there. Some closures couldn't be forced. "Poppy. Long time, huh?"

"Hi, Hassie." Poppy's usual exuberance was gone,

and I missed that light. This was the Poppy who left when life punched down. Could she trust in me a little longer? Figure this out together?

Hassie pointed a bright smile my way. "Erin said Saturdays are date night?"

I'd like to keep it that way. "Something wrong?" Might as well get straight to the point.

Her smile dipped. "I missed Auggie, and I have a break in my schedule." She sucked in a deep breath. "Actually, I'm on hiatus. I've been preparing for my next phase in life." She shrugged and stuffed her hands in the back pockets of her booty shorts. "It's a good time for the transition, so I'm opening a barrel racing training school. I can be closer to my son."

"Auggie?" The incredulity in my voice made her brows lift.

The sassy attitude that drew men like moths to her flame flared in her expression. "I don't have more than one."

How often did she remember she was even a mom? Each year, I anticipated Auggie's birthday phone call from her. Would this be the year she forgot?

Getting upset wouldn't help.

"I should go in." Poppy started for the house. She nodded between us. "Let you two talk."

I wanted to yank her back into me. I'd dealt with Hassie on my own for so long, and no one understood. She was the belle of the ball, and I'd always been the average Joe who should've been grateful for her scraps of attention no matter how much I'd had to scramble for them.

I watched Poppy disappear inside, then I caught Hassie scrutinizing me.

"Where are you moving to?" I asked, bracing myself for her answer.

She snapped out of her inspection and adopted a smile that held a hint of sexiness. "Here, silly. I'm coming home."

"What?" I'd carved out my own spot in Coal Haven, and Poppy was helping me secure it. Hassie moving back shouldn't change a thing. So why did it feel like my world teetered on an edge?

"Honey wants to sell." Honey was an older woman Hassie had befriended when we were kids. Honey raised horses and competed with them. Thankfully, our paths rarely crossed. "Said I can buy the house and the acreage the shop is on. She'll still rent out the pastures, and eventually, if she sells, I get first dibs. Then Auggie can get more experience with horses."

"What if he doesn't want more experience with horses?"

She scoffed. "My kid is not going to spend more time playing *soccer* than he does riding."

I ground my teeth together. There was nothing wrong with soccer, and it was a fuck ton cheaper. "He enjoys soccer. He's not scared of it."

She sauntered closer to me. "He just needs more time. Horses are therapy, and I'll work with him."

"It's getting late. We can talk in the morning." I started for the house, not letting her cross to me. Was Poppy talking to Mom? Did she retreat to the bedroom? How was Auggie dealing with his mom's arrival, or did she show after bedtime? And if she arrived when she knew he'd be in bed, why? Long day on the road, or was she up to something?

Poppy's form was in the window. She was chatting

with Mom. She hadn't gone to bed yet. I kicked up my pace and took the porch stairs in two bounds.

"Jensen, about that—"

I stepped into the house before Hassie finished. When I said we could talk in the morning, I meant it. I'd quit going by her schedule a long time ago.

Poppy glanced over, her smile tight. I wanted to cross to her and link our hands. To show her that nothing would change. But I wasn't letting my ex-wife force our hand in the tentative step forward we were taking in our relationship. Mom looked up from where she perched on the edge of the couch. Hassie crowded in the door behind me. I moved closer to Poppy.

"I was just asking how Bishop's was," Mom said as if she was oblivious to the tension, and I appreciated the effort. "It's been so long since I've eaten there. I might have to make it a grandma and grandson date."

"Auggie would love that," I said.

"He was asleep when I arrived," Hassie said. "I can't wait to see him."

Poppy inched toward her bedroom. "Good night, everyone."

"Speaking of that." Hassie's voice stopped Poppy in her tracks. "Dad's renters haven't moved out yet, and I thought I could crash here."

The room went silent. Shit. Renters were handy when I could talk Poppy into staying with me. Now, it sucked. The last thing I wanted was to wake up and see Hassie, but I also didn't want her to leave and have Auggie blame me. "Poppy's in the guest room," I said carefully, "and she's using the extra room upstairs for her office."

Hassie tipped her head as if she was waiting for me to

rearrange our situation just for her. Her pale brows drew together, and she let out a curt laugh. "It's a big house."

It was my house.

Mom clapped her hands together. "Well, I certainly have space. Why don't you crash with me? You can use the room Auggie uses when he sleeps over."

Relief washed over me. "Thanks, Mom. That's a great offer."

Hassie recoiled like she didn't expect me to give up on a solution to keep her under this roof. Her blue gaze darted back and forth between me and Poppy.

Poppy ducked her head and shrank in on herself. I had the urge to grab her hand, but that'd only make whatever was going on here worse. We had a deal, and I didn't want her to renege on it.

"Okay, then. Erin, you've got a roomie." She spun to me, standing in a way that made her tanned legs cross and all the muscles flex. Once upon a time, I used to live for that flirty stance until I saw the calculation behind it. It'd taken too many years to open my eyes. "How 'bout I bring lunch tomorrow? I can see Auggie then."

I glanced at Poppy, but she looked like she was trying to become one with the paint on the walls. "Yeah, that's fine," I said, hoping what I said next would dissuade her, "but I'll be working in the shop most of the day."

"That's fine," Hassie said. "It'll give me and Poppy a chance to catch up."

Poppy's flinch was subtle, but I caught it. Her confession about how my comments had made her so insecure ran through my head, amping up my remorse over it.

Before I could backpedal on my shop plans, Poppy caught my gaze and forced a smile. "Don't plan anything around me. I don't want to get in the way." She gave a stilted wave. "Good night, everyone. Thanks again, Erin."

She rushed out of the room, and it was all I could do to keep my feet rooted. If I chased her, she'd want to hide more. I'd give her this space while I got Hassie out of the house.

"Well," Hassie said with too much cheer in her voice, "it's a date. I'll bring lunch by."

"Glad everything worked out." Mom rose. "I'm not sure if you know where I live, Hassie. Why don't you follow me?"

Mom gave me a quick hug and a kiss on the cheek.

"Thank you," I said, hoping she could hear the depth of my gratitude. *Thanks for watching Auggie. Thanks for getting Hassie out of my house. Thanks for making this all easier.*

"Anytime." She cast a worried gaze toward Poppy's room, then slipped out the door, ushering Hassie with her.

Finally, I was alone. I watched their headlights disappear. The dread sinking through my gut didn't diminish.

Fuck.

I went straight for the guest room and knocked.

Poppy popped the door open. She had her bonnet on, and her expression was tired.

I reached for her, but she swayed back. Was this too intimate? The rebuff hurt, but with the drama from tonight, I couldn't blame her. Still, my old scars cracked open. "You okay?"

"Yeah, why wouldn't I be?"

The way she brushed off my question made the hurt more acute. "Because my ex-wife showed up expecting to stay here only minutes after we decided to explore where all this was going."

She let out a long exhale. "That was unexpected."

"More than a little." I rocked back and forth on my heels. "I don't want this to change anything."

"You don't?" she asked hesitantly.

"Of course not."

She nodded. "Okay. Me either. Um...thanks for the date."

Her lack of conviction burrowed its way into the husband who'd found himself home alone one too many nights. I was going to ask her about next Saturday, but that was too close to feeling like I was begging. "You're welcome. Good night, Poppy."

"Night, Jensen."

I turned away before she could shut the bedroom door in my face. Hassie would move on when she got bored. Auggie and I had never been enough for her to stay, and that likely hadn't changed.

Would we be enough for Poppy to stay?

Chapter Twenty-Two

Poppy

Clover: OMG!!! Is she there now?
   Clover: Did she sleep in his room?
   Clover: Did you sleep in his room?
   Clover. YOU CAN'T LEAVE ME HANGING!

I dropped my sleeping mask back over my eyes and rolled to my back. The incessant buzzing of my phone had woken me. I texted Clover last night when I was tossing and turning. She'd slept through it, but now she was clearly awake.

Seeing Hassie last night had me disconcerted in so many ways. The flirty way she stood around Jensen and the sultry smiles she aimed in his direction. Her legs were amazing. She was gorgeous from head to toe. If she wanted to get Jensen back, it'd probably work. Then she'd take him for granted again. But it'd be too late.

What was I going to do? I was supposed to marry the man, but his sexy ex-wife would be living in town.

I sighed and picked up my phone.

Poppy: She's staying with Erin, but she's bringing lunch and wants to catch up.

Seconds after I hit send, my phone vibrated. I fumbled and nearly dropped it on my face. Clover was calling.

"Hello?" I whispered.

"Are you being so quiet because you're sleeping next to Jensen? You're in his bed and that hussy is out in the rain, right?"

"No—and she's not a hussy. She's his ex." And it sounded like she had cheated on him. Perhaps not, but Jensen couldn't trust that she hadn't. "She's Auggie's mom."

"She's his mom when it works for her," Clover grumbled.

"She's hot." I blew out a gusty breath. "You should see her. She could do a decade of calendars and be all the months every year."

"Jensen thinks you're hot."

He'd never thought I was better looking than Hassie. We weren't kids anymore, but it didn't matter. "What if he goes back to her?" My concern should be losing my chance at the house. Having to come up with extra money for an office rental. Telling my family, just kidding, the wedding is off. The groom's back with his real wife.

"Does she want him back?"

I pressed my lips together. She wasn't reassuring me that he didn't want to rekindle what he and Hassie had.

"Obviously, he's into you," Clover said as if she was reading my mind.

He could be attracted to me and still want to try again

at everything he had with her. "We were just talking about...being more than pretend."

Her squeal filled the other end of the line. "Seriously? Poppy, I'm so happy. He's a really good guy."

"He's not *my* guy." I hadn't gotten a chance to try and make him mine.

"Make him yours."

"Sure." Wasn't one of my first lessons in love about how Jensen wasn't mine?

"Poppy, you're a competitive person. Make him yours."

I was competitive in sports. I liked competing with Jensen, but not for him. "I'm not demeaning myself by putting on a show for a guy. Either he wants me, or he doesn't."

"No, I totally get it. Sorry. You shouldn't have to make a guy notice you or love you. I'm just saying don't give up on him. He's into you, so don't convince yourself he's not just because you think Hassie's hot."

Hassie was the one I compared myself to. I never got self-conscious around women otherwise. I admired them. I also hadn't grown up getting compared to them by the guy I was falling hard for.

"Yoo-hoo!" someone called from outside the house and the doorbell rang. "Anyone home?"

"Oh shit." I hissed into the phone. "She's here, and I'm not even out of bed." I took the phone away from my face. "Oh my god. How did I sleep past ten?"

"Did Jensen wear you out on your date?" she teased.

Warm tingles spread over my body. I'd gone to bed smelling like him. I needed a shower and a beauty routine that included more than moisturizer with sunscreen.

The doorbell rang again.

I sat up and tugged my bonnet off. Where were Jensen and Auggie? "I've gotta go. Maybe I can sneak into the bathroom before she comes inside."

I hung up without waiting for her goodbye. After flying out of bed, I ran around the room, grabbing clothing that was at least clean. I didn't have anything that would rival Hassie's shorts and clinging tee.

Another ding-dong resonated through the house. Where was everyone? And why did I sleep so late?

I swung the door open. The house was quiet. I snuck out to the living room. Hassie was peering through the window. She waved, a big grin on her face.

My hair wasn't frizzed, thanks to the bonnet, but I hadn't even combed my fingers through it. Shit. I couldn't just leave her. But, oh, I wanted to.

I scurried to the door, opened it, and dashed backward as fast as I could go, aiming for the bathroom while hunching my shoulders because I didn't have a bra on. "Sorry, I don't know where the guys are."

"Jensen's pickup is outside." Grocery bags hung in her hands. "I thought y'all would be awake by now."

"Ah, late night." I winced at the way it sounded. "Um, I'll go clean up."

"I figured I'd bring the ingredients and make something." She set the bags on the island and sifted through them. "That's why I'm early. I know how Jensen appreciates a homemade meal."

Irritation prickled over my skin. "Sure."

Jensen and I had taken turns cooking and sometimes we prepared a meal together. With the nicer weather, we did a lot of grilling. He liked the sounds I made when I ate, but he didn't get that way when I cooked. Was that because no meal compared to a Hassie meal?

God, I was being ridiculous. I ducked into the bathroom and ran through the quickest shower of my life. I didn't bother with more than towel-drying my hair. It already looked better than it had when I answered the door. The rush was taking my mind off Jensen's ex-wife making him a homemade meal in the next room.

Hassie was humming in the kitchen when I flashed from the bathroom to the bedroom. While I was pulling my shorts on, I heard the front door open.

"Mom!" Auggie yelled.

I hopped on one leg and nearly fell over, grateful the door was closed all the way.

"There are my boys!" Hassie called.

This time, I flopped on the bed, my body heavy, like I had retained each drop of water from the shower.

There are my boys.

She sounded so...natural. Like she was meant to be here and I was the intruder.

But I wanted Jensen for myself.

I decided to marry him less than a week after reconnecting with him. Fake or not, that was a big commitment. Being with him since our deal only made it feel more right.

I fell for him. His smile. His unwavering support. The way he made me feel mentally and physically—I'd experienced nothing like it. I liked how he challenged me, but he also knew I just needed him to be there.

Tears poked hot into the backs of my eyes. A deep voice joined in the conversation in the kitchen. I pushed my hair out of my face and finished getting dressed before I found a hair tie and twisted my damp curls into a loose bun.

I was about to open the bedroom door when I

stopped. I could do this. Whatever happened, it would be fine. It might take some time, but I'd land on my feet.

I breezed out, leaving all my insecurities behind. Hassie had packs of chicken open and she was making a flour mixture to dredge them through. For fuck's sake, was she making homemade fried chicken? It wasn't even eleven.

Show-off.

Jensen was standing at the edge of the living room, his arms folded. He glanced at me and his expression lightened, but concern filled his eyes. "Morning."

"Morning. Sorry I slept in."

"Nothing to be sorry about," he said.

The tension was leaking out of me when Hassie popped her head up. "Early bird gets the worm, sleepyhead. I was at the store before it even opened. Since when do they keep the doors locked until nine?"

Any hunger I had vanished. I wasn't participating in this level of competition.

Jensen's lips were thinned when he faced me. "Auggie was in the shop helping me with the crown molding for the house." His voice was softer than his tone. "We'll get it measured and cut to install it tomorrow."

"I can help with that. Or I can do it even if you have stuff going on here." My gaze drifted to where Hassie was having Auggie beat a couple of eggs.

"You can give me a hand. Hassie said she'd come hang with Auggie tomorrow."

I almost said *it's a date*, but I held back. Awareness tickled down my spine. We were being watched. "I'll be there."

"I have to get back out to the shop so we have something to mount."

"You're all about the mounting," I muttered only loud enough for him, forgetting all the awkwardness of the last twelve hours. We snickered, and Hassie's focus burned into me. "Thanks for doing that."

He winked like he was oblivious to his ex. "Holding up my end of the deal. Do you want to come out and help?"

He was offering me an out. An escape from being stuck in the house with Hassie. I was a big girl. I could hang with her and save some pride. We'd been friends once.

"Dad—wait!" Auggie held his hands in the air. "Can I help again?"

"Of course, bud. Come on out after you wash your hands." Jensen disappeared outside. Auggie washed his hands and dashed out with him.

Now I was alone with Hassie. My stomach churned. We used to be friends. Maybe we still could be. It had to be better than this weirdness. "Can I help with anything?"

"I've got it." She smiled, but her eyes didn't sparkle at me like they did around Jensen. "So? How've you been?"

"Good. The normal. College, then work. Now I'm opening my own business."

She checked the pan of what I assumed must be oil on the stove. "I heard. Auggie has lots to say about his lessons."

"He's a wonderful pupil. I really enjoy working with him."

Her smile seemed genuine. "He's a good kid. Just wish we could work the same magic with horses that you can with reading."

Was she afraid the only thing that could link her and

her son was a love for the equine world? "I'm sure he'll come around. It's gotta be in his blood." I let out a nervous laugh.

She shrugged and dragged a drumstick through the egg and flour bowls she had prepared. When the meat was sizzling, she washed her hands and pulled out a chair at the table. She wasn't in booty shorts today, but her jeans barely hid how nice her figure was. Her blonde hair was thrown in a ponytail, and compared to mine, it looked like one of us walked out of the salon. It wasn't me.

"How have things been with you?"

"Oh, you know." She scrunched her face up as if she was debating what to tell me. "Jensen and I married pretty young, and that's probably why we didn't last. Two kids trying to act like grown-ups."

Two kids? If they divorced five years ago, they would've been in their late twenties. Still, I couldn't argue that age might've had something to do with the dissolution of their relationship.

She crossed one long leg over the other and bounced the heel of her square-toed cowboy boot. "For the last three years, I've been networking to open my own barrel racing school. I have clients willing to come from all over the country to learn from me." Pride shone from her blue eyes. "Look at us. Both going into teaching of some sort."

"We were always the bossy type."

Laughter chimed out of her, and I grinned. I needed this moment of camaraderie, but it didn't loosen the knot in my chest. She wanted Jensen back. She didn't have to say it. Showing up on the doorstep after hearing about his impending nuptials was the first sign. Add in the way she commented on how young and immature they'd been, that she was cooking for him in his kitchen, and the hard glances she shot my way when I had joked around with her ex, and I could only think one thing.

She let out a soft sigh. "Marriage, huh?"

"Yeah," I said slowly. "It seemed like a two-birds, one-stone kind of thing."

"Jensen always wants to care for those around him."

"He's a really good guy." I didn't know what else to say.

Not only is he nice, but he's good in the sack.

Your loss is my gain.

Your arrival is putting a cramp in our style.

I definitely couldn't say one of those lines, even though I keenly felt each one.

"He's the best. He's someone who's easy to take for granted." Her attention turned inward, and she dropped her attention to the floor. "I made a lot of mistakes." She lifted her gaze to meet mine. "But I intend to fix everything."

* * *

Jensen

Poppy had been quiet all day. We were attaching the last section of crown molding and then we were done for the day. I had looked forward to being alone with her in the Perez house, but if we weren't talking about carpentry, she wasn't speaking.

I'd already asked if everything was okay, and she'd shrugged and given me that *why wouldn't it be?* look. I hadn't pushed. We both knew what was going on.

Hassie had stayed at the house most of yesterday and

into the evening to tuck Auggie into bed. Poppy had disappeared into her bedroom before Hassie had left, and I'd had to kick my ex-wife out so I could get some sleep.

I pounded the last finishing nail in. "That's all she wrote." I tucked my hammer into my tool belt and stood back to study our work. "That really dresses the room up."

Admiration brushed across her face. "Some of the house's old elegance has been returned. Thank you," she finished, almost shyly.

I didn't like her shyness. Her quiet and subdued demeanor dimmed everything in my world. The fiery Poppy, ready to leap to any challenge, was the original Poppy. Hassie's arrival stole her sunlight, and I wanted to be the one to wrestle it back.

"You can talk to me." I loosely hooked my thumbs over my tool belt and waited. If she didn't talk, was there much hope for us? Were we a flame that couldn't survive a breeze?

She didn't speak for a long time. Neither of us moved as we stared at the new crown molding.

"She wants you back," she finally said, then shook her head, the ends of her puffy ponytail flying. "None of it is any of my business."

I barely had time to get over my shock from the first part of her statement. The second half kicked my feet out from under me. "How can you say that? We're getting married."

"But it's not real."

"My feelings for you are real. My feelings for her are dead."

Poppy's hazel eyes shimmered when she looked at me. "Are they?"

I almost answered with a succinct *yes*. End of story. But Poppy deserved more, and I needed her to understand. "It was death by a thousand cuts. A million erosions of love, trust, and respect. I wouldn't have gotten divorced if I was still in love with her. She kicked that emotion while it was down and then killed it dead for the last time right before I walked out, and she's done nothing to make me feel differently in the last five years."

"She said she wanted you back yesterday."

I barked out a laugh. "What?" I was sure I heard correctly. It sounded just like Hassie.

"Said you guys were young. She made a mistake. She wants to fix it." Her deadened tone bothered me as much as her subdued nature.

"Does it matter what I want?" It wasn't my ex. What I wanted was right next to me.

She let out a long, heavy exhale and prodded her temples. "You have to remember, Jensen, I've really only known you as having a major thing for her. Ninety-nine percent of the time I've known you, she's been the center of your world."

The pressure of the last two nights shot my anger up higher than normal. "You have to remember, Poppy, that you only knew me for a fraction of my life, and none of that was when I was an adult. No one knows what an adult Jensen is like when he dates except for you."

Her brows drew farther together the longer I spoke. She nibbled on her lower lip, and I wanted nothing more than to draw her into my arms. I'd been there before, and I'd gotten pushed back, both by Poppy and my ex, so I stayed in place.

"So what do you wanna do?" I asked more harshly than I intended. My frustration wasn't toward her. It was at my ex and at me for not getting through to Poppy that there was no competition between her and Hassie anymore.

Dismay filled her gaze when she glanced up. "You don't wanna get married anymore?"

"I'm not the one telling the other person that they must want to get back together with their ex-wife just because she's interested." Poppy recoiled, and yeah, my words were filled with heat. So many emotions tangled in my chest, hooking on my lungs and making it hard to breathe. "Shit. I'm sorry. I'm upset at all this. You and I had a plan and now it's slipping through cracks that I can't seem to fill fast enough."

"I don't want..." She stiffened and straightened her spine. "I don't want to be caught in the middle, and I don't wanna feel like I'm holding you back."

"For the first time in a long time, I feel like I'm going forward, and that's because of you."

Her gaze softened. "Really?"

This time, I pulled her into me. "You can trust me, Poppy. I don't want what I used to have. I want what I was hoping to get back then. But I'm not putting pressure on you. Yes, my ex-wife is in town, but I don't see why anything should change between us."

"When I saw her, it felt like everything changed." Her voice was muffled against my shoulder.

"Nothing did for me." She stiffened slightly, and I hugged her tighter. "Not when it comes to you."

"So we're still going to see where this goes?"

"Yes," I said into her hair. Stark relief was cool on the back of my neck. "We keep those Saturday date nights, and we keep sneaking around. We keep going like we were, but you and I know what's changed. No one else gets to interfere. Not anymore. But maybe we can cuddle a little more?"

Soft laughter shook her body. "Is that what we call this?"

"A standing cuddle? Sure."

She snuggled into me more.

Holding her wasn't something I got to do nearly enough, and with my ex around and juggling Auggie's feelings about that, it might be harder to squirrel away these moments between us.

Poppy was sensitive to Hassie and me, and I wasn't sure what the arrival of my ex meant when it came to my peaceful existence with my son. Add in Poppy, and anxiety churned in my gut. "This is new for me."

She pushed back to look at me again. "What is?"

"All of it. I had a pretty quiet life until you breezed into town." When uncertainty flickered in her gaze, I pushed a springy lock of hair behind her ear. "Suddenly my quiet, single dad life became fun and exciting. I got to date and live with a sexy woman, but I was worried how Auggie would take it. I still am, and I'm concerned over how it'll disrupt things between us. I don't know what I'm doing." But I was terrified of getting it wrong and sending Poppy careening to another state.

"Just talk to me, okay? We need to talk to each other."

"It won't be easy."

"Why?"

"Talking never worked before." Over and over, I'd ask to have a discussion. I'd ask for validation. I'd ask for love. I'd gotten a divorce for all my attempts.

"Maybe it'd work now."

"I'll promise to if you promise not to make plans to move on me."

"I don't just move when—" When I cocked a brow, she chewed on the inside of her cheek. "Fine. No moving and all the talking. Deal?"

"Deal. And you have to build a client list. And come up with a name."

"You can't tag stuff on after we agreed," she joked, but the alarm in her eyes told me the humor was superficial.

She wasn't keeping her roots shallow to ditch me. Another failure terrified her. "I know you are. But you have something you didn't have then—us. Support. We've got your back. You want to change your center's name? I'll make a new sign each time. You lose students? Auggie will do a commercial gushing about you. You've got this. We've got this." I flattened my hands on the small of her back and smoothed them up and down her body. Between the waning adrenaline from the last couple of days and having a beautiful woman in my arms, my dick stirred to life.

"You're amazing. You know that?"

"It means a lot to hear it."

She snaked her arms around my neck. I got harder, and she ground into me.

I moved us to the wall until her back was against it. "I'm gonna take your pants off now."

"I was hoping you would. It feels like it's been forever."

It had been. I was supposed to hold her after that night in the field. Two days and I was a starved man.

I claimed her mouth and swept her shirt up. I had to feel her satiny, soft skin before I dragged her shorts down. I dropped to a squat as I did it. Damn, she was right at face level. Perfect. A growl left me.

She knocked my cap off and pushed her fingers through my hair. I was hitching her leg over my shoulder when a series of knocks resonated through the house. I jerked and nearly toppled us both over. Her fingers locked around my hair as I steadied us.

"What the hell?" I muttered.

Then the front door cracked open and Auggie's yell filtered upstairs. "Dad? Poppy?"

Crap. Auggie couldn't catch us. One problem at a time.

"Yoo-hoo!" Hassie called.

This time, my groan resonated with all my dismay.

Poppy shoved my head back, and I landed on my ass. Shit. I grabbed her shorts and tossed them to her. "Yeah? Uh, be right down!" I shouted.

Her eyes were wide as she danced around to get back into her shorts. She caught my eye and the absurdity of almost getting caught like two teens hiding from Mom and Dad hit me. I grinned, giving her a wink.

She rolled her eyes, but a smile played over her lips.

"This is going to be an exciting couple of weeks," I said and left the room to run interference with my kid and my ex. They might've interrupted us now, but I could be a creative man.

Chapter Twenty-Three

Poppy

Auggie hadn't shown at practice yet. Jensen was catching up on work at the shop since Aspen and I didn't need him to fill in with coaching. I passed a ball back and forth between my feet, shuffling a few steps to the left and right. The boys I coached were spread around the field, doing their warm-ups. In a crooked line, they jumped up and down, switching the foot on the ball, doing toe taps.

I checked my phone. Not only was Auggie gone, but three kids hadn't returned. I glanced at Aspen's group. How small had hers gotten? At least four of Hadley's friends hadn't returned either.

I stayed anxious through all of practice. We would not survive our first season at this attrition rate. My stomach twisted on itself. How embarrassing would it be to hang the sign for my school—Uplifting Minds? No, not quite right. But how embarrassing to hang up my sign—whatever the title might be—only to have people wonder if I was the one who couldn't recruit enough kids for one soccer team?

The hour went by both slowly and quickly. No Auggie and no Jensen. I'd text them as soon as I was done. Everything was probably okay. Maybe they got involved at the shop and lost track of time. Maybe Auggie didn't want to play anymore.

"Bring it in," I called to the kids.

They surrounded me, and we all took a seat on the grass. I waved a few little flies out of my face. The city had sprayed for mosquitoes, so at least we weren't getting eaten alive, although it'd give me more to think about than my second failing soccer club attempt and how I had to lie about my fiancé to open a business. I used to tell the kids that winning wasn't a priority. But winning in life was a little more important.

"Tell me what you liked and what you didn't?" *And tell me if you're not coming back on Thursday.*

They all talked at the same time until I held up a finger. "Left to right." The two kids on the ends spoke together, and I chuckled. "My left. Sorry." I gestured to Jaxon.

"I liked getting it in the goal."

I smiled. "It's a good feeling."

"And I didn't like that Matthew's on vacation."

A small wave of relief cooled me off. "He's on vacation?"

Jaxon nodded solemnly. "With Davis. Their families go camping together."

Okay, that explained two. After all the kids told me they liked making goals and they missed their friends, I cut them loose.

Aspen had let her kids go at the same time, and she jogged toward me. "You had lots of kids gone too?"

I nodded. "Didn't look good, but a couple are on vacation."

She squinted at the parking lot. "A few of mine were too. To be expected, I guess." She waved at a swarm of tiny bugs. "Oh well. We can always enroll a coed team in the tournaments that allow it. Registration is still open on a couple, but I wanted to wait to see if our numbers were stable." She lifted her arms in a shrug and slapped her thighs. "Oh well. First year, we don't know what to expect."

"What if more kids drop?"

"Then no tournaments and we try again next year," she said brightly.

I nodded. There weren't thousands of other families' dollars on the line, so she could be cavalier about it. And it wasn't only my name attached to the Coal Haven Kickers.

I talked my blood pressure down. Crisis averted. I wouldn't have to move in shame. I could hold my head up high when I hung that Brain Power sign.

No, still not quite right for a name.

I just had to pick one. But the house wouldn't be ready until after the wedding, when I could actually open in my office. When I could actually order a sign. Jensen said he'd make it. And he'd make another.

I just needed a name.

After I helped Aspen load her bag of balls in her SUV, I jogged to my car. I checked my phone. Nothing from Jensen.

Worry gnawed at my stomach lining. I drove home, but his pickup was gone. Now what? I stayed in the car and stared at the house. Concern continued to eat at me, but so did envy. Hassie probably knew exactly where Jensen and Auggie were.

I could drive all over town looking for them and act like a jealous girlfriend. Or I could call Jensen. And talk. Which was what he'd asked me to do. I was tempted to text, but waiting for a reply would kill me.

He answered on the first ring. "Hey, how'd it go?"

I frowned. He sounded like nothing was wrong. "Uh, good. Auggie couldn't make it?"

"What?"

"He wasn't there. I thought maybe something happened."

"Shit," he hissed. "Hassie said she'd bring him, so I came to work. Let me call you back. I gotta make sure he's okay."

The line went dead. Dread filled me. I wanted everything to be fine, but if it was, that'd also mean that Hassie was using her son to drive a wedge between me and them.

I was still deciding if I should stay in the house or go when my phone vibrated. Jensen.

"Hey," I answered. "Is everything okay?"

"Yeah." The word came out exasperated. "She said he was having too much fun on the farm to stop him for soccer."

"Okay?" He had really been looking forward to it. Anger blazed a path across my cheeks. She had to have known how excited he was for practice.

"I know," he said grimly.

"I've worked with a lot of kids, and he's got so much passion. I'd hate to think she's..." It wasn't my place to say.

"Manipulating him? That's what I'm upset about. I

don't give a fuck if he wants to watercolor or learn to cross-stitch, but I won't tell him he gets to do something and then withhold it because I don't think he loves what I like enough. That's fucked up."

"Maybe he really was having a good time, and he suddenly can't get enough of horses or family friends." Call me surprised. I wasn't defending Hassie, but the fury would get too hot.

"Family friends who haven't reached out once since I've moved home."

Auggie didn't fit their lifestyle. My heart went out to him. If Hassie was trying to control his interests and then flitted from his life, he'd know. If he didn't realize it now, then he would in five years, ten years. Even twenty.

Jensen had to be seething. I was buffered during my time in the school system, but I'd seen enough antics that happened between divorced parents. It could get ugly, and while that wasn't Jensen, I didn't know it wasn't Hassie. "Let's assume he had fun until we learn differently."

His exhale gusted over the line. "You're right. Are you at home?"

The way he said home curled like a whisper through my insides. Home. I looked around the yard, from the proud farmhouse to the sprawling land behind it. The shop Jensen worked in where we'd made some steamy memories. The spot where he usually parked and we had our first time together. I'd never had a house before, and even if the Perez house became mine, if our wild plan worked, then I would, but that wouldn't change how I felt about this place.

"Yeah. I'm home."

●●●

Jensen

It was nearly dark before Hassie rolled up with Auggie. I was on the porch with Poppy, having a mineral water and enjoying the beautiful night. I'd stayed away from the beer so I could have a clear head to deal with any soccer fallout.

My heart dropped like a stone when I saw Auggie's tear-streaked face. He spotted Poppy and cried even harder. I was out of my chair and crossing the lawn in seconds.

"What's wrong, buddy?"

"I-I'm sorry. I-I forgot." He hiccuped.

Hassie rounded the back of her pickup with a sheepish look on her face. "The evenin' got away from us."

She was putting the charm on. It'd always saved her in the past. I felt Poppy's calming presence behind me.

Auggie slammed into my stomach, sobbing. "I'm sorry."

I hugged him and patted his back. "It's not your fault, bud."

Defensiveness flashed in Hassie's eyes, but I didn't care.

"I let Poppy down," he cried.

"It's not a problem, Auggie. There's always Thursday." Poppy looked at me, eyes wide. *Right?* she mouthed.

"Yes," I said firmly. "Thursday."

Hassie held her hands up. "Absolutely. Thursday. I

won't swoop in to take Auggie to see Honey's new goats. But they were really cute, weren't they?"

Auggie sniffled and nodded. He stepped back. "I liked the goats."

Hassie shrugged. "We're getting closer to horses, aren't we, hon?"

He stuffed the toe of his boot into the grass. When the hell did he get boots that fit him? He hated wearing anything but his athletic shoes.

"I petted Calvin." Pride shone from Auggie's face.

"That's cool." I rubbed his shoulder. Hassie was determined to get Auggie on horseback, and if she was willing to put the work in, fine. But she couldn't manipulate him. "Calvin's a good horse."

"He's my old horse," Hassie explained to Poppy. "Honey's been boarding him for me. Remember when I got him?" she asked me in a familiar, sultry tone.

I ground my molars together. She'd gotten Calvin after graduation. I'd hung out while she bonded with a two-year-old Calvin. That night was our first time together. Was that why she was bringing it up? "I think I remember. Maybe."

Her mouth dropped open. She snapped it shut. "So. Tomorrow? More goats, Auggie?"

"Yeah." Auggie whipped his head toward me. "Can I, Dad?"

"That'll be fine," I said, "but right now, it's bedtime. Go get cleaned up, and I'll be right in."

She glanced back and forth between me and Poppy, then at the house. "I'd like to tuck him in."

Auggie's evening had been dramatic enough. I wouldn't make it worse by confronting Hassie where he might hear. I lifted my chin toward the door. "Go ahead."

She gave me a sweet smile, but I didn't return it. My anger from the evening hadn't faded yet.

When my ex and Auggie were inside, I spun toward Poppy. "She's playing games."

"Which part?" She pretended to think. "With Auggie, or when she pointed out that I don't have a history with you?"

"She brought it up because it was our first time together that night, if you want to call two teens fumbling around memorable."

"It must be something because so many teens are still trying to fumble around, but I don't think they call it that these days."

Laughter trickled out of me. One little joke and she'd undone several tangles in my gut. "I'm so glad you can see what she's doing, and I'm really glad I don't have to deal with it alone. I just really want to hug you right now."

She smiled and lifted her gaze to the second level, where Auggie's window was. The bathroom light was on in the window next to it. "We might get busted."

"It's not Hassie seeing us that I'm worried about."

"But she suspects."

"Most definitely." I started for the porch, putting my hand on her lower back. A small touch, one I could take with me to bed.

We sat in our seats, and I took a long pull of my mineral water. "I'm glad you were here."

"I feel like I made it more awkward."

"I feel sane." When her brows lifted, I nodded. "When this happened before, I thought I was crazy. Overly jealous, too insecure. Whatever. But you saw what she was doing before me, and that means a lot."

The corner of her mouth lifted. "She's right. She

made a mistake and let a really good guy go. But that doesn't mean you're her good guy. Maybe you two weren't right for each other, and that's okay."

"I should've seen it sooner."

She lifted a shoulder and took a pull of her water, so accepting of me and my feelings. "You have a way of making me second-guess everything. When we talk like this, I always see my life more clearly."

She gave me an understanding but inquisitive look. "How do you mean?"

I propped my elbows on my knees. I'd never shared this moment with anyone. It'd been mine and mine alone, but it hadn't just been me. She'd been there. "Remember the day of my dad's funeral?"

The middle of my chest warmed when she nodded right away. She didn't have to think.

"When we sat on the hill and talked?" she asked.

"Yeah." I'd needed to get away from the crowd. The laughter. It'd been a sad day, and after days of seeing my mom's pale face force a smile, I'd needed to process our new normal away from everyone trying to make me feel better. "You just sat with me, and we talked about nothing and everything. It was the first time I thought that maybe I'd be okay. Life would be different than what I planned. My future might be a little different, but with the right person, it wouldn't be so scary. It wouldn't be so lonely." Her eyes were luminous when she looked at me, lit by the glow of the yard lamp. "Then you moved."

Her pink lips parted, and I had to look away. Back then, I hadn't been able to admit these thoughts to myself.

"But you never liked me like that," she said, barely above a whisper.

I studied a spot on the porch in front of me. "I didn't think there was another option until then. Before Dad's death, I coasted through life doing what I always did. Then I had to stop and rethink everything, and when I did, you were there. I wouldn't have wanted anyone else."

She turned in her seat. "And then I moved."

"Then you were gone, and it was easier to go back to what was familiar and continue my infatuation with *her*." I tilted my head toward the door. "I think if you had stayed, I might've chased you."

"Until she noticed and beckoned for your attention."

"You would've had it. Just like you do now." Without a doubt. I'd have been in Poppy's orbit. "I've always liked you, Poppy. You were one of my favorite people. Still are."

"And Hassie wasn't?"

The front door opened. Hassie stepped out, adding an extra swing to her hips. "He's asleep. I really am sorry about tonight."

I didn't trust her doe eyes.

Poppy picked up her can of mineral water. "I'll let you two talk."

Was she running, or was she sick of the weirdness when all three of us were together? Perhaps she wanted me to tell Hassie there was no chance we were reconnecting. Regardless, I let her go.

"I'll apologize a million times if you'll quit being mad at me." Hassie smiled, sticking a hand in her back pocket. She'd been on her friend's ranch, so she was in jeans, but that didn't stop her from kicking a hip out. I used to live for those moments. It had meant she noticed me. It had meant she wanted my attention. It had meant that maybe I hadn't made a horrible decision marrying Hassie Heart.

Now, I craved conversation. I craved someone

checking in because they wanted to. Like when Poppy called tonight, worried that something had happened to me and Auggie. When she would come into the shop to hang out. When she'd talked about me with her sisters and came up with guidelines for us to mess around because she couldn't help herself.

"I really didn't want to ruin the moment," she continued when I didn't give in to her flirtation, "but I had no idea that he'd take it that hard."

"You had some idea."

She blinked. Her frown was instant. "Jensen, it's not a big deal. It's just soccer."

"When you were his age, what would you have done if someone said the same thing about horse shows?"

She scoffed. "Where is this coming from? Was Poppy that upset? She's not his—"

"She has nothing to do with this," I said hotly, "but don't minimize her role in Auggie's life."

She drew back, giving me an aghast look. "And what is that? His *fake* stepmother?"

"A person who's been around him for the last six weeks, who hasn't broken her word to him, and who will continue to play a role in his life as his tutor and coach, and yes, as his fake stepmom."

"She can be all that, but she won't be Auggie's mom."

"What does being his mom mean to you?"

Hassie's mouth dropped open. "Jensen, I have been building a life for myself for the last five years. I've worked and competed and managed to build a reputation that'll let me move closer to my son. Yet you stand here and act like I'm a deadbeat mom? You know how many times I wanted to call, but I was in a different time zone? I didn't want to wake him up or promise that I'd call at a certain time only for an event to run long." She crossed her arms. No hips were cocked out. "I did the best I could until I could get here."

I narrowed my eyes. She talked a good game, but then she always had. The problem was that I'd bought into her claims each time. She hadn't cheated on me; she just had to flirt to get ahead. Don't hate the player; hate the game. She had to go to the tailgate parties. I no longer believed her, but *she* believed it. In her mind, Hassie was always right. "Okay."

She pouted, not hiding her disappointment. "You never gave me credit." She took a step forward, and I took one back. Her gaze turned shrewd. "Are you and Poppy a thing?"

I didn't want Hassie to interfere with the flame flickering between me and Poppy. As much as I wanted to confess, I'd honor the agreement Poppy and I had. "I told you the deal, and we don't have to be a thing for her to be important to me and Auggie."

"But you're not committed?"

She was nothing if not persistent. "We're helping each other, and Auggie likes her."

Fire flashed in her eyes. Should I have left the last part off?

She worked her jaw back and forth as if she didn't like that answer. "Okay. Well. I'll pick Auggie up tomorrow. He said he wants to ride a pony, and Honey has a few that would be good for him."

"Good night." I didn't watch her leave. I had a bedroom door to knock on and a shower to invite Poppy into.

Chapter Twenty-Four

Poppy

In the week since the missed practice, Hassie hadn't been around at all on practice night. She'd gone out of her way to be accommodating, but she hadn't stayed away from the house.

Jensen and Auggie had ridden to practice with me. Our player numbers had stabilized. Aspen was unloading two bags of balls. Jensen grabbed both of them and started for the fields. He'd been helping more when he didn't have quick jobs in his shop to do or clients to meet with.

I walked with Auggie, and Aspen fell into step next to us.

He kicked a small pebble across the gravel parking lot. "Who's all coming next weekend?"

"Clover will be here to see your practice next week, and Jasper will arrive on Friday. He's staying with Alder and Daisy." Clover and "The Douche" would get a room.

I didn't ask if it was our other sisters who didn't want him at their home or if Clover subconsciously didn't want them to witness how he treated her.

"I like Clover. What's Jasper like?"

"He's funny but serious."

Auggie scrunched his nose, then nodded.

"Ooh, that's right—it's right around the corner." Aspen gasped and she clutched my arm. "I never checked on how much time you need off for a honeymoon."

"No, it's fine." Heat licked across the back of my neck. I hated to lie to a friend and do so in front of a kid who was also in on the lie. "We're not going anywhere for a while. Maybe we'll see what next summer holds, but since I'm just moving and opening my center, you know..." I let her fill in the rest.

I peeked at Auggie, and he almost looked relieved that I didn't fib that much. We would have to see what next summer held. Maybe Jensen and I would want to stay married.

What a crazy thought.

Was it?

Or had we been inevitable? Had we had to grow up and learn who we were as individuals?

It was too much to think about in the minutes before practice.

Jensen had dropped a bag off at one of the goals where Aspen and her team practiced. Then he'd kicked a few balls to Hadley and her crew. She spotted me and her face lit.

"I hope you don't mind," Aspen said as she veered toward where her team was gathered in a loose group. "I told her to talk to you about a tournament in South Dakota."

A pit formed in my stomach. Before I could ask where, Hadley had reached us. Auggie ran off, and Jensen nodded toward me. A silent signal that he'd get warm-ups started.

"Hey, Coach," Hadley said. "Ready for the big day?"

I'd just been talking about the wedding, but my brain scrambled to keep up. Yes. In a little over a week, I was getting married. We had resumed our sneaking around, and we'd had to be a little sneakier since Auggie was present most of the day and we never knew when Hassie would appear. "Getting there."

The house would be finished this week. I'd confirm the food with Alder, but honestly, they could flake, and we'd be fine. Our ceremony was small. Intimate but casual. Instead of dreading fake nuptials, my excitement grew every day. I might even be daydreaming about how Jensen would look at me when I walked down the aisle. Then I had to wonder when I'd quit pretending to others that my feelings were fake.

I was falling in love with the man I was going to marry.

"So, there's this tournament in the Black Hills next month, and we can sign up just our team, but we need an official coach because I'll have to play."

A thrill rose inside me like a helium balloon. I'd love to coach a competitive game. Hadley and her friends knew how to play, and I'd been watching them practice. With some targeted guidance, they could be formidable.

"Aspen has summer school," Hadley continued, "so I thought we could ask you. Aspen even said that she'd have to get us the extra cost to pay for your fees and travel."

Ohmigosh, it would be like a coaching job. I was

donating my time for the evening practices, but it was a couple of hours a week. This was the most basic of a coaching position, but it meant that I was doing it again. "I would love to. Send me the dates and times that would work for you, and we can find some around my lessons."

She grinned. "Nice." But her tone said it was more than nice. She sprinted back to the girls and yelled something I couldn't make out. All the girls whooped and cheered.

Aspen laughed and trotted to meet me at the neighboring field. Jensen had the boys doing penguins, kicking it from the inside of one foot to the inside of the other, for warm-ups.

"You'll do it?" she asked.

"Yeah, I'll do it." Now that I had committed, it felt right. This was what I wanted to be doing.

Her grin was radiant. "I'll figure something out for jerseys, but I won't bug you with anything until after the wedding."

"Hey, do you wanna come?" I shrugged. "Sorry, I didn't send out invites because it's small, but I'd love to have you."

"And I'd love to go."

"The Perez house at seven."

"Is that to party all night or so you two can get away by yourselves earlier?"

I wished. Actually, I really did. The idea of a honeymoon poked at my brain, planting suggestions in the dirt of my fantasies. A weekend away with him? Even a trip with him and Auggie where we could openly hold hands or something.

I was getting ahead of myself.

I had to marry the man first. Then we'd see if we wanted to stay that way.

●●●

Jensen

I walked through the first floor of the Perez house. The wedding was tomorrow. Poppy, Auggie, and I had cleaned all day, windows open and music blasting. All the surfaces gleamed and the floors were freshly polished. Poppy had run to the furniture store in town and purchased some area rugs and a few seats to make a homey waiting area for when she had in-person students.

A part of me was nervous that she hadn't recruited clients yet, but she had several kids she worked with each week. But if she named her learning center, I'd feel better that she was staying.

"Does it pass inspection?" Poppy asked as she came down the stairs. Yesterday, we ran to the store to get supplies for the wedding. The bathrooms were stocked, the kitchen had backups of napkins and silverware, and she'd gotten a small table and chairs for the dining room. Three stools lined the island.

It wasn't homey, but the aesthetic wasn't clinical.

"I think it does." I fought the urge to pull her into my arms, to push a stray curl behind her ear, and claim her mouth. Auggie was still upstairs.

"My desk and shelving won't be delivered until after the wedding and then it's ready."

We hovered at the base of the stairs. The weekend had been low-key fun. Hassie had gone to Montana with her friend to look at a horse. I hadn't realized how much she'd changed the atmosphere around the house, infused it with an ever-present tension that didn't dissipate until she was out of city limits. Even Auggie had seemed more relaxed. Poor kid had been on a journey to please his mom since she'd arrived.

I didn't want this moment to end. The wedding had pulled together with little planning, and I wanted to enjoy the ease. "Should I grab a couple of pizzas from the gas station and bring 'em over?"

Poppy pressed a hand to her stomach. "Mm, I think we worked up an appetite."

"Can I get a root beer?" Auggie asked, coming down the stairs.

"I think we all deserve a root beer." I plugged the order into the phone, then ran to the store for some drinks and precut fruit. While I was out, I marveled over how this could be many nights. For many years. I liked that thought.

By the time I was done with that, our order was ready. I walked up to the house with the pizzas and the bag of goodies. Poppy and Auggie peered out the living room window, grins on their faces. First, Poppy waved and then Auggie followed suit. My heart damn near exploded. They were waiting for me, watching. A small moment like this was everything I had wanted. Poppy had no idea how often I'd walked into an empty house.

I was in love with Poppy.

She whipped open the door and lifted the grocery bag from my fingertips. "Let me get that."

She and Auggie had already set the table. We sat around it and dug in. Auggie peppered us with questions on how the week would go.

Poppy patiently answered them all. "Alder and Evander will be hauling tables and chairs over in the morning on Friday. Apparently, Evander stocked up for when they do pumpkin harvests." Poppy's eyes brightened. "Hey, maybe we can participate this year. He has quite a party—all of his cousins and their kids show."

"Do we get to pick the pumpkins?" Auggie asked, hopeful.

"He even lets you keep a few." She stiffened, then caught my eye. "I mean, if that's okay with your dad."

It was more than all right. "Absolutely. I'm not going to stand in the way of a pumpkin harvest."

I'd heard about the pumpkin gathering from clients. Evander and Violet were growing the event, and pumpkins showed up everywhere in town afterward. Auggie had wistfully commented on them before, asking if we could grow some. We had, but when it was just him picking them, it wasn't as fun. Now Poppy was inviting him right into the center of the whole thing. He'd be thrilled.

We cleaned up, and when the kitchen was returned to its shiny state, Poppy went for the sliding door. She stepped onto the porch that overlooked the expansive backyard. Auggie sprinted past us and charged into the middle of the grass.

We stopped at the railing, and I stood close to her.

"It's really going to happen," she murmured.

"Afraid you won't be able to get away after you say I do?"

She turned and put her butt against the railing. We were still close, a breath apart, but far enough away that Auggie would think we were only talking. Her eyes searched mine. "I am a little afraid."

Worry spiked in my blood. "Of what?"

She took in the house. "This weekend has been so..."

"Perfect."

Her gaze met mine and a small smile graced her face. "Yeah. Perfect." She licked her lower lip, and if Auggie wasn't around, I'd lean in and bite it.

When could we go public with our loved ones? When would it be less confusing for my son? Mom likely wouldn't have an issue. She'd been polite about Hassie staying with her, but she'd seen long before I had how our relationship really was. Would Poppy's family mind? Would she tell them?

"Have you got a name yet?"

She turned sheepish. "No. I'm so close to being official, it's just... No."

Since she was still scared, I didn't bother to ask if she'd lined up clients. She could keep subbing when her doors opened. It just seemed as temporary as our nuptials, and my anxiety and pride were not comfortable with that after my first marriage.

"I'm opening the center," she continued. "I'm getting married. My dad and Aunt Linda still have to sign off on us. I dunno, it just feels like there's a lot out of my control on how things will go." She tapped a finger to her chest. "And it's giving me that panicky feeling again."

I stroked my fingers down her cheek, uncaring of who saw. She was opening up to me, and I wouldn't brush her off because my feelings were hurt. "Hey, it's okay. It'll be fine. You're a good tutor. I don't have to see you work to know you're a hell of an occupational therapist."

"But it won't matter if people don't trust me not to scam them."

"They'll trust you. All they have to do is see you with Auggie, watch you with your team, to know."

"Kids are easy." Her eyes shimmered, and she scrubbed both hands over her face. "Why did I think I could start a business reliant on fundraising and not have my past haunt me?"

"Because you were innocent, and the people in charge threw you under the bus."

"Pushed me right off the train platform."

I gripped her shoulders. "There's no Amtrak stop here. All we have are coal trains, so you're safe."

"But Dad and Aunt Linda have to sign off on us. That's so unfair."

"It'll be fine." I peeked over her shoulder. Auggie was stalking a bug or frog and wasn't paying attention. He was too far away to hear. "They'll see how much I love having your legs wrapped around me."

"That would be awkward." Her cheeks turned pink. Good. I was getting her out of her head.

"They'll see that I think about kissing you all the time, and I count down the minutes until I can have you naked again."

Her flush grew darker. "You're incorrigible."

"It sucks that people have to sign off on us. But you know what?" When she gave her head a small shake, I continued. "It means we care. When we first made this deal, we only cared about faking it enough to pass. But now we're concerned that they won't actually see what's going on."

"You're worried too?"

"I wasn't until you brought it up."

She laughed and tipped her head back. One day, I'd

be able to kiss up her neck and along her jaw and not care who the hell saw—and it wouldn't be fucking fake.

She ran a finger down my chest. "There's no use worrying about it until we get married."

"You doing okay with that?" I grasped her hand. Her ring twinkled in the sunlight.

"I am. You? Is wedding planning bringing up memories?"

I let her go and caged her in. Auggie was chasing what looked to be a frog jumping through the grass. "No, actually. I'm looking forward to seeing everyone and just having a relaxing day. Auggie will be around a ton of kids, and he'll see what it's like to be part of an involved family."

"I'm looking forward to it too." Her soft smile burrowed right into my heart.

Was she eager for more than seeing her family? Did her stomach fill with butterflies when she thought of facing me in front of the justice? Was she wondering how we'd celebrate the wedding night?

That was a good question. Auggie was on his way back. The frog had gotten away.

I didn't move away from her yet. "Should I ask Mom if she can take Auggie for our wedding night? Make it look more believable?"

"I like that idea." Her sultry grin went straight to my dick. I'd have to drag her into the shower tonight.

"It's a date," I said.

One thing was different between this wedding and my first one. I looked forward to Saturday.

Chapter Twenty-Five

Jensen

I coached the boys' team tonight so Poppy could work with Hadley's team. She was showing the goalkeeper how to dive while the rest of the older girls were practicing their goal shots with Clover. Poppy's voice reached me with shouts of "good" and "that's it." Clover's boyfriend had stayed at the hotel in Bismarck for work. Good. The night was too beautiful to ruin it with assholes.

Hassie's silver pickup pulled into the gravel lot. Mom said she wanted to come watch Auggie, but Hassie had stayed far away from anything soccer. When she parked, she hopped out and Mom exited the passenger side. She waved when she saw me. I nodded back and jogged to the middle of the field.

"Line up!" I called.

I ran the boys through one more line of cones using the outside of their shoes and the bottoms before cutting them loose.

"Bye, Coach," rang out from each one as they high-fived and fist-bumped me. Auggie sprinted for the fence line, where Mom waved at him.

Poppy wasn't done with her team, so I followed Auggie.

"I think you found another calling," Mom said.

Hassie didn't look impressed, but she smiled and gushed about Auggie's skills.

"It's fun, and I think the community needed something local so kids didn't have to travel and then feel like a stranger on another community's team."

"Look at you three," Mom gushed, but she wasn't indicating Auggie. Her gaze was on where Poppy was kicking with the goalie. She wasn't ruthless, but she wasn't taking it easy on the teen goalie. "Giving back to the town you grew up in. It's really something. I remember the kids who used to argue but then complain when they had to leave the playground."

Hassie gave her an indulgent smile, but she didn't appear to be thrilled about giving back to the community she was raised in. "Well, I can't speak for Poppy, but for me and Jensen, it's definitely our pleasure."

Subtle. "I think Poppy feels the same. Hey, Mom, can Auggie stay with you this weekend?"

"Oh." Surprise lifted Mom's brows. "The wedding, yes."

"If it's not real," Hassie asked, not bothering to keep her voice down, "then why do you need the whole weekend?"

Mom frowned. "It's definitely fine to have Auggie over. It's not a problem of space. He can take the couch. We'll make it a campout."

"Sure, sure." Hassie's lips were in a troubled line. "But isn't it fake?"

It was supposed to be. When did I think about how the wedding tomorrow felt more right than my first one? None of that was Hassie's business. Our shared interest was our son. That was it. "We thought it'd look more real to have the weekend off. She's been telling people that we're not having a honeymoon because she's launching her center and she just moved. It's my busy season. But her aunt might think it's weird that we're not taking at least one night for ourselves, much less the weekend."

The furrow across Hassie's brow deepened.

Mom nodded. "Of course. Like I said, space isn't an issue. Hassie can keep the guest room. I might even go find a small tent for Auggie. Make it exciting."

"Thanks, Mom."

The group of older girls were chatting and laughing as they strolled toward the parking lot. Poppy was helping Aspen haul the ball bags.

"I'll be right back." I ditched Mom and Hassie and sprinted toward the others.

Poppy's sunglasses hid her eyes, but she smiled. "My knight in shining Under Armour." She handed her bag over but walked with us. I took the bag from Aspen too.

Aspen loaded the balls and shut the hatch. "Well, see you on your big day, then."

"I can't wait." Poppy reached for my hand.

I grasped her warm fingers. This was for show, but I wasn't missing my chance.

Aspen squealed. "Me either. I've been to so many weddings, you'd think I'd be sick of them, but I love it."

When she pulled away, I kept hold of Poppy's hand. Just a little longer. She clung to me back, and we shared a smile. Then I released her, and we started for the little group waiting for us.

Hassie's frown hadn't vanished as she watched us. Maybe it was a good thing Poppy and I were pretending to pretend for a little longer. No one needed a riled-up Hassie right before all of Poppy's family came to town.

She wouldn't do anything though...right? I couldn't imagine that she would. But the look on her face sparked some anxiety.

"Dad! Shoot on me. Grandma wants to watch." Auggie kicked his ball toward me. It went wide, but Poppy stopped it, jumped, and kicked it toward me.

Just for fun, I kicked it back. She put her foot on the top, jumped to the side, and punted it back with her other foot.

Auggie's laughter rang in the air, and he sprinted for the goal. I dribbled the ball until I was in front of the goal. Poppy posted at the corner to be a ball shagger. Auggie shuffled back and forth. I booted the ball, using only a fraction of my power. He stopped it and sent it back.

I kicked again and again. Auggie either hit my shots out of the net, caught it, or Poppy retrieved it and sent it back to me. Our laughter rang across the pitch. Mom would clap each time Auggie blocked a shot. Hassie studied us, an unimpressed expression on her face. As for me, it was amazing not to be driven to impress her.

Mom looked at her watch. "I hate to be Cinderella, but tomorrow's going to be a long day."

"'S all right," I said and softly tapped the ball to Auggie. He stopped it with the bottom of his foot, then practiced switching feet, jumping lightly as he switched back and forth. "It's getting to be Auggie's bedtime."

"It's not that late," he argued.

I ruffled his hair. "We've got a wedding tomorrow."

His eyes lit. "I get to carry the rings."

Hassie's gaze went to Poppy's left hand, and a cloud passed over her expression. She pushed off the fence. "Come give me a hug." She avoided looking at me or Poppy when she said her goodbyes to Auggie.

As Hassie walked with Mom back to her pickup, Poppy chewed on her lower lip. She glanced over and flared her eyes wide, making a grimace. I snorted, and she giggled.

Hassie looked over her shoulder, cast an even stare at us, then gave Auggie one more wave before they loaded up and left. Auggie climbed into my pickup. He chattered about practice all the way home and then about camping out inside with Grandma all weekend.

"Go get cleaned up," I said to Auggie after we parked at home. He ran inside, and I waited by the pickup with Poppy.

"So," she said, standing close, "that was tense."

"It was. Is she going to be a problem tomorrow?" Hassie had told Auggie she'd be there *"since it was fake and all, it shouldn't be an issue."*

Poppy pointed at herself. "You're asking me? She's not my ex."

"It's your wedding."

She opened her mouth, shut it again.

Ah hell. What did I say wrong?

"Right. Yes. My wedding."

I cupped her elbow and drew her closer to me. "Hey, I didn't mean it like that. We're in this together, but I'm used to having her suck the fun out of weddings. You're not."

"Was it really that bad?"

Yes. Back then, I didn't think so. I didn't want to think so, or I'd have had to admit a lot more than I was ready for. "That day wasn't about us. It was about her, and I was an accessory. She was more interested in hanging out with the wedding party than me. I kept her happy that day, and it was at the price of my sanity. A drunk Rodeo Barbie isn't easy to deal with."

She laughed. "I'm really sorry it didn't turn out well for you."

"Some lessons take longer to learn." I glanced at the front door, then up at the window. I tugged her in for a kiss. It was quick, and I let her go.

She kept going, backing up. "I'm gonna wait to shower until Auggie's in bed."

"What a coincidence. Me too."

She grinned and turned around to walk to the house. I watched her the whole way. When she was inside, I stared into the distance. Tonight was worlds different than the last time I was getting ready to marry a beautiful woman. I was relaxed. I had no qualms. My only worry was that one year from now, we'd be getting ready to divorce.

Chapter Twenty-Six

Poppy

The Perez house was bustling with people. My brothers were out on the lawn, milling around with my dad. I was in the room that would be my office. We'd hauled a few chairs up and the tub of hair styling supplies that Clover had brought was covered in curling irons and spray bottles. Violet had brought a full-length mirror that rested against the wall.

This morning, I had gone out to breakfast with my sisters. When our parents had gotten to town, they went straight for the diner. All my family was in city limits and were here to watch me get married.

My stomach fluttered, and I was so damn excited for tonight I was tempted to rush to the justice, say my vows, and hide away in the house with Jensen where we didn't have to pretend we were crazy about each other.

He really liked me.

But he hadn't said he loved me.

I wrestled with one unruly curl. Should I have kept my hair down? I plumped the stray lock, but the damn thing hung right down the middle of my forehead. I twisted it and tried to secure it in the delicate pile Clover had made on the top of my head.

More curls slipped loose.

"What are you fussing with that for?" Clover was in front of me, a frown line bisecting her forehead. She wore a pale-green summer dress. All my sisters were in their dresses, each having picked out the same style but in the colors they preferred. Violet and Lily both had chosen a lilac shade, and Daisy had a light yellow. They were like a bouquet of wildflowers in my future office.

I scowled. "There was a line going right down my forehead."

Lily's hair was pinned off her face, and she had a leg crossed under her skirt, her heel bobbing. "She was thinking about tonight and getting the house to herself with her man."

I let out an indignant gasp. "How did you know?"

Daisy smirked and exchanged a knowing glance with Lily.

Violet chortled. "We've each had the same thoughts on our wedding night."

"Well, not mine," Lily said. "I *wondered*, then I found out soon enough. But the excitement to have him and the house to ourselves never fades."

Lily and Eliot were married by the same justice as I would be today, but it'd been an office ceremony. Then they'd gone their separate ways. Their one-year anniversary celebration was different. They'd been the picture of wedded bliss, and I was certain they had snuck off at least once while we'd all been there.

"Did you…" I brushed my hands down my shorts. I hadn't changed into my dress yet, thankfully, so I couldn't get sweaty handprints on it.

Lily tilted her head, waiting for me to finish.

The thoughts swirling in my head were chaotic. Wishful. Fanciful. Should I even be thinking of this? It didn't matter. I was. "Did you feel like your first anniversary was the real start?"

Her teasing smile faded. "Are you wishing this was the real start?"

So much. "What if it's just a little real?"

Both Lily and Violet leaned forward in their chairs.

"You and Jensen?" Violet prompted.

"It felt inevitable. We couldn't help ourselves."

"Aw." Violet's blue eyes shimmered. "That's so sweet."

I pressed a hand against my belly. "I'm really excited, but if you look at it, we only just started dating. Will this whole year be a wait-and-see thing? Will we be afraid that we're not doing enough to get Aunt Linda and Dad to sign off on us?"

"You don't have to do anything," Clover said, fussing with my hair. She pinned the rogue curl in place. "We can see that you two like each other."

"But it's only like." I huffed out a breath. There, I said it. "I think I'm in love with the man I'm going to marry, but he hasn't said it."

"Have you?" Lily asked.

I shook my head. I might be a hypocrite, but I wanted to hear it first.

The four of them stared at me.

Understanding filled Daisy's eyes. "It's hard to put yourself out there when you've been hurt before. I almost ruined things between me and Alder because I didn't trust myself to open up."

"I've only dated duds." I didn't realize how dudly they were until Jensen.

"I'm not talking about you," Daisy said gently and went to stand by the window.

Oh. I worried the inside of my cheek. "I'm rushing him."

"You're getting married today." Clover gave my shoulder a squeeze. "It's hard not to feel like today should signify more than the start of the clock."

Violet crossed to the window. "And Hassie's here."

She was here because of the wedding. Because of me. "We're not rekindling our friendship anytime soon."

"Right," Daisy said, "but also, Hassie's *here*."

The butterflies in my stomach careened to the sides. "Yeah, it'd have looked worse to not invite her. I'd invite her a million times for Auggie, but I hope..."

When I didn't finish, Clover narrowed her eyes. "Has she been saying shit?"

"Not directly." I twisted my fingers together. "But she was double-checking that all this was fake yesterday. I think she hated seeing me, Jensen, and Auggie playing together."

Violet clucked her tongue. "And I'm sure it digs under her skin to think about you and Jensen *playing* together."

We played so hard together. "She doesn't know a life where he's not obsessed with her."

"Linda and Darren just arrived," Daisy said.

The nerves in my gut went wild. "It'll be fine. Right?"

"Why wouldn't it be?" Violet asked, and since she was the logical one, I calmed.

Why wouldn't today go all right? Everything was in place, and I was in love with the groom. He might not be there yet with me, but my aunt and uncle didn't have to know and neither did my parents. Maybe when the year was over, we'd get our own one-year anniversary celebration.

"It's starting soon." Clover took my dress off the hanger. "Once he sees you in this dress, he's going to haul you away in front of everyone."

It was go time. I looked at my empty ring finger. The ring and band would be on it before the end of the day. A symbol of our deal, but I was no longer satisfied with that. Marriage first. Hopefully, the love came later.

●●●

Jensen

The justice of the peace was chatting with Poppy's dad. Alder and Jasper had veered into talk of cattle ranching and horse breeding, and while I was mildly interested in both, I couldn't concentrate. I kept scanning the small, intimate crowd for Poppy.

I was comfortable. No tight western vest. No new pair of boots pinching my feet. I was in an old polished pair of cowboy boots, loose gray slacks, and a comfortable dress shirt. No pinching ties. No clinging suit coat. Just me.

Awareness prickled over my skin, and the jitters were right there, threatening to make my hands tremble. I yearned for the calming presence of Poppy. She'd understand how I felt with this almost-but-not-quite sense to the day. How I wanted to be excited and then remembered I wasn't supposed to be while also considering that everyone should think I was, so why couldn't I be excited again?

Poppy knew how I felt.

Did she know how I felt about her?

She knew I liked her. I couldn't keep my hands off her. But she didn't know how much I liked her. She had no idea that times like now, I craved her, and it wasn't just sexual. She didn't know I loved her.

Her aunt wandered by, looking uncertain.

"Hi, Linda," I said. "Thanks for coming."

Her salt-and-pepper brows lifted. "Hello, Jensen." She glanced around. "Is the house open for guests? I'm afraid I have to use the restroom."

"Absolutely it's open for guests. Poppy and I were hoping to show you the renovations."

Pleasure filled her face. "Of course. I'm looking forward to it. I hope I'll still get a tour when the ceremony is done." She walked away, picking over the grass in her low-heeled sandals. The wind fluttered her wide-legged pants.

I really did want her to see the place. In the next few weeks, I'd go over the pictures of the cabinets I made and installed and write up a description. Poppy would look at it, and we'd carry on like we'd been doing for the last two months.

I couldn't wait.

As I was turning, Hassie approached. She wore a backless pink dress that was more like a long nightgown with sheer fabric and a thigh-high slit. I didn't recognize the cowboy boots, but she had needed a horse trailer to haul all her footwear, and she likely hadn't pared down.

She'd been talking to Auggie. He was brandishing our rings to anyone who would stop long enough to admire them.

Hassie's features were pinched. "Can I talk to you for a minute?"

I suppressed a groan. "Yeah, What's up?"

Laughter rang up from the group of my future brothers-in-law.

Hassie twisted her lips. "Is there somewhere a little more private?"

Ah, hell. What was this about? "I want to stay out here, but we can move closer to the house. The porch?"

That way, I wasn't going off alone with my ex on my wedding day.

"Yeah, I guess that'll do." She walked ahead of me, her steps determined.

I lifted my gaze to the window that would be Poppy's office. I couldn't see movement, but the ceremony was supposed to be starting soon. Was she at the stairs? I'd love to see her descend, in whatever dress she had chosen, with those twinkling eyes.

Hassie didn't go up the porch stairs but angled to the right by some bushes I didn't get trimmed. Wrong time of year and Poppy hadn't cared if they looked a little shaggy.

Hassie folded her arms and leaned in. "Are you sure about this?"

"About what?"

She shook her head in that *duh?* way that had rankled when we'd been married.

"The *wedding*? Why wouldn't I be?"

She gave me a pointed look and then turned to the line of chairs. Aspen was chatting with Auggie. She'd already seen the rings. My future father-in-law, Weston, ushered his wife to the chairs. Poppy had invited Eliot's family, and knowing about the trust requirement for a marriage, they'd gathered with us to make it more believable.

Mom took a seat next to Magnolia and grinned. She hadn't looked so relaxed at my first wedding. That whole time, she'd kept her mouth in a tight line and had smiled congenially. Today, she acted like she was happy.

"This looks serious," Hassie hissed, fluttering her hands to take in everything around us.

"Because it is." I gave my head a shake. Why would she care so much? We were done. "We're both adults. We know what we're doing."

"Our son doesn't. Look how excited he is."

"What's wrong with that?"

"You can tell him this isn't real, but it is. It's a real wedding. There are real guests. You and Auggie and Poppy playing a happy family isn't real, and our son can't tell the difference."

Anger heated the back of my neck. If I'd been wearing a tie, I'd have to remove it. "I can worry about us just fine, like I've been doing for five years before you suddenly decided to show up and act like you're a good mom."

Her gasp probably drew attention, but I couldn't look. "How dare you drag my parenting into this conversation? I'm not the one who hit up a practical stranger to get married so he could work. I'm not the one who's getting married, so someone he barely knows can get a house. I'm not the one who's going to stand up there in front of everyone and say very real vows in order to fake a marriage so she can get this house."

A squeak resonated from behind me. Linda stared at us from the top of the stairs, her mouth gaping open.

My world went cold, ice crystallizing in my veins. *Shit.*

The door opened, and Poppy's sisters spilled out. They stilled when they saw me, Hassie, and Linda. I saw a stack of curls and a white dress moving behind the women on the porch.

"Geez, stop right in the way, why don't cha?" Poppy spotted us as she muscled her way through. She took in the tension, and her eyes widened.

My shock was wiped away. Goddamn, she was gorgeous. Curls framed her radiant face, and her white dress hinted at all the lush curves underneath.

Linda stared at her and her expression went stony. "Is it true?"

Hassie put her hands on her hips, a smug look on her face.

"Is it?" Linda snapped, and we all jumped. She was such a low-key person I hadn't thought it was possible for her to make a whip-snap sound. "Are you two doing this only to fool me?"

Her voice carried over the lawn. The guests had gone quiet. Auggie was frozen in place at the end of the row of chairs.

Poppy opened her mouth, but nothing came out.

Weston rose and started in our direction. Linda's husband was hot on his heels.

"This whole evening is a farce?" Linda's voice pitched up. Hurt was etched into her face.

Despair filled Poppy's expression, and it gutted me. She was losing everything, getting humiliated, and it was because of my ex. Because of a childhood crush I'd been too afraid to leave behind.

"What's this?" Weston asked.

Linda's expression was aghast as she stomped down the stairs. "It's a scam. All of it. For the house! Well, no need to go through with it on my account." She tucked herself into her husband's side. He glowered at us.

I circled around Hassie and took the stairs to Poppy's side. She was still frozen, devastation sinking into her lovely features, and I didn't want her to feel alone. "Can we talk about this?"

"What's there to talk about?" Darren blinked rapidly. "I can't believe this. My wife is not a fool."

"I didn't think she was," Poppy said hoarsely.

"How 'bout we find out what they have to say," Weston said. A heavy line crossed his brow, but he at least seemed willing to listen.

"Well, the secret's out now." Linda huffed. "They took me for an idiot and—"

"I love her." I slid a hand around Poppy. She was stiff as a nail.

There. I was doing it. Putting myself out there for a woman to cast off. Once again, I'd laid it all out there. I was free-falling, and Poppy was the only one with a safety net. But this time, I wasn't doing it for me. I didn't need the confirmation. I needed her to know. I wanted everyone else to know.

A small gasp came from Hassie. Weston tipped his head, and his gaze softened. Linda huffed, and Darren rubbed her back. Everyone's stares prickled across my skin, but the only one I cared about was Poppy's.

"You do?" she whispered.

"So damn much," I continued, opening myself wider in front of the crowd, and she relaxed into me. "Maybe we came up with this plan to get into the house sooner.

You have to admit, leaving a trust like that is a shitty thing to do to grandkids."

Linda rolled her lips in. No, she couldn't argue.

"But I also wish I could tell Annie Duke that the unfair trust was the best thing to have happened to me." My time with Poppy streamed through my head. All of it. Since I'd met her on the first day of kindergarten. How she smiled when she sauntered into the shop or when I appeared at her office door. Every time she didn't make me work for her affections, she showed me how she really felt. Poppy made love easy. "It was a way to keep Poppy in my life. I could help her, and she'd help me." I turned her toward me. My heart could've slammed out of my chest from the emotions exploding inside it. "You're the most beautiful thing I've ever seen."

Her lips parted and some of the fear got wiped out of her eyes.

"When I saw your face on that screen," I said, ripping the rest of myself wide for her, "I wanted more. I haven't quit wanting more. Poppy Duke, I want everything."

Her big eyes grew watery. "You really fell in love with me?"

"I fell so fucking hard, four-ten, and I've been a scared idiot about telling you, but I'm saying it now. I love you. So much. I want to spend the rest of my life with you. I want the last two months to be our next fifty years."

"I've been wanting today to be real," she whispered.

Euphoria filled me. I could float away. "It is." I tilted her chin up and kissed her. "It will be. Will you marry me, Poppy Duke?"

"Yes," she said with a brilliant smile.

"We can wait." I wanted this day to be special for her. I knew what it was like to look back on a wedding with less than enthusiastic memories. "We can invite more people. Do it bigger and better if you want."

"Everyone I love is here. Including you, Jensen Hollis. I love you." She put her hands on my shoulders and ran them down my arms to intertwine our fingers. "I'm going to make sure you always know it. You'll never have to ask, and I want to announce it in front of the world tonight."

I pulled her closer. This woman was everything I had ever wanted. "You already did."

"Dad?" Auggie's voice interrupted us.

I blinked and my emotional high dipped. How bewildering was this moment for Auggie to witness?

Hassie put her arm around his bony shoulders and scowled at us. "You're confusing him."

"He's a smart kid." I looked her in the eye when I said that. Then I turned a smile to Auggie. "Hey, bud, I fell hard for Poppy, and I want to marry her. She'd be my wife and your stepmom."

He scrunched his face up. "For a year?" His gaze darted back and forth like he was worried he'd spilled our secret.

He didn't need to worry, and I gave him a smile to let him know. He'd done nothing wrong. "No, Auggie. For forever."

He cast a worried look at Poppy. "Would you still tutor me?"

"Absolutely," Poppy said. "You're still going to be the first student at Poppy's Brilliant Minds Tutoring."

"Poppy's Brilliant Minds?" I asked.

She nodded and placed her hand on my chest. "You're making my sign, like you said, and Auggie will be my first official kid getting tutored in my new office. I've talked to five families who are changing centers officially, and two more queries are waiting in my inbox. I haven't been able to tell you with everything going on."

This woman drove me wild.

Auggie grinned at Hassie. "Mom, I get to have Poppy as a stepmom."

My ex's expression flickered through shock and dismay before she forced a pleasant facade. "Yeah, hon. I heard." The muscles in her jaw popped. "It's...exciting." She swallowed. "I hope it works out."

"Thank you," Poppy said to her and gave my fingers a squeeze. "It means a lot."

Hassie offered a small smile. "I should take my seat." She tugged Auggie with her and led him back to his spot.

Poppy turned her attention to Linda. "I'm sorry for the trouble, Aunt Linda. Next year, you might feel like you're in a tough spot, but it won't matter if you don't sign off. I'll find another space to rent. Do what you feel is right. No one is telling us whether we're legit or not."

Indecision rippled over Linda's delicate features. Her gaze softened. "I really do want the best for you."

"When it comes to Poppy," I told Linda, "my competitive side comes out. I'll make damn sure there's no one better. Now, if you all don't mind, I'd like to watch a gorgeous woman walk down the aisle to me."

Chapter Twenty-Seven

Poppy

The sun was sinking. Most of my family hung out chatting with each other. The kids played outside, kicking around soccer balls, throwing frisbees, and hunting for fireflies.

I was sitting on Jensen's lap on the porch of the Perez house. He was chatting with Alder, but the whole time, he held me as I talked to Clover. Elijah, now—ugh—her fiancé, had left early, claiming he needed to get online in the morning for a meeting. He'd probably been bored when he saw he was unable to impress my family with his business acumen.

Hassie had left already. Erin was grabbing Auggie to get him to the fort she'd made in her living room. Hassie had been stiff all the way through the ceremony, and when Jensen and I had been presented as husband and wife, her eyes had misted over.

Hopefully someday she'd find her person, but he wasn't Jensen.

He was mine.

I leaned back on him. The sheer pleasure I'd gotten out of holding his hand in public, kissing him when I wanted to, and cuddling with him made me think I was part exhibitionist.

"Ugh." Clover rose and smoothed her skirt. "You two are making me miss my man."

She would be the only one.

She gave me a quick hug and lightly punched Jensen on the shoulder. "Welcome to the family, brother."

One by one, my siblings left, all indicating that Jensen was now part of our big, unwieldy crew.

Mom took the key to the house from Jensen. "We'll clean up the place tomorrow. You two take the weekend for yourselves." She tapped the metal against her palm. "Does the 'no honeymoon' thing still stand? I can always come babysit if Erin can't take Auggie."

I exchanged a glance with Jensen, excitement building.

"I'd love to go away with you," he murmured.

"Me too, but maybe we should do a family-moon first. Then plan something for us."

So much love filled his eyes, it was staggering. "I'd like that. Auggie will be thrilled."

"I'm always on call for grandma duty." Mom gave me a hug.

Soon, we were standing alone on the porch of the Perez house.

"Your family is amazing," Jensen said.

"Yeah, they're pretty great. And they're all yours and Auggie's now too."

"Other than you, that's the best wedding gift a guy could ask for. Wait here." He went inside, shut off the lights, and locked up. When he returned, he swooped me into his arms.

I whooped and held on to him, laughing.

He didn't go down the stairs right away. "Did I tell you that you look amazing?"

"Once or twice." Five times, to be exact. His smile when he'd seen me being led toward him by my dad erased anything negative he'd said to me in childhood. The look I'd wanted from a man had been right there, and it had been familiar. Jensen had been looking at me that way all along.

"I've been thinking about peeling that dress off you all night."

"Then what are you waiting for?"

My breath whooshed out of me when he jumped down the steps and charged toward his pickup. He didn't speed, but he kept a proprietary hand on my thigh all the way to the house.

My feet didn't hit the ground. He was there to carry me inside all the way to his bedroom.

"I'm moving you in when we wake up." He set me on the edge of the bed. "If I can quit fucking you long enough to do it."

"I bet we won't get me moved in tomorrow because we're going to stay naked all day."

His grin was feral. "That's a bet I'm going to make sure you win."

He tugged me up to standing, held my hands, my ring twinkling in the ambient light, and stepped back. "Prettiest damn thing I've ever seen. If you can wear a dress or shorts every day, I'd be a happy man."

"Winter might get a little cold."

"I'll keep you warm."

He pulled the dress over my head before skating his hands down my body and dropping to a squat. He palmed my ass cheeks before dragging my underwear down with his teeth. A shocked giggle escaped as a shiver traveled over my fevered body.

Carefully, I stepped out. Desire swam under my skin. I needed him. I pushed my hands through his hair. "I love you."

He tilted his face up, his gaze sincere. "I love that you tell me you do."

"You'll never have to beg for my attention."

He pressed a kiss to my abdomen. "Did you know I have a major thing for soccer coaches?"

"No, but I have a thing for one of my students' dads."

"Mmm." He gripped my hips and brushed his thumbs along the crease of my legs. "My soccer coach has got an ass for days and thighs that crush my head, and when she boots the ball, the power turns me on." He laid a kiss along my bikini line. "I get all that strength at my fingertips."

He rose and unhooked my bra as he went. It dropped to the floor and I was naked.

"I have one problem." I started unbuttoning his shirt.

"Yeah?" he asked gruffly. The bulge behind his slacks waited for me like my own special wedding gift.

"You're overdressed for our first marital night together."

He ripped the fly of his pants open and shoved them down, taking his underwear with them. His cock bobbed out. I flipped his shirt down his back and arms. He stepped out of his clothing and shook it away. Then we faced each other, neither of us wearing a stitch. We had privacy, but we weren't hiding.

I slipped one pin out of my hair and another, continuing until my curls fell around my shoulders.

"It's like Christmas, my birthday, and Valentine's all in one," he said gruffly.

The way he made me feel precious wrapped around me like I was a porcelain figure, waiting for the right admirer to keep her forever. It was our wedding night, and he was handing me all my dreams. A simple ceremony with my family. The sense that I was the most valuable treasure he could hold. And a future where I didn't have to weather problems alone.

He lifted me again and placed me in the middle of the bedding, coming down on top of me. His kisses were melting and consuming. I wrapped my arms and legs around him. If we fused into one right now, I'd be perfectly content.

He rocked against me, his erection slicking through my heat. I shamelessly ground against him. He adjusted himself but didn't plunge inside me. We moved as one, rolling against each other, demanding more but not taking it, as if we were showing each other that there was no rush. The night was ours. Forever was ours.

I framed his face with my hands and tangled my tongue with his.

He broke away from my mouth to kiss a path down my neck. "You know what you get to be?"

I arched into him, pleasure tingling through my body all the way to my toes. "What?"

"Loud. I'm gonna make you scream, Poppy." He nipped the sensitive skin at the base of my neck.

The throbbing between my legs grew stronger, more demanding. "You able to back up those claims, Hollis?"

He growled and shifted his pelvis. He held still for a moment, long enough to make me squirm, and then he thrust inside.

I cried out. Finally. I was filled with him and I paused just to enjoy the moment, to feel the connection.

"I love you." He kissed my lips. "Wife."

"I love you too, husband." I let out a breathy giggle. "So formal."

"You're mine, four-ten." He drew back and thrust again.

I hitched my knees higher and widened them. He plunged in and out, and the force made my clit brush against him, and when he hit just the right angle, I pushed harder into him. I was going to come stronger than ever.

"You feel like home." He hooked his arms under my knees. I was open as wide as could be, and we slammed together, each bump and scrape an electrical shock straight to my clit.

"Jensen!"

"Fuck, Poppy, you feel so good."

"Yes!" I chanted that word over and over.

"Fuck." One more time, he rammed into me, and we catapulted together through our climaxes.

My heart raced, but he held me. I was secure with him, so loved and cared for that I couldn't possibly be dreaming. Nothing in my imagination had summoned anything this good.

He released my legs, and I wrapped my arms all the way around him. We lay like that together, our heartbeats in sync.

I ruffled his hair. "Okay, you lived up to that promise. I got loud."

"You're going to be louder," he said into my hair.

"Really? Because I think I can make you shout louder than me."

"Oh, my lovely wife—that's a challenge I'm happy to accept."

Chapter Twenty-Eight

Jensen

One year later...

"Dad? Poppy? Are you awake yet?"

I cracked an eye open. Another gorgeous June day tried to push its way past the darkening blinds on the bedroom windows.

"Yeah," I croaked, clearing my throat and checking the time. My alarm would've gone off in five minutes, but my son was super excited for this weekend. "We're up."

"'Kay. I'm gonna feed Luna." His footsteps receded.

A groan came from the other side of the bed. "It's so early."

It was a first for him, but he was getting better. Poppy had gotten him timers to use, and it'd helped him be more punctual. "He's excited for his first tournament. I'm excited we don't have to travel."

Last summer, Aspen had set up some friendlies, but none of the tournaments had worked out, except for the team Poppy took to the Black Hills. She'd coached all weekend, and we'd stayed longer for our family honeymoon. Auggie still talked about that weekend. He also wouldn't quit going on about the pumpkin picking. If Evander ever had a fan, it was Auggie. In fact, all of Poppy's siblings were adored by my kid, and he had cousins to run and play with.

Hassie hadn't set up her riding school here after all. She was looking for places in Wyoming instead. No big surprise, and while Auggie was disappointed, the Dukes had swooped in—no one more than Poppy. But Hassie called more, and she paid for riding lessons for him. She'd even asked when his games were so she could watch a few this summer.

I rolled over and wrapped my hand around the waist of my wife. "Happy anniversary, Coach," I murmured into a nest of soft hair.

She put her hands over mine and snuggled back into me. "Happy anniversary." She exhaled. "Tell me it's going to go well."

Poppy and Aspen planned a small tournament. The city had been supportive, and there was no reason to worry. They'd even asked if a rec program could be formed in the evenings during the fall.

"It's going to be amazing," I said, meaning every word.

"And if it's not?"

"Then we'll walk through town in shame, and it'll affect your center, and you'll have to close. But I won't leave you. We'll order everything to be delivered so we don't have to be seen in town for years. You'll recruit new students from the East Coast and West Coast, but Auggie will always want you to tutor him."

She chuckled. "Fair enough. But he's going to be done with his lessons soon."

"He's a well-connected dyslexic."

"Happens when you're the model for a tutoring center pamphlet."

"And a cabinet shop." My business was busier than ever. When the town got to see the inside of the Perez house, with a cohesive look on the woodwork that matched the shaker cabinets, word spread and I got more inquiries than ever.

Poppy didn't have to proof all my marketing materials anymore. Word of mouth was all I needed now, but I liked having her input whether she was making corrections or not. Likewise, she came to me to talk over plans she and Aspen made for the soccer club. She was even thinking of bringing on another instructor so she could host workshops for local teachers.

Her phone buzzed, and she groaned. "Don't tell me trouble's already starting." She tucked her head under her pillow.

"Want me to check?"

She nodded, still hiding.

I grinned and reached over her for her phone.

Clover: Get your tickets for Vegas!! I'm getting married!!!

"You might want to see this for yourself."

"Is it bad?"

I clicked my tongue. "Not in the way you think."

She sat up, eyes closed. I propped myself on my elbow and handed her the phone. She cracked open an eyelid.

Shock crossed her face before disgust. "She's *marrying* him?"

She tapped away on the screen. Clover and Elijah had waited a year, long enough that Poppy hoped the relationship wouldn't go anywhere, thinking that Elijah must not want to marry for the house. I was surprised he wanted to marry at all. It'd require him to think about more than himself.

"I can't believe it." She blinked at me, and her phone buzzed. She frowned. "She claims she's not marrying for the house. He's branching out on his own, and she wants to as well."

"Think they waited so it didn't seem suspicious to Linda?"

"Maybe. I don't like it."

I wrapped an arm around her. "She'll be fine. Whatever happens, she'll land on her feet."

"And maybe the flake won't be there when she does."

"He does flake on her a lot."

Poppy couldn't talk to Clover without hearing a story about some way "The Douche" let her down, only Clover talked about getting ditched or stood up like it was just another Monday.

"I wish she'd find someone who treats her better."

"She will. I never thought I would. Then you hung up as soon as you could on an online tutoring session when you saw it was me."

She flashed me a mischievous grin. "I checked you out first."

"Only 'cause you saw me first. Now I check you out the most."

She chuckled, then grimaced at the screen and set it aside. "That mess will have to wait."

"But we're going?"

She nodded. "She'll need me." She curled around me until we formed a ying-yang with our torsos. "Like I'll need you."

"You've got me all day, every day, four-ten."

"Forever, Hollis."

I smiled. My last name was now hers. Forever.

———

Thank you for reading! You're cordially invited to Clover Duke's Las Vegas wedding. She's left her job, her home, and has jump-started a family. The last thing she needs to do is marry her boyfriend and get access to the house her grandma left her. Only when it's time to say "I do" there's no groom, just his brother, Van, who's willing to make a deal that'll help both him and Clover out in Clover Dreams.

Want a day in the life of Poppy and Jensen one year later? You can find it when you sign up to my newsletter at mariejohnstonwriter.com/newsletter.

About the Author

Marie Johnston writes paranormal and contemporary romance and has collected several awards in both genres. Before she was a writer, she was a microbiologist. Depending on the situation, she can be oddly unconcerned about germs or weirdly phobic. She's also a licensed medical technician and has worked as a public health microbiologist and as a lab tech in hospital and clinic labs. Marie's been a volunteer EMT, a college instructor, a security guard, a phlebotomist, a hotel clerk, and a coffee pourer in a bingo hall. All fodder for a writer!! She has four kids, cats, lots of cats, and a corgie.

mariejohnstonwriter.com

Follow me:

Also by Marie Johnston

Return to Coal Haven

Violet Promises

Daisy Whispers

Poppy Kisses

Clover Dreams

Crocus Valley

A Reckless Memory

A Temporary Memory

An Unfinished Memory

A Fearless Memory

An Endless Memory

Coal Haven

Make Me Whole

Make Me Shiver

Make Me Blush

Make Me Dream

Make Me Exhale

King's Creek

King's Crown

King's Ransom

King's Treasure

King's Country

King's Queen

www.ingramcontent.com/pod-product-compliance
Lightning Source LLC
Chambersburg PA
CBHW061630190726
48289CB00006B/1549